Dream When You're
Feeling Blue

ELIZABETH BERG

Dream When You're
Feeling Blue

A NOVEL

RANDOM HOUSE  NEW YORK

Published in the United States by Random House,
an imprint of The Random House Publishing Group,
a division of Random House, Inc., New York.

RANDOM HOUSE and colophon are registered
trademarks of Random House, Inc.

ISBN 978-1-4000-6510-3

LIBRARY OF CONGRESS CATALOGING-IN-PUBLICATION DATA

Berg, Elizabeth.
   Dream when you're feeling blue: a novel / Elizabeth Berg.
     p. cm.
   ISBN 978-1-4000-6510-3
  1. Sisters—Fiction. 2. World War, 1939–1945—United States—
Fiction. I. Title.
   PS3552.E6996D74 2007
   813'.54—dc22   2006036747

Printed in the United States of America on acid-free paper

www.atrandom.com

9 8 7 6 5 4 3 2 1

FIRST EDITION

Book design by Judith Stagnitto Abbate/Abbate Design

FOR MY FATHER, ARTHUR P. HOFF,

WHO TAUGHT ME THE MEANING

OF

TRUE COURAGE

AND GOOD CHARACTER

Dream When You're
Feeling Blue

IT WAS KITTY'S TURN TO SLEEP with her head at the foot of the bed. She didn't mind; she preferred it, actually. She liked the mild disorientation that came from that position, and she liked the relative sense of privacy—her sisters' feet in her face, yes, but not their eyes, not their ears, nor the close, damp sounds of their breathing. And at the foot of the bed she was safe from Louise, who often yanked mercilessly at people's hair in her sleep.

Tonight Kitty was last to bed, having been last in the bathroom. Everybody liked it when Kitty was last in the bathroom because, of the eight people living in the house, she always took the longest. Apart from the normal ablutions, she did things in there: affected poses she thought made her look even more like Rita Hayworth—she *did* look like Rita Hayworth, everyone said so. She filed her fingernails, she experimented with combining perfumes to make a new scent, she creamed her face, she used eyebrow pencil to make beauty marks above her lip. She also read magazines in the bathroom because there, no one read over her shoulder. Oh, somebody would bang on the door every time she was in there, somebody was always banging on the bathroom door, but a girl could get a lot done in a room with a locked door. Kitty could do more in five minutes in the bathroom than in thirty minutes anywhere else in the house, where everyone in the family felt it their right—their obligation!—to butt into everyone else's business.

When Kitty came out of the bathroom, she tiptoed into the bedroom, where it appeared her sisters were already asleep—Tish on her side with her knees drawn up tight, Louise with the covers flung off. Kitty crouched down by Louise and whispered her sister's name. Kitty wanted to talk; she wasn't ready to sleep yet. But Louise didn't budge.

Kitty moved to the bottom of the bed, slid beneath the covers, and sighed quietly. She stared up at the ceiling, thinking of Julian, of how tomorrow he would be leaving, off to fight in the Pacific with the Marines, and no one knew for how long. And Michael, Louise's fiancé, he would be leaving, too, leaving at the same time but going in the opposite direction, for he was in the Army and shipping out to Europe. And why were they not in the same branch of the service, these old friends? Because Julian liked the forest green of the Marine uniforms better than the olive drab of the Army or the blue of the Navy. Also because James Roosevelt, the president's son, was in the Marines.

It seemed so odd to Kitty. So frightening and dangerous and even romantic; there was an element of romance to this war, but mostly it just felt so *odd*. As though the truth of all this hadn't quite caught up with her, nor would it for a while. No matter the graphic facts in FDR's Day of Infamy speech after the bombing of Pearl Harbor: the three thousand lives lost, the next day's declaration of war on Japan, then Germany's declaration of war on the United States. Kitty's facts were these: she was Kitty; he was Julian; every Saturday night they went downtown for dinner at Toffenetti's and then to one of the movie palaces on State Street. Sometimes, after that, he would take her to the Empire Room at the Palmer House for a pink squirrel, but her parents didn't like for Kitty to stay out so late, or to drink. Now his leave after basic was up and he was shipping out, he was going over there. And both boys foolishly volunteering for the infantry!

Kitty rose up on her elbows and again whispered Louise's name. A moment, and then she spoke out loud. "Hey? Louise?"

Nothing. Kitty fell back and rested her hands across her chest, one over the other, then quickly yanked them apart. It was like death, to lie that way; it was how people lay in coffins. She never slept that way, she always slept on her side. Why had she done that? Was it a premonition of some sort, a sign? What if it was a sign? "Louise!" she said, and now her sister mumbled back, "Cripes, Kitty, will you go to *sleep!*"

It was good to hear her sister's voice, even in anger. It soothed and anchored her. She breathed out, closed her eyes, and in a short while felt herself drifting toward sleep. She wanted to dream of Julian on the day she first met him: confident, careless, his blond hair mussed and hanging over one eye, his short-sleeved shirt revealing the disturbing curves of his muscles. She tried to will herself toward that.

People were packed in so tightly at Union Station that Kitty had to hold on to her hat lest it be jostled off her head and trampled. Elbows poked her; suitcases banged into her legs and she feared mightily for her very last pair of silk stockings. The noise level was so high, Julian had to lean in toward Kitty and practically shout to be heard. "Gonna write me every day?" he asked, grinning, and she nodded that she would. "Are *you* going to be *careful* for a change?" she asked, and he told her not to worry. He looked so handsome—there *was* something about a man in uniform—standing there with his duffel bag over his shoulder, his hat rakishly positioned at the side of his head.

Earlier that morning, Kitty and Julian and Louise and Michael had taken a Green Hornet streetcar to the train station and then breakfasted together at Fred Harvey's. Both men ate every bite of food on their plates, but the sisters could hardly swallow their coffee. Now it was time to say good-bye—Julian was on the 8:11 to San Francisco; Michael would leave just a few minutes later, on his way to New York City.

"*Boooard!*" the conductor cried, then made his announcement again, more urgently. "Okay, kid," Julian said. "I guess this is it." He waved at Michael and Louise, who were holding hands and standing nearby, then kissed Kitty quickly. "Take care of yourself." He spoke seriously, his voice thick, and for the first time she saw a glint of fear in his eyes. She stepped back from him and made herself smile brilliantly. She tossed her black hair and stuck out her chest. Already she knew how she'd sign the first photo she sent of herself: *Hi, Private.*

Louise was holding on to Michael and crying her eyes out, though she and Kitty had agreed *not* to do that, *under any circumstances.* They had agreed to look as pretty as they could, to wear their best outfits, to be cheerful and smile and wave at the boys as they pulled out of the station. They had agreed that it was their patriotic duty to behave in this fashion, and they had vowed to help each other be strong. But now Louise sobbed as Michael pulled away from her and ran for his train, and finally Kitty pinched her to make her stop. *"Ow!"* Louise said and pinched her sister back.

"Is this what you want him to remember?" Kitty asked.

Louise wiped at her nose with her sodden hankie. "I can't help it."

"You can!" Kitty told her angrily and then looked at Julian's train, where she saw him hanging out a window and motioning for her to come over to him. He was packed in among so many other men, all those boys with all their caps, sticking their heads and their arms out of the windows, but she could have found Julian in the middle of ten thousand men. She ran over and grabbed his hand. "Good-bye, Julian. Be careful. I mean it."

"I will, I promise. But Kat, listen, I almost forgot, I need you to do something for me. On Monday afternoon, go over to Munson's jewelry store and tell them to give you what I left for you there."

"What?" She laughed. "What do you mean?" A *ring?* Oh, it would be just like Julian, to do it this way! No bended knee, no flowery words of love. Instead, a cocksureness that Kitty found irresistible. Only a girl who had wrapped many men around her finger would be delighted by such cool assurance.

The train hissed loudly and began moving forward. Kitty ran alongside, mixed in with a crowd of mostly young women, some smiling, some weeping, all reaching up toward the hands of the boys who were leaving them behind. "I love you!" Kitty shouted. "Julian! I love you!" The words were new, shiny inside her.

"Munson's Jewelers, on Wabash near Harding's," he shouted back. The train picked up speed, and Kitty stopped running. Then she and the others on the platform stood still, watching the train grow smaller and finally disappear. It had become so quiet; a place that moments ago had reverberated with sound was now still as a chapel. Pigeons fluttered up onto steel beams and sat silent in rows, their feathers ruffled in the morning cold. Kitty became aware of the dampness of the place, the basementy smell, the spill of weak sunshine through the high, dusty windows onto the tracks below. And then, slowly, people began walking away, talking quietly to one another. One woman was holding a brown bag and crying to her husband about their son forgetting his lunch. "The other boys will share their food with him," the father said, and the mother said but she wanted him to have the lunch she had packed, his favorite cookies were in there. "Someone else will have cookies," the man said, and the woman said no, no one else would. She bumped into Kitty, crying hard, and apologized. Kitty touched her arm and said it was all right.

Louise stood forlorn and dry-eyed, holding her pocketbook hard against her middle. Kitty linked arms with her. "*Now* you stop crying," she said, and Louise said, "I know. I'm a dope."

They took a cab home, an extravagance. But they didn't want to wait for the next streetcar, and anyway, Julian had given Kitty money so they could do exactly that. At first she'd thought about using the money for something more practical, but now she luxuriated in the fact that the cab would take them exactly where they were going, directly from where they had been. It was swell. She was Rita Hayworth, and Louise was Dorothy Lamour. She leaned back and looked out the window. There were their fans walking down the sidewalk, wishing they'd come out and sign autographs.

At a stoplight, Kitty pointed to the spring dresses in the window of Marshall Field's. "Look how boxy sleeves are getting," she said, and Louise snapped back, "Jeez! How can you even think about that now?"

Kitty fell silent, but in her head, she started the Mills Brothers singing "Paper Doll." You couldn't think about those boys and where they were going. You had to think about something else. Louise began to weep again, and the driver reached back over the seat to give her his handkerchief, frayed at the edges but clean and neatly folded. "Dry your eyes now, darlin'; he'll be back before you know it," the man said. He was Irish, as they were.

Louise cried harder, but through her tears she said, "Thank you very much. I'll wash it and iron it and send it right back to you." The Heaney girls were nothing if not polite—their mother made sure of that. The Dreamy girls, the sisters were called, for their considerable beauty; and their mother seemed to feel it was her duty to prevent their good looks from going to their heads. You didn't want to be caught lingering before a mirror when Margaret Heaney was anywhere nearby. "Well, now," she'd say, her arms crossed. "Don't we find ourselves a fascination." And then she'd suggest that if you had so much time on your hands, you might find a way to make yourself useful; and if you couldn't think of something to do, she'd be glad to help you. Rugs didn't beat themselves, you know, there was that. The refrigerator needed defrosting, the bathroom and kitchen floors had to be scrubbed.

But their mother was also proud of them. And she not infrequently remarked on how the beauty found in all her children—the dimples, the long lashes, the thick, lustrous hair, the clear skin—didn't come from *no*where. Whereupon their father would inflate his chest, stick his thumbs under his suspenders, and say, "'Tis true! And no need to look any farther for the source!"

"You're going to give yourself a headache with all that crying," Kitty told her sister, and Louise said, "I don't care! I *want* a headache!" Indeed, Michael's mother lay at home on her living room sofa with a sick headache, a cold rag across her forehead, a throw-up bucket at her side—she'd been unable to come to the station, and Michael had told his father to stay home and take care of her. Julian's parents had not come to the station, either. They'd said they wanted to give Kitty and Julian that time alone, but Kitty knew that, although they were proud of their only son, their hearts were broken at his leave-taking. They needed to keep their good-byes—and their anguish—private. Kitty turned to stare out the window again. Louise really ought to look at the beautiful things in the store windows: the hats lodged nestlike on the mannequins' heads; the red open-toed shoes with the ankle straps. Or she ought to think about what she might say in her letter to Michael that night. They had agreed they would write to their men every night until they were safely back home: they'd put each other's hair up and get into their pajamas and then sit at the kitchen table and write at least two pages, every night, no matter what. Tish was already writing to three men she'd met at USO dances.

Kitty snuck a look at her still-weeping sister. What weakness of character! Louise needed to stop thinking about herself. She could think about her job as a teacher's aide, or her friends, or their three little brothers, only eight, eleven, and thirteen but out almost every day with their wagon, collecting for the metal drive. They got a penny a pound, and they'd raised more money for war bonds than any other kids in their Chicago neighborhood—they'd even had their picture in the newspaper. It didn't do any good for Louise to carry on this way. It didn't help Michael or even herself. But then Kitty's throat caught, and she reached over to embrace her sister, and she began to cry, too. Julian with the sun in his hair, saying good-bye, perhaps forever.

"Ah, now, girls," the cabbie said. "Get hold of yourselves, won't you. We'll take care of them Japs in short order, don't you doubt it! And then wait and see if I'm not the very one taking you all home again! And won't we be celebratin'! You keep my handkerchief; I'll collect it from you on that far happier occasion."

"Germans," Louise said, her voice muffled by the handkerchief.

"What's that, now?" the cabbie asked.

"Mine will be fighting the *Nazis*!" she wailed.

"Well, I meant them, too!" the cabbie said. "Germans, Italians, Japanese. What d'ya think any of them scoundrels can do against our fine boys?" He looked into the rearview mirror at the girls, and Kitty saw the worry in his blue eyes, the doubt. It came to her to say, "My boyfriend will be fighting the Japs." But it didn't seem to make much difference, really. She and Louise stopped crying, but they held hands the rest of the way home.

IT WAS THEIR YOUNGEST BROTHER'S HABIT to nearly run over people when he was excited, then call out their names as though they had failed to see him. As soon as Kitty walked in the front door, Benjamin came skidding around the corner and his head butted her stomach. "Kitty! Kitty! Guess what?"

She lowered her face level with his and quietly acknowledged him. Sometimes this worked to calm him down. Not today, though, for he continued to yell and hop on one leg, saying, "We collected for rubber today? And guess what? Old Lady Clooney gave us her *girdle*!"

"Well, that was nice of her," Kitty said, and Louise, hanging her jacket on the coat tree, said, "Don't call her Old Lady, Binks."

"She *is* old! And also she's a lady. So? Old Lady. It's just the same as Mister."

Louise yanked at his brown hair, grown longer than usual. "You know what I mean."

"You're a young lady," Binks told Louise. "Does it bother you to be called Young Lady?"

Louise tilted her head, thinking. "No."

Binks showed her his upturned hands, the physical equivalent of saying "*So?*"

"You're exasperating," Louise said and moved toward the kitchen.

"What's that mean?" Binks called after her. "Louise! What's *that* mean?"

"It means you're interesting," Kitty said and followed her sister. She felt guilty having her grief superseded by hunger, but there it was: she was ravenous.

Tish was kneeling before the oven, her head stuck in through the open door. Her blouse was hiked up on her back, and you could see two safety pins holding her skirt closed. She was terrible about mending. When it was her turn to sew buttons on Binks's shirts, she'd say, "Oh, just wait a day or two and he'll be too big for them anyway."

"Hi," they heard her muffled voice say.

"What are you *doing?*" Kitty asked.

"Drying my hair," Tish said. "It's murder. But this is what I have to do because Ma won't let me get a permanent wave." She pulled her head out, sat back on her heels, and smiled at her sisters.

"A permanent wave is too expensive, and besides that it would ruin your hair," Margaret said. She was standing at the counter, briskly stirring the contents of a mixing bowl with a wooden spoon. "Now shut that door, Tish; the oven won't heat properly, and my cake will fall."

Kitty clapped her hands together. "We're having cake?"

"Make-do cake," Margaret said.

"Oh." Kitty hated the eggless, milkless, butterless recipe so prevalent now. She longed for the burnt-sugar cake with caramel icing they used to have for dessert every Sunday dinner. She wanted cookies around the house again: pineapple nut and pecan fingers, blond brownies and coconut dreams. She wanted jam squares and ginger cookies, chocolate drops and raisin crisps. Ah well. *Use it all, wear it out, make it do, or do without.* Kitty reached for an apple from the bowl on the table.

"Don't eat that," her mother said. "I need it for the red cabbage I'm making tonight."

"I'm hungry!" Kitty said.

"You had breakfast not two hours ago."

"Yes, but I'm *hungry.*"

Her mother said nothing; the wooden spoon went round and round.

"I'm *suffering,*" Kitty said.

"I'll remember you in my prayers along with the poor souls in purgatory," Margaret told her. And then, "Tish! I told you to—"

"I *am!*" Tish shut the oven door and came to sit at the kitchen table with her sisters to sulk; she was a champion sulker. She reached up to adjust one of her pin curls and cried out, then blew on her fingers.

Kitty tsked and rolled her eyes. "What do you *expect* when you touch hot metal?"

"Why don't you just let your hair dry naturally?" Louise asked.

"She can never wait for anything," Kitty said, and Tish said, "I can so! You're the one who can never wait for anything!"

"Are those my bobby pins, anyway?" Kitty asked, leaning forward to inspect Tish's head.

"Is your name written on them?" Louise asked.

"Girls," their mother said and poured her mix from the bowl into cake pans.

Binks had plunked himself in the middle of the kitchen floor to hold his knees to his chest and spin around in circles, singing in his high boy's voice. Now he rose lightning fast and attached himself to his mother's side. "Can I lick the bowl? Ma! Can I lick the bowl, please? Can I?"

"*May* I."

"May I lick the bowl, please?"

"No."

"The spoon?"

"No."

"Aw, gee whiz. Why?"

"Why *not*. Because you already had some. Remember, I gave you a spoonful? The rest goes to your sisters. You go outside now, find your brothers and play with them. But first run over and see if Mrs. Sullivan will trade me some of her coffee coupons for sugar. And wear your jacket. Zipped *up!*"

Their father complained mightily about "Roosevelt coffee," the watered-down version they'd been drinking since the war began. According to their mother, the only coffee Frank Heaney liked was the kind his spoon would stand straight up in. She couldn't make coffee like that when they got only a pound every five weeks. But oftentimes Mrs. Sullivan would make a deal, and then Margaret could at least occasionally offer Frank the rich-flavored brew he so liked.

Binks ran to the hall for his jacket, then raced out of the house, slamming the door so hard it made all the women jump. Margaret brought the mixing bowl over to the table for the sisters to share. Then, her voice low and careful, she asked, "How was it at the station?"

Tish pulled her finger out of the bowl and sat still to listen respectfully. Tears trembled in Louise's eyes, so Kitty answered for both of them. "There were so many people there!"

"Did you cry?" Margaret asked.

"No," Kitty said. "But Louise did."

"Ah, well." Margaret sat down heavily at the table with her daughters. "They're fine boys, both of them." Subtly, she turned the morning paper over, but not before her daughters saw the headlines. So many more lost. Every day, so many lost.

It grew silent then; there was only the steady ticking sound of the grandfather clock in the living room. And then Tish, reaching into the bowl to get a good fingerful of batter, suddenly froze. "Kitty. Is that . . . Are you wearing my *new blouse*? And *eating* in it?"

"It was just for this morning. I'm going to change in one second."

"You didn't even ask!"

Louise, ever the peacemaker, spoke soothingly. "She just wanted to look nice for Julian. You were sleeping, and she didn't want to wake you."

"My foot," Tish said. "She never asks! She just goes in and takes whatever she wants! She thinks just because you're the first one up, you can—"

"Girls!" Margaret said.

Kitty pushed away from the table. "Fine. I'll go and change right now. But leave me some batter." She hated the cake, but she was hungry, by God.

Tish sat back in her chair, her arms crossed, glaring at her sister. Then her eyes widened as Kitty stood. "And is that my *skirt*?"

Kitty bolted for the stairs, Tish right behind her, yelling about how she bet Kitty hadn't even worn *underarm* shields and Kitty yelling back that she had too and that *she* wasn't the one who perspired like a *pig* anyway. Louise looked at her mother and shrugged. Then she said, "Ma? Michael and I are sort of engaged."

ON THE RADIO, BOB HOPE, entertaining at a California boot camp, was doing a skit with a woman who had a most flirtatious voice. It was the kind of voice that sounded like a cat looked when you petted it and it arched its back in pleasure. The women was a blonde, Kitty thought as she dreamily mashed the potatoes. A starlet with a cherub bob, wearing a skintight sweater and an equally tight skirt. Kitty wanted to dress that way, but if she did, her mother would never let her out of the house. The girl was saying she'd been meaning to ask Bob if there were any sharks near San Diego. And here came Hope's droll response: "Did you ever meet a Marine with a pair of dice?" Loud laughter from a large group of men. Kitty could imagine them, all those young men sitting on chairs and on the ground, looking up and smiling, all those white teeth, all those handsome faces.

"Kitty!" her mother said.

"Yes?"

"Get the potatoes on the table, I said. Here come the boys. I want you to make sure Billy gets his hands clean."

That would be a challenge. Every night, the boys were meant to wash up in the metal pan in the kitchen sink before dinner. Binks complied, though frantically, and there was never a problem with freckle-faced Tommy, whose nature was so gentle it worried the rest of the family. But everything was an argument with Billy. His black hair was always a tangled mess, his shirt untucked, and his shoes unshined. He had difficulty finding nice friends; his latest companion was a boy named Anthony Mancini, who at eighteen was far too old for him. "But what do you *do* with him?" Margaret once asked, and Billy shrugged and said, "Nuttin'." To which Margaret responded, "What was that? It sounded like English, but I'm not quite sure. Check your mouth and see if you don't have Binks's marbles in there."

The back door flew open and here the boys came, moving together across the kitchen floor like a human tornado. Billy was first to the sink. "I don't need that," he said, pushing away the floating cake of Ivory. "I ain't that dirty."

"Billy," Margaret said.

"What."

"Language."

"Oh. Sorry. *Me* ain't that dirty."

Margaret looked up from arranging pork chops on a platter. "Just keep it up."

"Sure, whatever you say, Ma, I'll do my best." He pulled his hands out of the pan and reached toward Kitty and the towel. Kitty shook her head no. "C'mon, sis," he said. "I'm starving."

"Use the soap," Kitty said. "Your hands are *black*."

"They ain't black," Billy said, but then the back door opened and their father walked in. Billy put his hands back in the sink and grabbed the soap. There was one person he would obey, and that was Frank Heaney, not out of fear but out of great love.

"Hi, Pop," Kitty said.

Frank stopped dead in his tracks. "Why . . . is it *Kitty Heaney*, then? For the love of Mike, what are you doing here?"

She smiled at him. Always a joke with Frank Heaney.

"Hey, Pop," Billy said. "Did you hear about Alan Betterman?"

"What about him?" Kitty asked. She had gone to school with him.

"I know him," Tish said. "He's dreamy. I used to have a crush on him."

"Him and half the civilized world," Louise said, from the table where she was laying out silverware. She got irritable when she was nervous: at dinner, her mother was going to tell Frank about her and Michael's engagement. That afternoon, Louise had told her sisters about it, and she had said that if their father objected, she didn't know what she'd do.

"Why would he object?" Tish had asked. "He loves Michael."

"Lots of people say you should wait until the boy comes home to get married," Louise had said. "I know a girl whose parents got really mad that she eloped with her guy who was going overseas, because what if he doesn't come back? Then she's a *widow*. And who would want a widow?"

"What do you mean?" Kitty had asked.

Louise had turned to stand so that Tish couldn't see her. Then she'd whispered, *"Experienced."*

"I heard you!" Tish had said. "And I know exactly what you mean. You mean she's not a virgin anymore, 'cause she had marital relations. Don't worry, I know the score: she had *sexual intercourse*."

"Quiet!" Louise and Kitty said together. Heaven forbid their mother hear any of her children say such a thing. Heaven forbid she find out that her daughters knew exactly what it meant. Not for nothing had Louise and Kitty pored over a book "for the married woman" they'd found one day when they were supposed to be cleaning out the attic. As for Tish, well, she always knew everything she wasn't supposed to know.

As both Binks and Tommy waited their turn for the drying towel, Billy said, "Alan got killed in New Guinea. Got shot in the forehead."

Kitty drew in a sharp breath. "Billy! Don't *say* that!"

"It's true!" he said. "His old lady told me. She started crying when she told me. She sure is sad."

"Well, of course she's sad!" Margaret cried.

"But wait," Billy said. "She's sad, but she said she's also proud. And now her other son's enlisting. In the Navy."

"Pete?" Tish asked.

"Yeah, that's his name."

"I went ice skating with him!" Tish said.

"Tish," their mother said. "Must *everything* have to do with your *social* life? Oh, poor Edith. I can't imagine. Two sons. Poor woman."

"Pete ain't dead!" Billy said. "He's joining the *Navy*!"

"I shall visit her tomorrow. And girls, I want each of you to write her a note tonight. Oh, right from our own neighborhood, God help us."

Kitty thought of an incident in fifth grade, a time on the playground when she had enlisted other boys to tie Alan Betterman to a tree using the ribbons from her hair. It was because she was angry at him for trying to pull up her skirt. At the time, having Alan tied to the tree for the whole of recess seemed fitting—even mild—punishment. Now Kitty was sorry. Alan Betterman, with his brown eyes and high coloring. She wasn't close friends with him—she'd seen him around, she'd always waved and said hello, but she'd known nothing about him, really. Only now she felt she'd lost a friend. And when she wrote the condolence card, she would mean it most sincerely. Last time she saw Alan, he'd been in line at the Majestic, his arm around a girl. Who? And did that girl know? And . . . *Julian.* She swallowed hard, then moved to take her place at the table.

She sat unmoving, the voices of her family distant things. Alan Betterman was dead, her sister was getting married, and all the world was such a tender place. It was impossible to be careful enough.

"I'll bring her a spiritual bouquet," Tommy said. "Shall I?"

"'*Shall I.*'" Billy snickered at the proper usage and reached across Binks for the red cabbage.

"Mind your manners!" his mother told him.

"'Bout what?" he asked, honestly confused.

"A spiritual bouquet would be lovely, Tommy," said their mother, looking away from all of them, out the window toward the Bettermans' house.

"FINE WAY TO SPEND A SATURDAY NIGHT," Tish grumbled. The sisters were sitting at the kitchen table dressed in their flannel pajamas and

woolen robes, all of them with mugs of hot water and lemon. It was unseasonably cold out tonight, the famous Chicago wind howling. Kitty
and Louise had put their hair up in rag rollers; Tish had combed out her
beautiful blond hair and complained that all the wonderful waves were
going to waste. "You'll look very nice for Father Fleishmann at mass tomorrow," Margaret told her, and Tish rolled her eyes. She'd been planning on going to a USO dance that night, but her mother had decided
she should stay home and write letters instead. "Enough is enough,"
Margaret said. "You're only seventeen years old. You don't need to be
gallivanting all over town every night."

"It's not every night," Tish said. "And it isn't all over town. And I'm
doing it for the war effort, Ma. Knitting isn't the only thing to do, you
know. It helps the boys' morale to dance with beautiful girls."

"Ah, so it's *beautiful* we are now. And never mind leaving it to someone else to offer the compliment! Should it be warranted in the first
place!"

Tish made a show out of opening the letter she would answer first.
She shook the page and put it down on the table to press out the creases.
"Well, well," she said. " '*Dear Beautiful,*' Sam Wischow writes."

"Beauty is as beauty does," Margaret said. "It wouldn't hurt you to
learn to knit as well as dance, Tish. God forbid those boys are still fighting in Europe this winter, they'll need scarves and mittens and socks.
Peg Bennett knit a vest for her son last winter and he very much appreciated it, 'twas a wonderful gift. Now, you write your letters, and I don't
want to hear another word about where you'd rather be."

She went into the parlor to sit with her husband and listen to the
radio. Edward R. Murrow was a must for both of them. Frank liked *I
Love a Mystery,* with its A-1 Detective Agency, whereas Margaret preferred Fred Allen and Jack Benny, or Amos 'n' Andy and their Fresh Air
Taxi, courtesy of the missing windshield. Most times, though, they'd
talk over the radio shows. Occasionally there was an argument, but of a
friendly, swat-fly variety that always ended the same way. Frank would
say, "Ah, I should have married that willowy blonde I used to see on the

streetcar every morning. She could never keep her eyes off of me." And Margaret would counter with "No doubt she was mesmerized by the breakfast crumbs on your face. *I* should have married Howard Kresge, he had such gorgeous curls. And I'll bet he's worth a million dollars by now."

They would sit silently for a while, Margaret rocking and knitting, Frank sucking at his pipe. And then they would forget about any argument and start talking again. Tonight, no doubt, they'd be discussing Louise's engagement. There was some doubt about how Frank felt: he'd congratulated Louise, but he'd looked like an elephant was standing on his toe when he did so. As for Margaret, she couldn't have been happier: she loved Michael like a son already.

Kitty wondered how her parents would feel when she told them that she, too, was engaged. She hadn't told her sisters yet; she wanted to surprise them with the ring.

As though sensing her thoughts, Tish asked Louise, "So what do you think your ring will look like? I hope it's a big diamond, emerald cut, just like Judy Garland's."

"Round," Kitty said. "More elegant." She hoped hers was round. And she hoped it was big, too; Julian could afford it—or at least his parents could. She couldn't wait to show her ring to the girls at the insurance company. Every morning, there was a big get-together before the typing and the filing began, all the women gathering near the watercooler to catch up on one another's lives. Kitty had it all planned: just as they were ready to get down to work, she'd say, "Oh, girls? One last thing." And then she'd hold up her hand. Tuesday morning, she'd do this, after having picked up the ring on Monday. She'd make sure she did a good manicure Monday night—Tish would help her. Although Tommy was also good at manicures, and he'd help anyone do anything.

"I'm not going to get a ring," Louise said. "We're going to save for other things."

Tish looked up from the letter she was signing off on. *With hugs and kisses and lots of love,* she'd write. Next she'd put a big kiss mark on the page with red lipstick—she kept the tube handy on the kitchen table. She signed off that way to every guy on her list, even though her sisters had told her it was improper—a kiss made with an open mouth, no less! But now Tish was the one preaching propriety. "You have to have a ring!" she told Louise. "That's what makes you engaged!"

"It's not the ring that makes you engaged," Louise said. "It's the promise."

"Welllll," Tish said, and her voice was high and singsong. "I don't *know.* A girl needs a *ring* to know that it is a *prom*ise. Or maybe the guy's just *fool*ing."

Then, when both Kitty and Louise looked over at her, she looked away, embarrassed. Michael wasn't that kind of guy.

But Julian was, Kitty thought. Julian was the kind of guy who called you "baby" while watching another girl—or, worse, a fancy car—go by. But things were different now. A ring changed everything. A ring was what every girl waited for. It was the oddest thing, the way getting it made you so excited yet also serenely calm. It was as though you could finally stop holding your breath.

In only two days, Kitty would have proof that Julian loved her. She hadn't wanted to put pressure on him, but she had just turned twenty-two. With a yearlong engagement, she'd be twenty-three when they were wed. It was time. For Louise, at twenty, it wasn't as critical; she was nowhere near being called an old maid.

"When I get married," Tish said, "we're going to eat by candlelight every night. Twelve loooong white candles, in a silver candelabra. Two candelabras!"

Louise said, "I'm going to make a pie for dinner every day; Michael loves pie more than just about anything. I'll make all different kinds. And I'll always have fresh flowers on the table, even if it's just one little blossom. One flower can make such a big difference!"

"I'm not putting anything on the table," Kitty said. "We're going to go out to dinner every night. And then to a club for drinks and dancing."

"That would get old," Louise said, and Tish and Kitty answered together, "No it wouldn't!"

It was quiet, then, both girls writing their letters, Louise lost in thought, Tish with the tip of her tongue sticking out as she labored away. Kitty was having a hard time thinking of something else to say: for heaven's sake, she'd just seen Julian that morning. She could talk about plans for their married life once she had the ring on her finger, but that hadn't happened yet. She'd already told him about Louise and Michael, which he probably knew anyway, since he and Michael were such good friends. What else was there to write about? What they'd had for dinner? She certainly didn't think she should mention Alan Betterman. She wrote, *I guess you'll be plenty busy, but I sure hope you'll have time to write now and then.* Then, shyly, she added, *honey.* She sat back in her chair and regarded the word on the page. Maybe it was wrong. Maybe *hon* would be better. Or some newfangled word of endearment: Julian was always up on the latest slang. Last time they were trying to have some private time at her house, Julian had told Billy, "Go climb up your thumb, wouldja?"

Kitty stared at her letter, and decided to leave *honey* in. It would look worse to scratch it out. Then she wrote, *Say, I know this is awfully short, but Louise is calling me to help her with some crazy thing. Remember me in your dreams, as I will you.* She'd write a longer letter later, after something had happened.

Tish licked an envelope, sealed it, and set it aside, then put the letter she'd answered back in its packet tied with red ribbon. She had three different colors for the men she was currently writing: red for Roy Letterman from Oakland, California; yellow for Bill Carson from Bayonne, New Jersey; and blue for her favorite, Donald Erickson from Madison, Wisconsin. She'd had pink for Whitey Nelson from New York City, but the letters from him had recently stopped. No one wanted to think why. At least Tish's last letter to him had not come back marked DECEASED. Yet.

"You guys?" Tish said. "Do you ever wonder . . . Do you think there's any danger that we'll get attacked?"

Louise sighed. "Who knows?"

"Because I have a plan," Tish said. "If we get attacked, we put a line of red nail polish across our throats like blood and play dead. I have the polish under the bed; it's all ready in case we need it. Becky gave it to me, that girl who sits behind me in school. She has two bottles under her bed. She's going to pour it all over her forehead like she shot herself."

Kitty and Louise exchanged glances, and then Louise spoke reassuringly. "That's a good plan, Tish. But I don't think we'll need it. I think we'll win the war, and the boys will come home. It's all going to be over soon."

Silence but for the sound of the radio in the parlor, and then Tish opened another letter and laughed. "Listen to what this guy said: '*I hope I didn't embarrass you, praising your charms this way. Or make you mad! If I did, don't be sore, it's just with a puss like mine, I thought the only woman I'd hear from would be my mom. I'm the luckiest man in my company, everyone agrees.*' See that?" She smiled at her sisters, then read the lines again, silently this time, but with her lips moving.

"Guess you're a good knitter after all, Tish," Louise said. And then she got them all more hot water and lemon, and they worked quietly until their mother came into the kitchen and announced that, as she was tired, it was time for all of them to go to bed.

After the sisters were in bed, the lights out, Kitty whispered, "Hey? You know Mrs. O'Brien, that young woman whose husband's been gone since Pearl Harbor? The real pretty one? Well, she had the grocery delivery boy inside her house for *half an hour* the other day! Mrs. Sullivan told me—she lives right next door. I'll bet she got an eyeful!"

When her sisters didn't respond, she thought at first they were ignoring such unkind gossip. But when she leaned up on her elbow and looked at them, she saw that they were sound asleep, Tish with her mouth open, Louise with covers flung off, a dark lock of hair loose from the rag roller. Kitty had a thought to fix it but didn't want to wake her.

They were home, she and her sisters. They were safe, three in a bed, but it was a comfortable bed. High above them, the sky was full of drifting clouds and stars. But across both oceans, boys not much older than her own brothers slept in the dirt, and the skies above them exploded regularly. It comforted Kitty to think that the letters she and her sisters wrote would soon be in their hands. But it was a small comfort, and mostly inside herself she felt the hollowness of fear. Her mouth grew dry; she wanted water. A trip to the kitchen? No. She would wait until morning. What luxury, the choice.

RIGHT AWAY ON MONDAY MORNING, Kitty knew something was wrong. Rather than the usual loud and cheerful banter of the women at her office, there was silence. A knot of women was gathered around the desk of Maddy Pearson, and she had her hands to her face and was crying.

Kitty swallowed against the sudden tightness of her throat, lay her jacket and purse on her desk chair, and moved over to the group. "What happened?'" she whispered, and Polly Dunn whispered back, "Her brother Walter was killed. His plane was shot down. He parachuted out, but then the Jerrys got him on the ground. The family just found out on Saturday."

Tears started up in Kitty's eyes, and she blinked them away, then moved forward so that she could kneel at her friend's side. "Maddy?" she whispered.

Maddy turned toward her and took Kitty's hands into her own. She squeezed them so tightly, Kitty had to draw in a breath and clench her teeth to keep from crying out. Maddy spoke between hiccuping sobs. "I thought I was better off coming to work but, golly . . ." She shook her head. "I guess it wasn't such a good idea after all."

"Want to come outside for a minute?" Kitty asked, and Maddy nodded.

They rose together, and the other women parted silently to make way for them. As she and Maddy left the room, Kitty could hear the women start to talk again in the low tones of sorrow.

"Now I'm the one," Maddy said. "I'm the one they're all talking about because my brother is gone."

Kitty linked arms with her. "Shhhhh," she said. "Let's go outside. We'll sit for a while." She smiled. "It's real nice out." As soon as she said the words, she regretted them—how callous to turn the conversation to the weather! But her friend only tried to smile back.

Down the block and across the street was a small park, and Kitty led Maddy to a bench there. "He'd been dead for well over a week before we found out," Maddy said. "Can you imagine? We're all just going on like normal, and he's . . ." She looked at Kitty. "I'd just written him a letter the day before we got the telegram, and I told him all these things he never . . . he never got to read. I guess that letter'll just come back. And it will seem so silly, won't it? All I said?" She put her hand over her heart. "Oh, boy. It hurts. It's real pain. Right here."

"I know," Kitty said.

They sat in silence for some time, and above them the birds chirped and hopped busily from one branch to another. Maddy sighed heavily. She looked up and watched the birds for a while, then reached in her pocket for her hankie. She blew her nose loudly, and it honked, and the girls smiled in spite of themselves. "It's awful," Maddy said then, and Kitty nodded.

"I just don't know what to do. My mother won't get out of bed. My father sits at the kitchen table and stares. Just . . . stares. Bobby's coming home for the funeral, and I don't know if he should go back. One's enough, isn't it?"

"One's enough," Kitty said, and then she sat quietly, holding her friend's hand until she stopped crying.

Finally, Maddy took in a long breath and said, "Okay. I'm okay now. Thanks for coming out here with me, Kitty. I think I'll just . . . I think I'll go home. I'll make Ma some soup; she's got to eat, and she likes my cabbage soup. Or I'll just . . . I'll just be there. I'm not ready to go back to work yet."

"Take your time. And if you need me to do anything for you, let me know."

"There are some invoices on my desk. If you could—"

"I'll do them right away." Kitty hugged her friend and then watched her move in and out of the shade of the trees, walking slowly toward home. All over the country, this just kept happening. And over and over again, Kitty had to straighten her back and remember why. It probably wasn't right to say so, but this was how she felt: at home, bombs were falling, too.

She started back for the office. After lunch, she'd tell the girls about her ring, she'd show it to them. They needed good news, too. Did they ever.

THE BELL OVER THE DOOR at Munson's Jewelers tinkled gaily when Kitty walked in. It was as though it, too, wanted to join in the excitement of what she was about to do. So much for the remark Kitty had overheard Julian make to Michael recently: "I'd like to see any quail try to put the bite on me!" All the pressure men felt to try to avoid being "trapped." And all the pressure women felt to trap them! You couldn't look at a ladies' magazine without being beaten about the head with the message that if you weren't engaged you were nothing. The ad Kitty had looked at most often said, "She's lovely! She's engaged!" and she wasn't even lovely! Kitty had stared and stared at the woman's face (she looked a little stuck up, too), and thought, *How come* she *got a ring?* Something Bob Hope had said on the radio was going around: "You know what a husband is, don't you? A bank account with pants and an empty stomach. Easy to catch one, though, all it takes is a flashy car with a bear trap for a bumper. Your only competition is twenty-three million other women—and the draft board." Another joke going around said they were beginning to draft scarecrows. Well, Kitty didn't have to worry anymore.

She could feel her heart pounding in her chest, and across the top of her forehead was a thin line of perspiration. She had walked to the store so quickly she'd nearly tripped over the last curb. She'd tell Julian that, in her letter to him tonight. *Jeepers, hon, I was in such a hurry I nearly fell flat on my face on my way over to Munson's. But it would have been worth it to take a tumble for the incredibly beautiful ring that now sits on that finger!* She'd say something like that. The diamond was bound to be big; Julian would never settle for anything under a full carat. It might even be two carats! She'd say he needn't have done that, but then she'd say how happy she was that he did. She'd heard that if you caught a diamond in the light the right way, you could cast huge rainbows on the wall. She'd wait to do that until her sisters could see it with her. They'd be so excited for her, and they'd love her ring, Tish especially. No stone could be too big for Tish. Louise might think Kitty's large diamond was crass, but she'd have to admire its great beauty. Everyone would.

Around her parents, Kitty would be more subdued. Already she could hear her mother's response: "So it's finally an engagement ring, is it. And none too early, either!" She imagined her father inspecting the stone and saying, "Sure there's a year's worth of mortgage payments you're sporting on your finger!" But he would congratulate her, and he would mean it. He would embrace her, saying, "God love ya, you're my own shinin'—"

"*Miss?*"

Kitty started and looked up at the thin face of the man across the counter from her. He wore rimless glasses and a red bow tie, a neatly pressed blue suit and white shirt.

"Oh! I'm sorry, I . . . My name is Kitty Heaney." Her voice shook a bit, and she smiled. "Gosh, I'm awful nervous!"

"Am I to assume this is a holdup?" He smirked at his own joke.

Kitty stood tall and tossed her hair back. Then she lowered her chin and looked up at the man. There. She had him now; he was beginning to blush. Kitty loved it when she made men blush. "I'm here to pick up something that Julian Stanton—"

"Oh, yes!" the man said. "I have it in the back. Excuse me for one moment; I'll bring it right out."

Kitty's toes curled in her shoes. She wondered how he knew what size ring she wore. Had one of her sisters told him? Louise? Did she know all about this? It would have to be Louise; Tish couldn't keep a secret if her life depended on it. She admitted this about herself; if you wanted to confide in her and asked if she could keep a secret, she would frankly say no. Then she would ask you to tell it to her anyway.

Kitty inspected some of the jewelry in the case while she waited. Rings, brooches, necklaces, bracelets, all so bright and beautiful. And she was seconds away from her own diamond engagement ring. It wasn't happening quite the way she'd imagined, but it was happening. Part of her felt guilty for feeling such happiness on a day when her friend Maddy was suffering so. But when bad news came, you had to keep on going, just like the boys did.

"*Here* we are," the man said. He handed Kitty a silver bag. Inside was a long box, bracelet size, and a ring box, oh, black velvet! Perfect. There was also an envelope with her name on it, and Julian's handwriting: *Read this first.*

"Thank you!" Kitty told the man and rushed out of the store. *Read this first,* my eye. First she'd put on the ring. She took in a deep breath, pulled out the velvet box, and opened it. And stared. She tried mightily to hold back her feeling of disappointment. The ring was no full carat. It wasn't even half. In fact, you could hardly *see* the diamond. Still, it was a ring. More or less.

Far less enthusiastically, she opened the bracelet box. Only it wasn't a bracelet, it was a Lady Elgin watch. Now, here was something *nice!* She slipped it on her wrist and checked the time against the bank clock across the street. Exactly right. More slowly, then, she pushed the ring onto her finger. Or tried to. He had guessed wrong; the ring wouldn't go past her knuckle.

But wait. Kitty understood now. This ring was merely a substitute for the real ring, something she might wear on a chain around her neck.

Oh, that Julian! He must have ordered her real ring special; Munson's probably didn't carry diamonds the size he wanted. That was what the note would explain. She opened the envelope and read Julian's words eagerly. Then she read them again, more slowly. And then she put the note back into the envelope, the ring back into the box, and headed toward the office. There was time to stop at the Automat for an egg salad sandwich. She would eat her lunch and think about how to do what Julian had asked.

When she got back to work, she'd show the girls her watch.

"WELL, AREN'T YOU TOGGED TO THE BRICKS!"

It was Saturday night, still cool for the end of May, and another meat-stretcher dinner was finished. ("For the love of God, who ever heard of *wheat cereal* in *steak*!" their father had asked, and their mother had answered pleasantly, "'Tisn't steak anyway, Frank; 'tis ground beef. The recipe is only called 'Emergency Steak.'") The sisters had washed and dried and put away the dishes, and the usual argument between Billy and Binks had taken place over whose turn it was to flatten the cans and take out the garbage, until Tommy had quietly done it himself.

Now, up in their bedroom, Tish stood staring at Kitty, who was making adjustments to the thin straps of a white chiffon dress. Their mother had decided that Tish needed more chaperoning at the USO dances than her friends' brothers had provided, and she had all but ordered Tish's sisters to start accompanying her. With their men gone, they'd have time now.

Kitty's dress had silver sequins sewn here and there over the bodice and on the skirt; when she twirled around, she sparkled. She was wearing new shoes, too, white heels with little bows at the front, which made your feet look smaller. "Where'd you get all that?" Tish asked.

"Goldblatt's," Kitty answered nonchalantly. The truth was, though, that she was very excited to wear what she'd spent her entire savings—and her shoe ration stamp—on. She'd tried on a spaghetti loop dress, with its fabric half circles sweeping down princess lines from shoulders to concealed pockets, but $7.98 was too much to spend on it. She'd loved the Two-Timer, with its tightly fitted aqua-blue jacket embroidered with gold thread: the black pebble-crepe skirt had flared divinely. But it was the white chiffon she'd finally decided on. Might as well wear a white dress this way; it sure didn't seem like she'd be wearing the other kind anytime soon.

When she'd ridden the streetcar home, she'd kept putting her hand in her shopping bag, just to feel the fabric of her beautiful dress, just to feel the edge of the shoe box, where her heels lay nestled in tissue. She already knew where she'd hide her shoes so her sisters couldn't get at them: in the basement, beneath her father's fishing gear; he hadn't fished in ages.

Kitty had felt a little strange at first, looking at all the lovely dresses while Julian was so far away, pulling them off the rack and holding them up against herself while she swayed from side to side. But then she'd decided that, if she were honest with herself, she would have to admit that she was looking at those dresses *because* he was so far away, in more ways than one. His indifference to her wanting a ring—he had to know she was dying for one!—put her in the odd position of being angry at him at the same time that she was missing him terribly and worried sick about him. What to do about this confusing mix of emotions? Why, get dolled up and fawned over. That would fix Julian's wagon, and the best part was he wouldn't even know about it.

Kitty turned to the side and stood on her tiptoes, trying to see as much of herself as she could in the dresser mirror. She took in a deep breath and tossed her hair back.

"Don't you think you went a little overboard?" Tish asked.

Kitty stuck her tongue out at her sister.

"You did! You're supposed to be buying only the things you really need."

Well, who didn't know that? Everywhere you turned, you were reminded of all that the boys were doing for you. And one of the things you could do for them was "thoughtful buying." For Pete's sake, a person felt guilty if she ever put herself first for anything. But sometimes you just had to.

"Well, I *really need* this," Kitty said. "You're the one who said it contributed to the war effort to look nice."

"Nobody gets *that* dressed up!"

"I do."

Louise came rushing into the room with her robe tied tightly around her tiny waist—of all the sisters', hers was the smallest: nineteen and a half inches and holding. Not so much of a bosom, though, Kitty reminded herself every time she felt a twist of envy. "Be ready in a minute," Louise said. "Cripes, but that leg makeup takes a long time to dry! And this is Velva! Elizabeth *Arden*!"

When she saw Kitty, her mouth dropped open.

"What do you think?" Kitty asked and spun in a slow circle.

"I think . . . Well, jeepers, you look just beautiful, Kitty! That's the prettiest dress I've ever seen."

Kitty smirked in Tish's direction.

"She's too ginned up," Tish said. "She'll embarrass herself. Wait till Ma and Pop see her; they won't let her out of the house."

"I already showed it to Ma," Kitty said.

"When?" Tish asked.

Kitty moved to the mirror to adjust her hairpins. "When I brought it home."

Tish snorted. "In the bag? Sure. But wait till she sees it on you!"

"You're just jealous," Kitty said, and when Tish crossed her arms and said, "No I'm not!" Louise told her mildly she was, too. Tish was wearing their mother's faux pearl necklace and a nice skirt and sweater in a lovely blue color that set off her eyes, but she was nothing next to Kitty.

Tish went to the closet and pulled out one of the sisters' oldest cardigans, a saggy white one, the bottom button hanging by a thread. "Wear this out of the house," she told Kitty. And then, to Louise, "See? Would I help her if I were jealous?"

"I'm not wearing that!" Kitty said. "You still haven't tightened the button, and besides that you got a mustard stain on the elbow!"

"Uh-oh," Louise said. "I guess I got the mustard on it. I had a hot dog last time I wore it. Sorry."

"Just wear it out of the house," Tish said. "Believe me, I have experience in these matters."

On this point Kitty had to agree. She snatched the cardigan from her sister, then returned to the mirror to finish perfecting her hairdo. Maybe she'd cut her hair. A girl at work had told her about a hairstyle she'd seen in a magazine called the Bombshell. You cut your hair short, then curled it into tight ringlets that "exploded" all over your head.

Louise put on a plain blue dress that she might wear to work and pulled her hair back in a snood. "Okay," she said. "I'm ready. Let's go."

Her sisters stared at her.

"That's it?" Tish asked.

"What?" Louise looked down at herself.

"You're so . . . plain," Tish said.

"I'm engaged," Louise said.

Tish laughed. "So are half the fellows! You're not there to get involved; you're there to show the guys a good time for one night! They're scared, and they're lonely. Most of them just want to talk!"

Louise marched over to the mirror and yanked the snood from her hair. She put combs on either side of her head and halfheartedly fluffed her curls. She put on lipstick and blotted it, using the other half of a tissue Kitty had left on the dresser top, then threw the tissue pointedly into the trash. "Let's go," she said, "or we'll be late." To Kitty, she said, "And I wish that for once you would pick up after yourself. I'm not your maid."

Kitty said nothing. She had been wondering if this was the Moment. For almost a week now, she'd been waiting for it. In his brief note, Julian had told her that he had finished making the payments on the ring Michael secretly had on layaway for Louise. He'd done it at the last minute so Michael could do nothing about it—his pride would never stand for Julian doing such a thing. But Julian felt that if Michael and Louise were going to be engaged, let the girl have the ring. These were uncertain times. Let Louise have the ring.

Julian said he would tell Michael about it in a letter. Kitty was to give the ring to Louise when the moment was right, and then explain to her why Julian had done what he had. Well, the moment might have been right when Louise had said she was engaged, just before she started acting like Kitty's mother. But now Kitty would wait for another moment, a time when Louise was blue. Anyone would agree that that was a better idea. Her *maid*!

MAYOR KELLY'S SERVICEMEN'S CENTER was at Washington and Wells, one block from city hall, in a fourteen-story building that had been an Elks Club. But nearly two years ago, the building had been vacated and offered free of charge for the center's use. It had been renovated, then decorated by artists. Individuals and businesses had donated everything from furniture and board games to a pipe organ. The top three floors were dormitories with showers, a pressing room, and 150 beds, where men who signed up early enough could sleep. There was a library, a games room, and a music room with more than twelve thousand phonograph albums to listen to. There were rooms where men could dictate letters to "private secretaries" or make recordings of their voices to send home. Chicago artists offered to do men's portraits. There was space for jewelry making, pottery making, wood carving, and leatherwork. There were two dining rooms, where servicemen could have a floor show and music with their dinner. The mayor himself visited often, and his wife served cake. But the most popular thing had to be this very ballroom, throbbing so hard with the sound of music and voices that Kitty could feel it in her chest.

She stood still, trying to take everything in. The walls were draped with American flags, and the place was packed with servicemen in uniforms—all kinds of men, tall and short, handsome and not so. They were on the dance floor moving to the sounds of the live orchestra playing "Moonlight Serenade," and they were all along the sides of the room, sipping from punch cups and talking to one another or to girls or, sometimes, simply standing alone and staring. When the boys talked among themselves, it was bold and jocular, full of jabs to ribs and slaps on the back; when they talked to girls, it was different. Some of them looked painfully shy, standing far away and looking more at the floor than at the young women they were addressing. Others, in the dark corners of the room, leaned in close, one hand against the wall. They were saying things into the girls' ears, and the girls were laughing. Kitty saw one man reach out and caress a girl's throat, and the girl leaned her head back and closed her eyes. Well! If Margaret Heaney saw that, she'd escort all three of her daughters right out of the hall and never permit them to come to a dance again.

Mostly, though, people were just dancing. Madly. And Tish was wrong: lots of girls wore fancy dresses. When they'd arrived, Kitty hadn't been able to get out of her cardigan quickly enough. She'd had a thought to toss it right into the trash, but then she'd have to add wastefulness to her list of sins for next week's confession, so she stashed the sweater under a metal folding chair. And anyway, she'd need to wear the sweater home: Frank Heaney would be waiting up for them—asleep beside the radio, perhaps, but he'd wake up when his daughters came in and pretend he'd not been sleeping at all. He'd greet them and inspect them and kiss their foreheads before he climbed the creaky stairs to bed. And their mother, cold-creamed and hairnetted and in bed already, reading from one of the fat novels she'd checked out of the library, she'd be wide awake, and she'd know the precise second her girls crossed the threshold. No doubt she'd come down into the kitchen to make sure they did what they were supposed to.

After supper, Margaret had laid out writing paper and pens on the kitchen table for her daughters: they could go to the dance, all right, but they'd tend to their letter-writing duties as soon as they got home. So they'd better not stay out too late and get too tired. They'd better come home at a decent hour from that dance. A lot of girls were getting a reputation for being fast, going to those dances and staying out late, Margaret said. And a lot of them seemed to deserve that reputation, if the truth be told. Bad habits rubbed off, you know. A girl could be perfectly innocent, but put her around enough of those who weren't, and . . . Well. Lie down with dogs and you'll rise up with fleas. Remember where you came from, and get home at a decent hour. "Remember where you came from" was Margaretese for "Remember your morals." And "morals" was Margaretese for everything from unfolding your napkin to laying it properly across your lap to . . . much more.

The tall, redheaded girl serving as hostess at the refreshment table poured punch for Kitty and nearly missed her cup, so busy was she scanning the crowd. "Sorry!" she told Kitty, and Kitty said it was okay, although if the girl had spilled on her new dress there'd have been hell to pay. "Lotta cute guys tonight, huh?" the girl said.

"I just got here," Kitty said, and the girl, scanning the crowd again, said, "Well, take my word for it, sister, there's a surplus of droolies here tonight!" Kitty smiled; this one was what Julian would call "khaki wacky." But he would also say that she was Able-Grable. A blackout girl. A dilly. Good-looking, in other words.

Kitty walked back over to Louise and nudged her. She pointed with her chin to a couple getting amorous in the corner. The man's mouth was barely an inch away from the girl's. Louise drew in a breath and turned away. "Stop staring!" she told Kitty, but Kitty wouldn't. If they were going to kiss, Kitty wanted to see. But they didn't kiss. They joined hands and moved farther into the shadows.

Tish had hit the dance floor as soon as they arrived. It was so crowded, it was sometimes hard to move. But move they did. Kitty saw every variation of the jitterbug: the Lindy Hop, the Balboa, the Jersey Bounce. Some people were doing the Jig Walk and the Flea Hop. They were shagging, trucking, and Suzy-Qing. Some couples were conversation dancing, standing close together and holding each other's hands. Kitty moved her shoulders from side to side and tapped her foot. She knew all those dances, as well as the rumba and the fox-trot and the polka, too—people used to make admiring circles around her and Julian when they danced. It would be odd to dance with someone other than Julian, but Kitty couldn't wait to get onto the floor. "War is *fun!*" Kitty had overheard a girl at the office say today, and she had been horrified. But maybe, in some respects, it was true.

The band ended its rousing rendition of "Dipsy Doodle," and the dancers whooped and whistled. The boys mopped their foreheads, and the girls fanned their faces. Then a petite, dark-haired woman was pulled onto the stage, and people began to clap and cheer. "Hey!" Louise said. "I know that woman! I went to school with her. That's Dorothy Hermann!" She grabbed Kitty's hand, and they pressed closer. Dorothy, a pretty brunette with a dazzling smile, began to sing, "There'll be bluebirds over / The white cliffs of Dover / Tomorrow, just you wait and see," and the room quieted. The woman's voice was lovely, and the song, with its message of hopefulness for peace and for freedom, never failed to stir its listeners. Kitty felt a tapping on her shoulder. A man whom she'd noticed on walking in, a tall, handsome, serious-faced man who'd been standing alone, his hands in his pockets, was asking her to dance. Kitty nodded and stepped into his arms.

"WILL YOU HURRY UP?" Kitty told Tish. "We're going to miss the streetcar!"

"I can't," Tish whined. "I'm telling you, my dogs are barking!"

"Oh, stop," Louise said. "You've gone to dances lots of times before. You must be used to this by now. You're not even wearing very high heels!"

"It's not the shoes," Tish said. "It's that dead hoofer I got stuck with for the last two dances. He stepped all over my feet. And then he kept laughing. He didn't even apologize."

"He was probably too embarrassed to know what to say," Louise said.

"Aw, he was a creep," Tish said.

Both of her sisters stopped walking and turned to stare at her.

"Well, it's true. Oh, I know how you two feel. At first when you go to these dances, you think every guy in there is wonderful. Because you feel sorry for them, where they have to go and what they have to do. But after a while you realize that just because a guy's a soldier it doesn't mean he's a peach. Some of them are ugly on the outside, and some of them are ugly on the inside, and some of them are both."

"Tish!" Louise cried.

"It's true! Most of them are good guys, but some are drips! I noticed you only danced with handsome men, Louise. And Kitty stayed with the same guy the whole night! In fact, I'm going to tell Julian, and let's just see what he thinks about that."

"Good luck finding out anything from him," Kitty said. She'd gotten only one letter from Julian so far, and he hadn't said much—he'd said so little, in fact, that Kitty had the letter memorized: *Hi de ho, doll. All things considered, I'd rather be golfing. Off the rattler and onto the ship, off the ship and straight into hell. But don't worry about me; now that Michael and I have joined the party, licking these goons will be eggs in the coffee. It's going to take some time, though—a long time, I'm afraid. Well, kid, I've got to drift. More later. Love, Julian.*

It would take a long time, he'd said. How did he know? What was happening that he couldn't talk about? Of course, none of the men could talk about the specifics of what was going on over there, everyone knew that, and if you ever forgot, there'd be some gigantic face on a poster with her finger to her lips, warning you not to let any secrets fall into enemy hands. There was one poster of a drowning sailor, the caption at the bottom saying SOMEBODY TALKED! Oh, that was a terrible one. The sailor was a handsome blond man, and the sea was so dark and threatening. Another poster showed a motherly woman in an apron over the caption WANTED FOR MURDER. She'd blabbed to the enemy, and now look.

Sometimes, although she never told anyone, Kitty felt weary of it all. What enemies? Where were they? In line at the supermarket? Behind her in the movies? At a desk next to her at work? And what was the use of having plane spotters in Chicago? "Nobody knows how far they could fly in," her father had said, but he didn't fool Kitty—he didn't think for a moment that Chicago was in danger of being bombed. Still, he did his part as an air-raid warden. For how could you ever know for certain? So much evil was suddenly in the world, so many impossible things happening. She wished she could grab Adolf Hitler by his ear and say, "*Stop that!*"

Love, Julian had said, signing off. He'd said the word. Well, written it. He'd never done that before. She'd been with Julian a long time; certain things were assumed, but they were never said. Kitty was certainly not going to write "I love you" first, and neither was Julian, apparently. She'd asked Louise once if Michael ever told her he loved her, and Louise had said, "Well, of course! Doesn't Julian tell you?" And Kitty had said yes, he did. But not in those words. "He has to say *those* words," Louise had said.

Kitty had traced the word Julian had written with her fingers, thrilled and uneasy both. What did it mean, really? What was he thinking when he wrote it? How did he look? Was he alone? Was he smiling? Was his face serious? What did love really mean, anyway? Of course, she loved Julian, too, but what did it *mean*?

Kitty pulled the ugly cardigan more tightly around her. Now she was glad to have it. What had started out as a mild May evening had turned chilly.

Tish was still going on about squealing on her. "That's the first letter I'm going to write tonight," she said. "I'm going to tell Julian how you danced every dance with a handsome stranger."

"Go ahead," Kitty said. "I can never think what to say to him, anyway."

Louise looked over at her, frowning. "Really?"

The streetcar came then, and Kitty, grateful for the distraction, positioned herself to board. "Window seat, I called it first," she said. But there were no window seats. The car was packed, as usual. Servicemen were all over Chicago, all the time. There were sailors in training at Great Lakes Naval Training Center, pilots from the Glenview Naval Air

Station, inductees going through basic training at the newly enlarged Fort Sheridan, naval midshipmen training at Northwestern. Other area universities trained for specialty jobs: language, electronics, weather forecasting—even spying, it was rumored. Tish sat down next to a smiling sailor. Kitty and Louise squeezed into a bench seat at the back. "Did you see the dimples on that guy Tish sat by?" Kitty whispered. Louise nodded gravely, then whispered back, "Did you see his muscles?"

"Not on my watch, baby!" one of the sailors yelled to a woman riding with him. She giggled loudly, then kissed him, one hand around his neck, one holding on to her hat. Those sailors. They were the ones. They had the worst reputations. Kitty leaned forward, trying to see what the boy looked like. But then a thought of Julian came to her, and she felt how much she missed him. It was as though the center of herself suddenly became a cavernous, empty place, full of whistling wind. She tightened her grip on her pocketbook. Oh, Julian. Tonight, at least, she'd have something to write about. She'd tell him about the dance, about how Louise's friend Dorothy had sung so beautifully and in fact had told them later that she was on her way to New York City to audition for a Broadway play in which Jeanette MacDonald had practically guaranteed her a part. Although that might make him feel bad, to say she'd been to a dance. Better not mention that. She'd tell him Tommy had given away his Lionel trains for the metal drive and Frank had wanted to get mad at him but then couldn't. She'd say that her mother had made stuffed green peppers using SPAM and her father hadn't even known. And . . . what else? What else?

KITTY SAT CHEWING HER LIPS at the kitchen table while Tish rushed through letters to her now four men, and Louise filled page after page (front and back!) with her small, exceptionally neat script—in school, Louise always won awards for penmanship.

Kitty looked down at her paper, where thus far she had written three paragraphs. Oh, she had the guidelines beside her—"What the Boys Want to Know," the pamphlet was called. You were supposed to talk about them first, then say the family was fine and very busy with everyone trying to help with the war effort. If you had children, you were supposed to talk about them; then you gave a report on relatives and friends. ("Anyone get married?" the pamphlet helpfully suggested, and Kitty stared blackly at the question.) "Pets always make good reading," the pamphlet said, but her family didn't have any pets. "What's doing in town?" Well, obviously whoever wrote the pamphlet didn't live in Chicago—how would she even begin to answer such a question? Finally, the pamphlet suggested that she end her letter with a "personal message." How personal could a girl get when she didn't really know where she stood?

Kitty stared at her pen, checked the level in the Skrip black ink bottle, tightened a pin curl at the base of her neck. She stared out the window, then at the wall. She tried to see what Louise was writing, but her sister caught her and moved her pages away. Kitty watched her, writing and writing and writing with a little smile on her face. What was there to go *on* about this way?

"What are you saying right now?" Kitty asked, and Louise looked up at her. "It's personal."

"What about you, Tish?" Kitty said.

"Mine's personal, too," Tish said and kept right on scribbling.

"But . . . personal about what?" Kitty said.

Now Tish did look up. "You gotta make 'em feel better," she said. She raised an eyebrow. "You know? You gotta get their minds off the war!"

"But what are you *saying* to get their minds off the war?" Kitty asked, and Tish said loudly, "You've got the guidelines right there! I'm not telling you what I wrote! Make up your own letter!"

From the parlor came their mother's warning voice. "*Girls . . .*"

Kitty tapped her pen against her paper and Louise looked up, irritated. "Oh, for Pete's sake, tell him how you want to get a cat, or how fierce that thunderstorm was, or how much you liked some movie or book. Say what you'll do when he comes home. Gosh, Kitty, I never knew you were so . . . so . . ."

"So what?" Kitty asked. "You never knew I was so what?"

"Dumb," Tish said, and Louise laughed and said, "No, not dumb! Just . . ." She shrugged. "I don't know. I'm just surprised, that's all. I mean, you and Julian! Anybody would think you would have tons to say to him!"

"We do better in person," Kitty said. And she started a new paragraph about how annoying her sisters were. Yes. Julian used to laugh when she did that. But . . . She put down her pen and picked at a cuticle. Maybe it would be bad to say that now. Maybe she shouldn't complain about anything. Maybe he needed to hear only happy things. Had she already told him the salvage joke about how all the housewives were bringing in their fat cans, ha ha? She was pretty sure she had. In fact, now that she thought of it, she remembered it was Julian who had told it to her.

Kitty wound a lock of hair around her finger and sniffed at it. That Kreml shampoo smelled good; Margie Hennessey, who'd told her about it, was right. Margie said the John Robert Powers models used Kreml, and they always married millionaires. Kitty wrote, *Margie Hennessey says hi,* then shifted her eyes to the kitchen clock. Had it not moved at all since she last looked? She went over and smacked it.

"What are you *doing*?" Louise asked.

"The doggone clock's broken," Kitty said. But it wasn't. She came back to the table, flung herself into her chair, and crossed her arms tightly over her chest. "Well, fine, I can't think of a single thing more to say! Nothing ever happens here! It's all happening there! And I've gotten only one letter from him! There's nothing to respond to!"

Neither of her sisters dignified this outburst with an answer. Kitty leaned back and crossed one leg over the other. Swung it. Then she remembered something, and she sat up and bent over her page to write, *Susie Anderson left work to go and live with her aunt in North Carolina. She's painting airplanes. Can you imagine? She paints them white on the underbelly, blue on the sides, and green on the top. So if you look from underneath they look like clouds, and from the side they look like sky and from above they look like*—Here she stopped to think. What was it Susie had written to Maureen?—*like water!* she wrote, and then wondered if that was right. And wait—was it North Carolina or South Carolina? Oh, Julian wouldn't care, and anyway he surely already knew all about camouflage techniques. *I wish Ma and Pop would let me get a defense job,* she wrote. But she'd told him that before. So she added, *I still do wish that.* Then she sat lightly tapping her heel against the floor and staring into space while her sisters' pens scratched and scratched and scratched away.

They heard footsteps coming down the stairs, and their mother appeared in the kitchen to wash out her teacup. "Hey, Ma," Kitty said. "What should I write to Julian?"

"I'm sure I wouldn't know," Margaret said and turned to look over her glasses at Kitty.

"Well, if Pop were overseas and you were writing to him, what would you say?"

"I'd ask him how we were able to produce such an unimaginative daughter. Now, listen, girls. Write for another fifteen minutes, and then it's lights-out. I'm going to need some help housecleaning tomorrow. I can't go to Red Cross meetings twice a week and keep up with all the housework I used to do." Louise and Tish sped up their writing. Kitty sighed and rubbed at the back of her neck. She wrote, *Ma's busy with her Red Cross training. Last week, they laid someone out on the table to pretend she was wounded and suffering from shock, and Ma asked the other women what should be done next. One of them said, "Offer him a book." I swear it's true!* Kitty read over what she'd written, then wondered if it was wise to be talking about being wounded. Maybe it would frighten Julian. Maybe it was bad luck. She thought of what she might say to counteract what she'd written. Nothing came to her. Nothing. And look at the white space still at the bottom of her page. Kitty grabbed Tish's lipstick, smeared some on her mouth, and made two big kiss marks on her letter. "*My* lipstick," Tish said, but she didn't look up.

Oh, the kiss marks were a wonderful idea. They took up at least four lines. *With all my heart,* Kitty wrote next and signed off. In the blank space below, she drew a large heart. Surrounded by lace. Punctured by a large arrow. That took up six lines, and it brought her to the end of the page. Done.

Happily, she folded her page and put them into the envelope. She addressed the envelope with the strange Army address, licked the stamp, affixed it, and pounded it with her fist so that it wouldn't fall off. Wouldn't that just be the topper?

AFTER HER SISTERS FELL ASLEEP, Kitty lay thinking of Hank, the man she'd danced with. It wasn't until they were sleeping that she'd felt safe thinking of him—she didn't want things to come popping out of her mouth and set her sisters off asking ten thousand questions. She didn't know quite what to make of him. He'd told her such odd things, things very much out of keeping with what everyone else was saying about the war; but it was all so compelling and completely sensible. He'd told her about a young man who'd booed an image of FDR on a newsreel at the movies. The man had been beaten up by the other men around him and fined two hundred dollars in court. But wasn't freedom of speech one of the things we were fighting for? And the Japanese Americans— should such a violation of their rights be occurring here in the land of the free and the home of the brave?

A few months after Pearl Harbor, Hank had seen a crowd of Japanese Americans waiting to board a train that would take them to internment camps. One of them had been a little girl, no more than four years of age, who sat on top of a suitcase tightly clutching a child's purse. Huge, overstuffed duffel bags full of her family's belongings surrounded her. She had an apple in her hand, but she wasn't eating it; instead, she stared into space, looking frightened and sorrowful. He'd not been able to get the image out of his mind. "Know what I kept thinking?" he'd said to Kitty. "I kept wondering, what had she saved to carry in that little purse?"

On the newsreels, they made it seem as though the Japanese American evacuation was a vacation. But when Kitty told Hank that, he had said, "Some vacation. The day after Pearl Harbor, the Japanese Americans had their funds frozen and banks refused to cash their checks. Mailmen wouldn't deliver their mail and the milkmen and grocers wouldn't serve them, either. Insurance companies canceled their policies. They lost their jobs. And after Walter Lippmann's column—you know about that column, don't you?"

Kitty didn't. She'd made a sound that could have been interpreted as a yes and promised herself to read the paper cover to cover from now on.

Hank had gone on. "Well, after that column, 110,000 people, the entire Japanese community of the West, were driven from their homes. They had forty-eight hours to dispose of everything—their houses, their businesses, all their furniture. And their 'vacation' was to go to a barren camp surrounded by barbed wire."

Kitty hadn't known what to say. It seemed impossible. So she'd said that, and Hank had said yes, but it had happened. He had been an isolationist and a member of America First up until Pearl Harbor, because he didn't believe in war as an answer in supposedly civilized times. After December 7, he'd become a conscientious objector, doing public service as an orderly in a hospital. Then, because of an injured soldier he had cared for there, he'd changed his mind and enlisted. Why? Kitty had asked. What had happened to make him change his mind? He'd looked at her, contemplating whether or not to answer. Then he'd smiled and said he'd tell her another time, in a letter, how about that? How about if they corresponded?

He was an Army flier who had just completed training for aerial reconnaissance. These men dropped no bombs—they simply took photographs. He told her they flew at great heights and at great speeds, often in deepest night, and they flew completely unarmed. One reason was that the cameras added so much weight; another was the assumption that if a pilot had guns on his plane, he might want to fight back instead of quickly returning to base with those valuable photos.

Hank was on his way overseas. Overseas where? Kitty had asked. He'd leaned in toward her and said in a low voice, "Now, you know I can't tell you that." And Kitty had felt a zipperlike thrill run up her back, then felt immediately guilty. But what was a girl to do? It was a completely natural reaction. Although it had been only a few weeks, it felt like an eternity since a man's face had come near hers.

Mostly, Kitty had just liked talking to Hank. And she'd given him her address. Oh, he knew she was practically engaged—she'd told him all about Julian. She'd told him how they met, how they wanted four children: two boys and two girls. She'd told him about Frank and Margaret and her brothers; and she had pointed out her sisters, about whom he'd said, "Wow! Beautiful girls!" He hadn't said she was pretty, and she'd rather liked that he hadn't. She'd liked, too, the light way he put his hand on her back when they waltzed to the slow ones, the way he listened so intently to what she said, not only listened but asked questions in order to understand better. Henry was his name, but he preferred Hank in the same way that she preferred Kitty to Katherine. "I always think I'm in trouble if someone calls me Henry," he'd told her. "Me, too," she'd said, and then quickly added, "Well, I mean when they call me Katherine, not Henry!" She'd flushed at the foolishness of that remark; of course he knew that! But Hank had only said, "And if they call you by all three names, you're really in for it!" He had asked what her middle name was, and she had told him it was Grace; his, he'd said, was Carter, after his maternal grandfather. Kitty thought it was strange, telling a man you'd just met your middle name. In some ways it felt more intimate than a kiss.

Henry Carter Cunningham III, although about this last he'd said, "Not *that* kind of 'the Third.' I'm afraid my circumstances might best be described as modest. More dreams than dollars are generated in my family." Hank Cunningham, from San Francisco, California. Kitty covered her mouth and held back a laugh, and for the life of her, she didn't know why.

She closed her eyes and thought about Julian. Where was he, right now? What was he doing? Playing cards? Dodging bullets? Eating rehy-drated pears? When would she hear from him again? What if he . . . ? Her stomach dropped and her hands grew cold. You never knew. You never heard right away. And sometimes the information you got was false. She'd heard about a family who'd been told their soldier was dead when he was just as alive as he could be! She'd also heard about a guy who was said to have sustained a "minor injury," but he died from a mas-sive head wound.

Here she'd been complaining about not hearing from Julian, and he might not be able to write! How would she know? She felt like biting her knuckles, yanking at her hair. But what good would that do? She needed to be strong for him. Cheerful. She needed to be less selfish and to try much harder when she wrote to him. Surely she could do better than she had. She was never much of a writer—or a reader, for that matter—as Louise was. Even Tish liked reading a lot better than Kitty. Well, face it; everyone in the family liked reading better than Kitty. Even Billy liked his books. *"Geronimoooo!"* he'd yell, running through the house with one of his books about, well, Geronimo. But Kitty was not a reader. She was a *doer*—the kind of person books were written about, she thought, privately consoling herself.

She wondered what Louise's letters to Michael were like. And his to her. Already, Louise had gotten four. The first one was practically a novel. Kitty knew where Louise kept those letters—in her underwear drawer. If Kitty could read one, she would be better able to write to Ju-lian. She'd know the tone she should take, the things Julian might be longing to hear. Not that Julian and Michael were that much alike, but still . . .

"Louise?" she whispered to the still form beside her. Nothing. She sat up and looked at Tish, sprawled out at the bottom of the bed. "Tish?" Again, nothing. Slowly, she pulled back the covers, got out of bed, put on her robe, and tiptoed over to the bureau. Holding her breath, she soundlessly slid open the drawer and reached under a pile of Louise's slips. There. A pack of letters, a length of blue velvet ribbon holding them together. She removed the letter on top and slipped it into her pocket, closed the drawer, and tiptoed down the hall to the bathroom. She locked the door, sat on the lid of the toilet, and pulled the onionskin pages from the envelope. She reminded herself to put the letter back exactly as she'd found it—the folded crease toward the bottom of the envelope. She hesitated for a moment, shame burning at the edges of her stomach. This was such an invasion of privacy! Really, if she were going to do this, she should read Tish's letters. But those weren't real relationships that Tish had. They were flirtations, distractions. Good for the men's morale, Kitty agreed, but surely lacking the kind of thing that might inspire her to write more easily to Julian. Louise would never know Kitty had done this, and she would be glad if Kitty were better able to write Julian; she and Julian liked each other very much. And anyway, hadn't Kitty readily shown Louise the letter Julian had sent? Fair was fair. She tucked her hair behind her ears, opened the pages and started to read, then stopped when she heard a knock on the door.

Hastily, she shoved the pages back into the envelope, the envelope into her robe pocket. "Yes?" she said.

"Is that you, then, Kitty?" Her father.

"Yes, Pa."

"Well, hurry it up, girl, I've got a bit of an emergency."

Kitty opened the door. Here and there, her father's hair stood on end, as though he were being selectively electrocuted. His face was creased with elongated Xs, and his pajamas had shifted sideways. No one looked more comical rising from sleep than Frank Heaney. "Here's our Tom, come home after his nightly catfight," their mother said every morning. "'Tis our own Clark Gable," their father always answered.

"I can let you go first," Kitty told him.

"God love you. Ben Macalister, our venerable block captain, stopped over tonight. If that man were invited to a wedding, he'd stay for the christening. And me drinking the water and drinking the water just to stay awake." He squeezed past her and quickly closed the door.

Out in the hall, Kitty rubbed her fingers along the rough edge of the envelope in her pocket. Was this divine intervention? Was she being given a chance to reconsider her imminent misdeed? She leaned against the wall and stared up at the ceiling, debating. In the corner, she saw a huge spiderweb, the owner and occupant hanging heavy in the center. Tomorrow, she'd clean it away, although she was frightened to death of spiders. Penance. And here came the sound of the chain being pulled and the toilet flushing. Yes. God had made a deal with her. *Go ahead in there and read it, now that we understand each other.*

Frank came out of the bathroom and kissed her cheek as he passed by. "Night, darlin'. Give my regards to the wee ones." The fairies, he meant; those beautiful gossamer creatures he used to tell his children would visit at night, but only after they fell asleep. Which made them struggle to stay awake, of course, hopeful of seeing one. Only in the last year or so had Binks abandoned sleeping with a Mason jar by his bed.

"Night, Pa," she said, innocent as an angel. Really, she could be an actress. She wasn't the only one who said so.

Seated again on the toilet lid, she pulled out the letter and read.

26 April 1943
Somewhere in England

Dearest Louise,

I knew I would miss you like bing, of course, but the severity of my longing is taking me a bit by surprise—my heart is quite literally heavy all the time. Guess I'm homesick in a big way: I miss you and my parents and you and steak and you and fresh fruit and you and the baseball games with the gang and you and Lake Michigan and you and movies and you and you and you! (Remember how I used to tell my English students to avoid redundancy? Never mind—don't you know there's a war on?)

The train ride was largely uneventful—extremely crowded, of course, and boisterously loud at some times, then strangely silent at others. A lot of guys lost inside their heads, I imagine, wondering what their fates would be, myself included. A couple of times, waking up disoriented from a nodding-off kind of nap, I came close to regretting the day that Julian and I decided to enlist together. (Honestly, we were not drunk!) But as I tried to explain before, there are some things I just have to do. I want to feel at the end of this thing that I did my part, and not by staying at a job deemed essential to the war effort. I know it doesn't make sense to you, Louise, but I want to be on the front lines, with the infantry. If I'm going to be in this thing, then let me be in it. You can have all the air and sea support imaginable, but in the end a war is lost or won because of the foot soldier. I have a great deal of admiration for the Marines fighting at Wake Island who were being pounded by the Japs in '41. Do you remember that story? How when the Navy was finally able to get through to them and asked if they wanted anything, they said, "Yeah, more Japs!"? I confess I am not so interested in dying in battle as they seem to be (some Marine sergeant is said to have bellowed to his badly wounded platoon, "C'mon, you sons of bitches, do you want to live forever?"), but they do have my utmost respect.

Anyway, I got off the train at the New York Port of Embarkation and onto a huge ocean liner, painted a cheerless gray. It was something being out in the middle of the ocean, knowing that here, there, or anywhere could be submarines with entirely unfriendly intentions. I spent plenty of hours with my nose in my Service Bible!

We docked at a port that's about a day's train travel from where I am now. We were given a lunch for the train ride, and in it was a pie. Well, I saved it for dessert, of course. Turned out to be meat pie, all cold and doughy—not the flaky apple and cinnamon concoction I was so looking forward to. I ate the thing for the sake of the person who so kindly made it, but it didn't go down easy. I guess the English are real bad cooks. One guy said the way they served cabbage was to cook it a long time in too much water with not enough salt, serve it lukewarm in too much water, and if you're lucky a caterpillar would be thrown in.

I share a barracks room with three other guys in my squad. It's about fourteen feet square, and it's stuffed full of equipment and clothes. We have one window that we black out every night when the sun starts setting. I'm the one up first every day to take down that grim reminder of what might happen to us during the night, and on mornings when the mist isn't too heavy, there are the spring buds to greet me. Hitler can't stop everything.

There are four bunks, two straight chairs, a fireplace, and a rickety old table that serves as a desk. On the walls are maps, greeting cards from home, and the usual assortment of cheesecake: Rita and Rosalind and Greer and Hedy and Betty and Marlene. But the most beautiful girl featured is y-o-u. One of my roommates, Ted Fletcher, spends an inordinate amount of time standing before you. "Those her real eyelashes?" he once asked, and I told him everything about you was real. Good thing he talks about his wife so much or I'd start to get jealous.

Our training is going well—sometimes it seems as though we're really in combat. I may be using my antitank gun against mock tanks, but the explosives they plant in the field to get us used to shell fire are real enough. I know exactly when to give the "commence firing" command, and I've become a whiz at digging foxholes—so in case I don't stop a tank it can't roll over me. Sometimes when I dig, I find a piece of bone from the grave of some Roman soldier—I'm training on ground that's been fought on for over 1,900 years. It makes you think, Louise, about the nature of man and the inevitability of war. It makes you wonder. I lie on my bunk on these dark nights and think about all the men who battled on this ground and who kept their own silent counsel during other dark nights so very long ago. I wonder if they lay there thinking about the women they loved. If they thought of their families and the life they lived before they came to fight. If they prayed or wept or cried out. I hope that they believed in what they were doing, that the cost was worth the price they paid.

But listen, hon, I don't want you to worry about me. Nothing's going to hurt me. I'm as well trained as I could possibly be, and I'm in the best shape of my life. On days we don't practice battles, we go on twenty-five-to thirty-mile hikes through the countryside with sixty-pound packs on our backs. Little kids come out to beg from us, and we give them pennies and gum; they just love that gum.

I've seen some beautiful architecture in London. I've been to some pubs to play darts and argue with these blokes about who's got the better country, but a lot of times I don't go into town on leave—I'd rather stay here and read, or write to you. I want to save seeing London so that I can do it with you, in better times.

If I'm honest, I must admit I'm frightened of the real action to come— and I think it will be coming soon—but I'm also eager to get going. The sooner we fight, the sooner we'll win, and with the U.S. now in this war, it will be won. And then I can come home to you. What a sweet word "home" is; it has always been a sweet word to me, but never more so than now.

Take care of yourself, darling, and remember every day how very much I love you. It's for you that I do everything; I can't wait to be with you and start our married life. Sometimes I think of my coming through the door into the house where we live with our little ones, and it's all I can do not to cry. We will be so happy together, Louise. We were truly meant for each other. Here's a kiss to your mouth, and one behind your ear, and one everywhere else on your beautiful face, and   Well. I'd better stop here. I'd better go and take a walk, despite the rain. Gosh, it rains a lot here. I'll write more as soon as I can.

All my love,
Michael

P.S. *Say, sweetheart, if you get a chance, go and see my mother, will you? She's not been well and could use the company. Assure her that I'm fine now and will continue to be— Dad says she's got an eye permanently trained on the front walk, fearful of the telegram. If anyone can take her mind off things, you can.*

Kitty swallowed. Folded the pages tenderly. Put them back into the envelope. Used the toilet, as long as she was there. Washed her hands and looked at herself in the mirror. She was a black-haired girl who didn't know anything. A girl who'd betrayed her sister, never mind that spiderweb she'd promised God to clean away tomorrow. How could God have any time to listen to her now? Prayers must be shooting up to Him as fast and furious as a Fourth of July fireworks finale, times a million. Times a billion. More.

She had a different idea for penance. Monday, during her lunch hour, she'd run over to Field's and put a Montgomery beret on layaway for Louise—her sister loved those hats and she'd look fine in it. Well, all the sisters would. But Louise would wear it first, and Kitty would take her picture in it, and Louise could send the picture to Michael. As for now, she'd put the letter back in the drawer, then wake up Louise and give her the ring. She'd bring her back to the bathroom for a private ceremony.

KITTY CREPT INTO THE BEDROOM and successfully replaced the letter. She breathed out a quiet sigh of relief, then pulled open her own drawer. She put the ring box in her pocket, tiptoed across the room, and stood next to her sleeping sister. "Hey?" she whispered. "Louise?" She tapped her on the shoulder and Louise started, then cried out.

"*Shhhhh!*" Kitty motioned for her sister to follow her.

"What do you want?" Louise whispered. "I'm *tired*! Tell me tomorrow."

Kitty motioned more emphatically for Louise to come with her.

"Oh, all right!" Louise sat up and pushed her feet into her slippers. She pulled her robe off the chair and put it on, tying it neatly at the side of her waist. Kitty crossed her arms, clamped her teeth together, and waited. No point in trying to rush her. Louise had to get dressed for everything. Even as young girls in the middle of summer, they could never just fly out of the house barefoot and carefree—Louise would need to put on her shoes, and the laces had to be tied evenly. She would have to put bows at the bottoms of her braids. She'd have to step out onto the porch and test the weather to see if she needed a sweater.

Tish was always ready for action—she'd fly out of the house bare naked—but she was the baby. Nobody wanted the baby sister along, but there she always was. Sometimes Kitty and Louise, weary of caring for Tish, were cruel to her. As seven- and five-year-olds, they had taken scissors to Tish's curls as she lay sleeping, for they believed Tish's bright blond hair, so different from their own, was being too much admired. The wagon they were pulling her in would "accidentally" overturn. They would tell her they were playing hide-and-go-seek outside, then sneak inside the house to escape her, giggling as they watched Tish standing beneath the towering elm that was home base, calling around the thumb in her mouth, "I give *up,* now! Come *in,* now. Alley, alley in fwee!" Why must you treat her so? Ma would ask. She's your baby sister! And Kitty and Louise would look at each other and struggle to keep from laughing. Exactly. She was a stupid *baby.*

And now here came that baby sister's voice, thick with sleep. "What are you guys doing? What's the matter?"

"Nothing," Kitty said. "Go back to sleep."

Tish rose up on one elbow, blinked, and then let her head fall heavily back onto her pillow. "Well, *stop* it, then," she mumbled.

Kitty led Louise to the bathroom, pulled her in, and locked the door behind them. Louise, her eyes squinting in the bright light, said, "What is it? Do you have cramps?"

"There's something I need to give you," Kitty said.

Louise sighed. *"Now?"*

There was a knock on the door, and here came Tish's voice. "Hey? What's going on, you guys? Did something happen?" Her voice rose. "Are we being *attacked?*"

Kitty yanked the door open a crack. "Shhhhhhhhh! No, we're not being attacked! Go back to bed."

Tish pushed the door open and looked at Louise. "What's going on?"

Louise shrugged. *"I* don't know."

"Go back to bed!" Kitty said, and Tish crossed her arms. No.

Kitty sighed and grabbed Tish's arm, pulling her into the bathroom.

Might as well let her be here, too. There was no pushing around this baby sister anymore.

Again, Kitty locked the door, then turned to face her sisters. "I have something for Louise from Julian. Well, it's from Michael, but it's from Julian."

"What are you *talking* about?" Louise asked.

Kitty pulled the velvet box out of her pocket, and Louise's hands flew to her mouth. "No," she whispered.

"Yes," Kitty said. "Take it."

Louise shook her head. "No."

"For cripes' sake, *take* it!" Tish said.

Slowly, Louise reached for the box and opened it. Tish rushed to her side and began to squeal. "You got it! You got it!"

Louise stared in happy disbelief. "It's so *beautiful*," she said, and Kitty felt ashamed, remembering her own reaction to such a small stone.

"Put it on!" Tish said.

"I . . ." Louise began to laugh. "Gosh, I'm shaking!"

"I'll put it on you," Tish said. "Want me to put it on you? I'll pretend to be Michael. I'll even kiss you! Through a towel, though."

"Tish!" Kitty said. "Will you stop? Let her do it!"

Louise nodded, took in a breath, and pulled the ring from the box. She kissed it, then slid it onto her finger, where it fit perfectly. *Cinderella,* Kitty thought, instinctively clenching her own left hand into a fist. Where did Louise get such small fingers? Why were Kitty's so large?

Louise turned her hand this way and that, watching the diamond catch the light. Then, holding it out to show her sisters, she burst into tears. And her sisters followed suit. They embraced one another, laughing and crying.

Another knock at door.

The sisters sprang apart, and Kitty opened the door. Tommy looked up at her, his face troubled. "What's wrong?" he asked. "Who's crying?"

And now here came their parents marching quickly down the hall, Margaret's face determined and Frank's full of confusion.

"Who's hurt?" Margaret demanded. It was her Red Cross training coming through. In times past, Margaret would have been wringing her hands about a possible injury. Now she was ready to take over and manage the crisis. Kitty all but expected her mother to say, "Go and boil water, lots of it!" The knot in Margaret's hairnet had slid to the middle of her forehead, and her robe hung open; she tightened it now, distractedly but determinedly. As for their father, he'd apparently risen so quickly he'd forgotten both robe and slippers.

Louise pushed her way out of the bathroom and held up her hand, waving it around excitedly. "Look what I just got!"

Margaret grabbed her daughter's hand and inspected the ring. "Ah, Louise. That's grand. 'Tis lovely." She looked up at her daughter. "But what do you mean, you just got it?"

"Kitty just gave it to me."

"Why did *she* give it to you?"

"Julian gave it to me," Kitty said.

"What the devil are you *talking* about?" Frank bellowed, and now here came Billy and Binks down the hall, pushing at each other in their haste to get there.

"Let's go downstairs and celebrate," Margaret said.

"What are we celebrating?" Billy asked. "Ma? What are we celebrating? *Ma!*"

But Margaret was already in the kitchen; they heard the banging of pots and pans.

Louise knelt before Binks and embraced him, then stood to hug the other brothers. "I have just gotten a ring. A diamond engagement ring!"

Billy's forehead crinkled. "But Kitty said it was from Julian. Are you engaged to Julian now? Boy, Michael's going to be mad!"

"But I like Michael," Tommy said, alarmed, and Binks began to cry, saying he liked Michael, too.

"For the love of God, will someone tell me what's going on here?" Frank said.

Kitty clapped her hands. "Listen to me! Everybody! Julian helped

Michael get a ring for Louise. It was a secret; it was left for me to pick up at the jeweler's so I could give it to her. I just now did."

"Well, what in the world are you doing giving it to her in the middle of the *night*?" Frank asked.

Kitty sighed loudly. "It was supposed to be *private*!"

"Sure, a family's no place for privacy!" Frank said, hiking up his pajama bottoms.

From downstairs came their mother's voice. "Come down for cocoa and toast, everyone! Spread with real butter, by God!"

"Make me a cup of real coffee, Margaret!" Frank bellowed.

"You'll be up all night!" she answered.

Frank looked at Louise, tears in his eyes. "And wouldn't I be anyway? With such grand news arriving?" He took her into his arms. "I've been living for the moment to say this: 'May the saddest day of your future together be no worse than the happiest day of your past.'" Over Louise's head, his eyes met Kitty's. She looked away, then back at him. She, too, had thought she'd be first. But maybe her mother was right in saying that even as Billy, the oldest boy, was the least mature of the sons, she was the "youngest" of the daughters.

"Louise?" Billy said.

She stepped away from her father. "Yes?"

"I just wanted to say, 'As you slide down the banister of life, may the splinters never point in the wrong direction.'" He cleared his throat and reached out to shake her hand. Louise shook it solemnly. And then, as their mother yelled up at all of them that this was the last time she was calling or she'd eat every last bite herself, Louise said to Billy, "Race you downstairs?" He grinned.

"Wait, Louise, I have one!" Binks said. "I have one, too!" And he told her, "A turkey never voted for an early Thanksgiving."

"Ah," Louise said. "Well, thank you very much, Binks."

And then she and Billy raced for the kitchen, Binks and Tommy following close behind.

Frank held out his elbows for Kitty and Tish, and they moved slowly downstairs together. These were the steps that Louise would walk down with her father when she married Michael. Apparently Tish was thinking the same thing, for she began humming the Wedding March. Kitty broke loose to chase after her brothers. "I'll beat you all!" she cried.

AT THREE A.M., THE SISTERS WERE STILL AWAKE, too excited to sleep. They lay whispering to one another, Louise at the foot of the bed, Kitty and Tish at the head. Tish told Louise, "Now you'll have to do it, and you'll see what it feels like."

Louise laughed. "It's not a question of have to. I want to!"

"You do?" Tish asked. "You want his thing in you?"

"Of course!"

"Ew," Kitty said, yawning.

"He'll be my husband. I love him. Sex is part of love."

Tish sat up. "See? They just say that to make you feel better. But it really hurts. I know that for a fact."

"How do *you* know?" Kitty asked. She sat up; then Louise did, too.

"Because I heard *all about it,* that's how." Tish crossed her legs Indian-style and began picking at a toenail.

"Stop that!" Kitty said. "If I find another one of your toenails in this bed, I'm going to show it to every guy you meet at the next dance. I mean it. I'll carry it around in a little box like a science exhibit. Your creepy old toenail with a sign pinned next to it saying, 'This came from Tish Heaney.'"

Tish shrugged. "I don't care. They'll think it's cute. They think everything about me is cute."

"No they don't," Kitty said, disgusted.

Louise said, "Hey? How *do* you know it hurts, Tish?"

"Aw, don't work yourself into a tizzy, Louise; I'm no chippie. But I know some girls who have done it. Unmarried ones, too."

"Shame on them," Louise said, automatically. It was Margaret, speaking out of her mouth. "They'll live to regret the day." Margaret again. But it was true! Men didn't marry girls like that. Why buy the cow when you got the milk free?

Tish shrugged. "It's different now. A lot of these guys you meet, they might never come home again. You might be the last thing they remember."

"That's it," Louise said. "I'm telling Ma not to let you go to those dances anymore. I saw what goes on! You're too young to go, anyway; you're supposed to be eighteen."

"Oh, those old buffaloes don't even look at your birth certificate. They don't care who they let in or keep out; they just want to get their names in the paper for being hostesses."

"It's not a good place for you to be, Tish."

Kitty crossed her arms and set her mouth in agreement.

"*I* don't do anything!" Tish said. "Wise up, guys! Would I tell you all this if I was doing it? I just talk to people, that's all. All kinds of people! I'm not a snob like you and Kitty."

"I'm not a snob!" Kitty said, but privately she wondered if she was, just a little.

"I talk to everyone I meet, and I find out a lot of things you guys would never imagine."

"Such as?" Louise asked.

"Such as . . ." Tish said. "Just a lot of things you would never, ever believe. *Ever.*"

"*What* things?" Louise said.

Tish leaned forward and spoke in a whisper they could hardly hear. "One girl told me she kissed it."

A horrified silence, and then Kitty said, "Kissed what?" just to be sure.

"*It!*" Tish said. "It started in France; those French girls, they'll do anything. They put their mouths right on the wang wang doodle."

Louise began laughing, but Kitty grew unaccountably angry and whispered to Tish, "You stop your filthy lying! I can't believe those words came out of you! Wash your mouth out! That's a mortal sin!" Her fury grew as her sisters put their pillows over their faces, trying to smother their laughter.

Finally, when they had all settled down, Tish asked, "So . . . *do* you guys want to know about it? Regular sexual intercourse?"

Neither sister answered; the silence spoke for them.

"Okay," Tish said. "I'll tell you everything. *If* I get the green pleated skirt to wear to school on Monday. Agreed?"

"Okay," Louise said, and Kitty agreed glumly. She'd wanted to wear that skirt to work on Monday. Easy for Louise to give away clothing rights; her little first graders didn't notice what she wore unless it sparkled.

Tish stretched luxuriously, then said, "Well, first you have to get naked all the way—no nightgown, no nothing—and you have to let him lie on you and feel anything he wants. You have to touch him, too, even the testicombs."

"Testicles," Louise said.

"Right, that's what I mean. You have to touch them, too. Now. The boinger feels like a fat rubber stick, it gets real fat around, and the testicles feel like little water balloons. You touch them. And you have to rub the penis before he sticks it in. And when he sticks it in, it's really tight, and your skin gets all stretched, and it hurts bad."

"I feel like vomiting," Kitty said, but now she was laughing. She was excited, too, and she didn't know what to do about that. Remember the Holy Family, she told herself. The poor souls in purgatory. Remember, man, that thou art dust and unto dust shalt thou return. "All right, Tish," she said. "That's enough now."

"She can talk," Louise said. "I guess I need to know."

"You know!" Kitty said.

"Only from books, though," Louise said. And then, to Tish, "Okay, but so what does it *feel* like?"

"Kind of like if you pull on your earlobe *really* hard," Tish said. "It hurts bad, and also you bleed when your cherry pops."

"Hymen," Louise said.

"Who's that?" Tish asked.

"H-y-m-e-n," Louise said. "That's what the 'cherry' is called."

Tish contemplated this, then said, "That's disgusting. I like 'cherry' better. But anyway, it pops—"

"Breaks," Kitty said.

"Okay, that's it. I'm not telling any more if all you guys are going to do is interrupt me. And I'm not telling about childbirth, which I also know how that feels; it feels like an elephant going through the eye of the needle."

"It does not!" Louise said.

Tish punched her pillow and lay down. "Ha. Ask Ma, if you don't believe me. Now button it up; I'm going to sleep."

Louise and Kitty lay down, too, and the air grew dense with quiet. Then, "Hussy," Kitty whispered.

"Prude!" Tish shot back.

Kitty readjusted herself and closed her eyes. Then she opened them. Was she?

ON A SATURDAY MORNING IN LATE JUNE, Kitty was out in the back-yard pegging clothes on the line while, in a corner of their victory gar-den, Frank was explaining to Tommy that he needed to let the green peppers get bigger before he picked them. "Let them get to be as tall as your two fists put together, how's that?"

"Okay," Tommy said and put one of his fists on top of the other, then looked up at his father. "Like this?"

"Good lad, you're a quick learner."

Margaret leaned out of the back door and shook the crumbs from the breakfast tablecloth. "Frank! Arthur Waterstone's on the phone, wanting to know can you plane-spot for him tonight!"

"Jesus, Mary, and Joseph," Kitty heard her father mutter. "Not enough that the mail I deliver has gotten so much heavier or that I ful-fill my own duties in Civil Defense two times a week as well. No, I've got to do another man's job on top of it!" But he told Margaret, "Tell him I'll do it. But don't be too nice about it when you do."

"Tell him yourself if it's nasty you're wanting," Margaret said and then, to her daughter, "Kitty! What's the matter with you? Hang those shirts by their tails, not by their collars!"

Kitty looked at her father's white shirt before her. She had indeed hung it incorrectly; her mind was not on her work. She reversed the shirt, then thought again about what she was going to tell her family at Sunday dinner tomorrow. She had decided to apply for a defense job. She knew her parents would object, and she knew all the reasons why: it wasn't necessary; she made less money at her office job, but she made enough. It would ruin her hands. She would have to wear slacks. Women who took those kinds of jobs just weren't quite respectable, and the men they worked with at the factories knew it: she'd be fighting off their advances all the livelong day—or evening; as it happened, Kitty wanted the swing shift for the extra twelve cents an hour. A lot of the men didn't want you to do well; they resented your being there even though they knew the war effort needed you. She'd written to Julian about it, and he'd said he thought it was darby, so she was going to do it. If Julian had objected, that would have been one thing, but he hadn't. He'd said, Go for the kale; those jobs will disappear when the war is over and you'll be back to earning half as much.

She'd start with that: she'd say, Now, Julian and I have discussed this at length. . . . Really, she had discussed it more with Hank Cunningham, to whom she was writing more and more often; he seemed truly interested in anything she told him. He'd known some women who had built bombers in California; he'd also known some men who worked at the same factory. When she'd asked what he thought about women in defense jobs, he told her all the pros and cons he could without advising her about what to do. It seemed like a wash; she'd have to endure some hardships at a defense plant, but the benefits would make it worthwhile.

"Kitty?" Tommy said. "Can I ask you something?"

"'Course you can."

"Is war a sin?"

He was lying in the grass, poking idly at the undersides of the sheets hung U-shaped on the line. Since he was a toddler, he'd liked lying under the sheets this way. Kitty thought she understood; there was something peaceful about it; it made your mind slow down when you watched the breeze dance with those voluptuous pieces of fabric. She hung the last shirt—properly!—and then went to lie beside her brother. He turned to look at her. "Is it?"

He had grown older overnight, it seemed, or maybe it was just that, in the hustle and bustle of their family life, Kitty rarely had time to truly see anyone she lived with. All of a sudden, her mother's jaw had softened, or her father's hair had thinned, or Tish was emphatically less a teenager than a beautiful woman. Looking closely at Tommy now, Kitty saw that his face had lost its childish roundness; his cheekbones and jaw were those of a young man. Her heart lurched; she felt proud, somehow, but she felt sad, too. Where had little Tommy gone? Still, so much of him always remained. From the time he was a toddler, he'd been the same kind and earnest boy. He had extraordinary patience and a bottomless generosity that no one else in the family had or even understood—Frank sometimes referred to him as the milkman's son.

"I don't know if you could call war a sin, exactly," Kitty said. "It's more complicated than that." It *was* complicated. She'd been trying to pay more attention to the war news, confusing and depressing as it was. When Hank had asked if she'd read that article in the newspaper and she'd fibbed about it, she'd embarrassed herself. At least she wasn't alone; Hank had also told her that the men from other countries whom he'd met had told him they were surprised at the political naïveté of American soldiers, surprised, too, at their lack of philosophical inquiry.

"But killing someone is a sin," Tommy said. "And in war, they kill people. Every day!"

Kitty nodded. "Yes. They do." She supposed that Tommy's perception of the war was not all that much more sophisticated than Binks's: one man facing another and *Bang! Bang! You're dead!* She hoped Tommy wasn't aware that when Hitler blitzed England, he killed 43,000 civilians. The youngest was eleven hours old. She hoped—uselessly, she supposed—her brother would never know that.

She stared up into the sky. That pure blue. Those white, white clouds. The loopy flight of the bumblebees going about their business with no interference. She and Tommy were so lucky to be lying in the grass, alive and unafraid, their uniforms the soft cotton fabrics of summer. Newspapers full of terrible headlines landed on people's front porches every morning; but those people dressed, ate breakfast and went to work, went to visit friends, went out to eat and to dance and to church and to meetings and to weddings. The sound of bombs falling was heard only in movies, and people emerged from theaters yawning and went home to houses that were standing, to refrigerators that were full of food, to beds that had been made up with sweet-smelling linens—and to evening papers full of terrible headlines. Sometimes Kitty tried to imagine what the war would be like if women were fighting it. She didn't believe things would ever have gone so far as this. Vicious as women could be, things never would have gone so far as this. Women would . . . Well, they'd stop speaking to one another. That would translate into economic sanctions, she guessed. But bombing civilians? Never. Perhaps because women brought new life into the world, they felt more keenly the loss of it. She wondered what Hitler's mother would think of what he was doing. It didn't seem possible that he had a mother.

"I know it's hard to understand, honey," Kitty said. "But we are imperfect, we humans. We just have to try to fix our messes the best way we can. Sometimes that means we have to pick the lesser of two evils— you've heard that phrase, right?"

Tommy nodded.

"So," Kitty said, "we have to get rid of these guys because they want to do some really bad things to us."

"Do they all want to do that? Or just the leaders?"

"Hmmm. That's a very good question, Tommy. I guess sometimes people get brainwashed to believe what their leaders want them to believe."

"Are we brainwashed, too? By our leaders?"

Kitty rolled onto her side and looked at her brother. "I think there really is a right and a wrong side. And we're on the right side. But we have to pay a price to make the wrong side stop doing what it's doing."

"But what if . . . Do you worry about Julian and Michael?"

"Yes, I do. I worry about all the guys who are fighting." She spoke carefully then. "Do you, Tommy?" Had his face changed because he was losing weight? Was he taking all this too much to heart? It would be so like him to worry alone, not wanting to burden others with his fears. "Do you worry a lot about Julian and Michael?"

He shrugged. "I guess so. I sure *think* about stuff a lot." He smiled. "I got a letter from Julian yesterday."

"I know," Kitty said. "I saw it on the telephone table. I got one from him, too." Three pages! And another "Love." But nothing in the letter more intimate than a description of the Vienna sausages he'd had for lunch that day, and how the worst hash house in Chicago would taste like heaven to him now. How he'd finally beat the cardsharp he'd met in a game of poker, how exhausting the heat was during the day, how wearing iron (she figured he meant carrying guns) had become as natural as wearing underwear. How he hoped he didn't get zotzed and come home in a wooden kimono. She'd read this last to her sisters, laughing, but they hadn't laughed with her, and it had put her in a foul mood.

"Did Julian tell you he thinks his roommate is a nance?" Tommy asked.

Kitty laughed, astonished. "No! Did he tell you that?"

"Yeah," Tommy said. "He said he's really nice, but he's a nance."

"Well, Julian may just have been exaggerating a little. You know. Or kidding around a bit. You know Julian." What was he doing, saying such things to Tommy! She would have to find a way to admonish Julian without demoralizing him. It was tricky business, yelling at a guy who was fighting a war.

"It didn't seem like he was kidding," Tommy said. "He said the guy—Philip is his name—was real prissy. But he's nice, and he can play the banjo, and he gives Julian books to read."

"Gosh. He told you more than he told me!"

From around the side of the house came Binks, running at full tilt. He wore a colander as a helmet, he had clothespins in his hands that he was using for guns, and he was shooting at the sky. "You're done for now, you dirty Japs!" he yelled, and his friend Roland made a rat-a-tat sound and then whistled like a falling plane. How did boys do that?

Kitty wondered. How did they learn to make those sounds? It was in them from birth, she imagined, like a lust for lace in girls.

Louise had added a lacy slip to her hope chest the other day, a gift from one of the teachers when she heard about Louise's engagement. Kitty had watched her sister fold it carefully before putting it in the chest. She felt so far away from Louise now. As though she'd been living right next to someone who'd been hiding something dazzling beneath her blouse and now had triumphantly revealed it. In the days that followed Louise getting her ring, Kitty found herself trying to be like her sister. If she were like Louise, maybe she'd get a ring, too. But she wasn't like Louise. She was Kitty, up and down, front and back, through and through. Louise was going to start accumulating lacy things in her hope chest; Kitty was going to switch jobs and come home every night with dirt under her fingernails. Assuming she had any nails after she started working there.

From the upstairs window, Kitty heard Louise calling her name. She shaded her eyes against the sun and looked up. "What do you *want*?" She didn't want to be disturbed; she wanted to talk to Tommy some more. Funny to say about someone you saw every day, but she missed him.

"It's important," Louise said. "Can you come up here right away?"

Kitty sighed and got up. She brushed off her skirt and hiked the laundry basket onto her hip. One more load to hang, and then she was free. She was going to meet Dot Krug for a Coke at the drugstore, and then they were going to do each other's hair. Kitty had been planning on going to another servicemen's center dance with her sisters, but now she said, "Hey, Tommy, do you want to go to the movies with me tonight? Just you and me?"

His eyes widened. "Really?"

"You bet. And afterward, we'll ride out to Oak Park to Petersen's and you can have a turtle sundae."

"Wow!" He leaped up. "Wow!"

"Right after dinner," Kitty said.

And then, to the impatient Louise, who had continued calling her, "I'm coming! Jeez! Hold your horses!" What could be the problem? She was engaged, wasn't she?

Kitty raced up the stairs to the bedroom and flopped onto the bed. "Whew!" she said. "It's hotter out there than you think!"

"Why do you *always* have to race up the stairs?" Louise asked.

Kitty sat up. "What's eating you? I just *raced* up here because you were acting like it was some emergency or something!"

"You *always* run. You *never* walk. You should *walk*."

Kitty stared at her sister standing before the dresser, her back to her. She walked over and put her hand on Louise's shoulder. "Hey? What's wrong, Coots?"

Louise turned and started to speak, but then her eyes filled, and she wiped the tears away.

Kitty gasped. "Louise? Is it Michael? Did something happen to Michael?"

Louise shook her head, and Kitty breathed out, dizzy with relief. "Well, what, then?" Her mouth grew dry. "Julian? Did you hear something about *Julian*?"

"Michael's mother . . ." Louise said.

"Michael's mother told you? Is Julian hurt? Is he dead?"

"No, no!" Louise took her hand. "It's not Julian, it's Michael's mother. She's really sick, and she won't tell Michael. But I talked to the doctor, and I think she might be dying! I don't know what to do!"

"Why won't she tell Michael?"

"She thinks she'll improve, and even if she doesn't, she said it's better for him to just come back for her funeral than for him to worry about her. She said he has to keep his mind on his job."

"But what about his father? What does he say?"

"He says he wants to respect his wife's wishes. But Kitty, I don't think he knows what do to, either!"

Their mother appeared suddenly in their room; neither girl had heard her coming. "What's wrong?" she asked.

"Nothing," Louise said. And then she told her mother everything.

SUPPER WAS QUIETER THAN USUAL, with the news of Michael's mother seeming to hover above the table. Tommy barely ate a thing, and even Billy was affected, eating far less than he usually did. Margaret had said she would go and visit Mrs. O'Conner tomorrow on the pretext of consulting with her about dahlias—Michael's mother's gardening skills were legendary.

Kitty wanted to bring up working at a defense job, but now surely wasn't the time. And why did she have to ask anyway? Suppose the factory didn't hire her? Then she would have caused a ruckus for nothing. She'd apply after work tomorrow; then, if she was hired, she'd let her parents know. She wasn't a baby. She could make her own decisions. She stole a look at her father, gamely chewing his mystery meat. What a meal they'd have when the war was over! Kitty had envisioned it million times over: the thick steak, the mile-high apple pie, loaded with ice cream. When the war was over, when the war was over, sometimes it seemed that was all she heard. Everybody dreaming about how wonderful life would be when the boys came home. But when would they come home? How long could this war last? Some people thought only a few months more. Others were not so optimistic. Sally Kirk, a woman with whom Kitty worked, believed herself to have psychic abilities, and she was confident it wouldn't end for five years. But then, she had predicted she'd meet a tall man in the advertising business and become engaged last summer. So far, her ring finger was as empty as Kitty's.

Last night, Louise had read aloud from Michael's last letter: "*To those people who still wonder why we have to be in it, I would say it's because of our idealism. How can you look at what's going on and not step up to the plate? More than that, how could any American still be an isolationist after Pearl Harbor? Yes, I guess this war could last for years, maybe many years. It could change everything about the way we live, everything we're so comfortable with and used to. But there will eventually be a winner, and that winner has to be us and not Hitler. It has to be."*

"Dad?" Billy said. "My bicycle's worn out."

Frank nodded. "It sure is, son. But you know you can't have a new one."

"Cripes. I don't see why . . ." Billy pushed his food around on his plate.

Frank patted his mouth with his napkin and pushed himself back from the table. "Know what, Billy?"

"What." He stared glumly at his plate.

"There's nothing wrong with your wanting a new bike; sure it's only natural. I wish I could give it to you. But there aren't any new bikes to be had. That's because the metal's going to our soldiers. When you do without a bike, you're helping to put a gun in a man's hand. Understand? And when the house was kept a little cold last winter, why, that was nothing compared with the cold our boys suffer in their tents, or sleeping on the ground. I know it's hard to go without the food you want, but think about our soldiers with their lousy C rations, and how glad they'd be to get this . . ." He looked at Margaret. "What is this again, dear?"

"Ham croquettes."

"Ham, is it. Well, anyway, Billy, the point is, a fighting soldier rarely gets a hot meal of any kind. If one of our guys could sit at our table tonight, he'd think he was at the Palmer House itself."

"He wouldn't like the prune whip," Billy said.

"He'd love the prune whip!" Frank said, and Tish said, "I like prune whip. What's wrong with prune whip?"

"You're fighting the war, too, Billy," Frank said. "We all are. I can't think of anything more noble."

"What about the guys who are really there?" Billy asked. "The ones getting shot at and stuff."

"Well, of course, that's the noblest thing of all, and the thing I admire most. Those boys risking their lives every day, for us. Never knowing if—"

"May I be excused?" Louise asked.

"Of course," Margaret said.

Louise ran upstairs, and Margaret spoke quietly. "Can't you watch what you say, you two? Now you've gone and upset her." She shook her head. "'Tis a terrible thing, the kind of courtship young people have nowadays. Newly engaged and never even talking to each other. Writing all their hopes and dreams in letters instead of moonin' and spoonin' as they ought to be."

"What's moonin' and spoonin'?" asked Binks. He had moved from sitting to draping himself across the seat of the chair so that he could let his arms and head dangle. He liked to do this until he grew dizzy and his stomach hurt, and then he liked to complain about how dizzy he felt and how his stomach hurt him. "Ma? What's moonin' and spoonin'?" He slid off the chair and leaned against the table leg with his head in his hands. "Whoa! I'm dizzy!"

Margaret began clearing the table. "Never mind about things that needn't concern you. Let's clean up these dishes and get Louise down here for a lovely game of canasta."

"I'm taking Tommy to the movies," Kitty said.

"I want to come, too!" Binks said. "Can I come, too?"

"I'll take you another time," Kitty told him. "This time it's just me and Tommy."

"Yeah, but why can't I come, too?"

"Aren't you coming to the dance with us?" Tish asked Kitty. And then, to her parents, "I'll take Louise to a dance. That'll take her mind off things."

"Och, and what an angel you are, to make such a sacrifice," Margaret said.

Binks stood. "Kitty? Can I come, too?"

"I'm going over to Anthony's," Billy said.

"After you take the garbage out," Binks told him.

"I'm not taking the garbage out. It's your turn to take the garbage out. I'm going to Anthony's. I'll be home by nine or so."

"No 'or so,'" Margaret said. "On the dot."

Binks put his hand over his stomach. "I can't take the garbage out. I'm *sick!*"

"It's your turn!" Billy said. *"Ma!"*

"I'll just do it," Tommy said, and together his parents said, "No you won't!"

"I don't see that you have to spend so much time with that Anthony anyway," Frank said. "He's eighteen, way too old for you."

"I turn fourteen in two days."

"He's still too old for you."

"He tried to enlist yesterday," Billy said.

"And?" Now some admiration came into Frank's eyes; maybe Anthony was good for Billy after all.

"He has flat feet."

"Ah," Frank said. "Let me ask you something, Billy. What do you do with Anthony, anyway?"

"Nuttin'," Billy said. "I'll take the garbage out; then can I go?"

"May I," Margaret said.

Billy smiled. "Sure, you can come, Ma. Bring some prune whip."

"I GOT A NOTE FROM JULIAN, AND HONEY, *I guess it's okay what he did,*" Louise read aloud to her sisters. "*About the ring, I mean. I really wanted to put it on your finger myself, and at first I was sore about your seeing it without my being there, to say nothing about him paying for it. A guy likes to buy his girl a ring himself. But I'm going to pay him back the installments I was going to pay Munson's, so I guess it's all the same and you get to have it sooner. Gee, I sure hope you like it; I took a long enough time picking it out! And sometime I'm going to give you a bigger ring. And then I'm going to—*"

"Well, wait a minute," Louise said. She read to herself for a moment, smiling, then resumed reading from Michael's letter. "*I wonder what it's like where Julian is. Did you know the Pacific war covers nearly half the planet? From Panama to Singapore is 11,800 miles. It boggles the mind, doesn't it? Boggles and saddens it, I think. My love to you, my darling. My love, my all.*"

Louise put her letter down, and for a moment none of the girls spoke. Then Kitty said, "I don't know what else to say to Julian."

"Not this again," Tish said, sighing.

Kitty looked at the three-quarters of the page she'd filled. She was using the V-mail form, where the writing paper was also the envelope. V-mail was wonderful. It was free to service personnel, and it got preferential handling so that letters were no longer delayed—sometimes for months—because of the great volume of mail being sent. These form letters were photographed and transferred onto microfilm, and the film was taken to various destinations. At a processing center close to the addressee, the letter was printed onto photographic paper, then delivered.

V-mail was only one page long, and many people still used airmail so that they could write longer letters. But Kitty was struggling to fill this page. She could do it if she wrote big, but if she wrote big, Julian would know she was having trouble coming up with things to say, and that would make him feel bad.

"Tell him about the movie you saw tonight," Louise said.

Kitty sighed. "I did." The Paradise Theater had more than three thousand seats, and they'd all been filled, many of them with servicemen, who got to go for free. These boys got lots of things for free: tickets for ball games, boxing matches, and the theater. Rides on public transportation. All the food at the servicemen's center: hot dogs and sandwiches, cake and pie and cookies and candy. Hard-boiled eggs, cigarettes, coffee, and milk. Toilet supplies and canned goods and fresh produce donated from people's gardens. Kitty had read in the paper that, in a single evening, five hundred dozen doughnuts had been served. She felt proud of all Chicago was doing, but she wondered how it really felt to the boys: *Give us your life and we'll give you some doughnuts!* But maybe that was just her. The men seemed as though they truly appreciated everything. One USO center had gotten a letter from a grateful Marine stationed in Guadalcanal, saying, "You know what we talk about in our foxholes while the Jap bullets whiz over us? The Chicago servicemen's centers."

"Tell him about some stuff at work," Tish said, and again Kitty said, "I did." Helen Turnbull was p.g., she'd written. Rose Ellison had moved in with her sister. (Because her sister's husband had been killed, but she didn't tell Julian that.) She'd written that she was going to apply at Douglas Aircraft, so that she could help make the Skymaster. If they didn't hire her, she'd try the Studebaker Company, which made aircraft engines, the Pullman-Standard Car Manufacturing Company, which now made cargo planes, and International Harvester, which made torpedoes.

She wanted to ask Julian whether he was frightened, but she knew he'd never give her a straight answer. She wanted to ask him if he ever thought of her, but wasn't he supposed to tell her things like that automatically? Even Hank longingly alluded to their brief time together and how pleasant it had been for him, how he sure missed the scent of a nice perfume, the softness of a girl's skin. Kitty pressed down hard on her pen, and the tip snapped. "Darn it!"

"What's the *matter* with you?" Tish asked. She put down her pen—*she* was using *regular* stationery because she *never* ran out of things to say. Tonight she was writing to Warren Mueller, a banker's son from Albany, New York. Tall guy with curly black hair and nice shoulders. Before the war, he'd gotten a new car every year. He said he thought Tish was a dish, ha ha. Tish had known Warren for exactly one week, and here she was filling up page after page. "Do you say the same thing to every guy?" Kitty had once asked, and Tish had said, "Gosh, no. That would be rude! What if the guys ever met?" Kitty wondered: Was this possible? She supposed so. Tish wrote on and on, a little smile on her face. How could she be so sure the guy would be interested in what she said?

Tish got up for another cup of tea. "Julian is practically your fiancé, for cripes' sake. You love him! I don't get it; what's your problem?"

She sat down and blew on her tea. Louise looked at her expectantly, and Tish sighed. "If you wanted tea, why didn't you ask me when I was up?"

"Why didn't you ask *me*?" Louise answered.

Tish stood. "Okay. Who wants more tea?"

"I do," Louise sang out.

"Kitty?"

"No." Kitty didn't want anything. She wanted to go to bed. She wanted to go to bed and sleep until the war was over.

"Maybe you should try being really honest with Julian," Louise said gently. "Tell him what's in your heart."

Tish said, "Set the table, Mabel; tell him you want a ring."

"I can't tell him that!"

"Sure you can," Louise said. "Not directly, just . . ." Her face brightened. "You want me to write him? I can say something about how happy I am, and ask when he's going to propose to you!"

It might not be a bad idea. Julian liked Louise a lot. He wouldn't object to the question coming from her. Maybe he'd even give her a straight answer—he treated Louise differently than he treated Kitty. More . . . seriously.

Kitty shrugged. "Okay." Now she felt better. "Get me some tea, Tish."

"Kiss my foot." Tish continued reading another one of the letters she'd gotten that day. Then she said, "Hey, listen to this. This guy, Ron Berman, he's stationed in Malaysia? And the natives there say 'light belong cloud' for lightning. Isn't that funny? And when they want a haircut, they say, 'Cut-im grass belong head belong me.' And a mirror is 'glass belong look-look.'"

"Pidgin English," Louise said, continuing to write her letter to Michael.

"How do you know?" Tish asked.

"Read something sometime, why don't you?"

Kitty busied herself putting a new nib on her pen. She hadn't known, either.

Tish laughed loudly. "'New fellow moon he come up!' That means the first of the month. Oh, brother."

"You couldn't speak their language at all, Tish," Kitty said. She thought of how, in one of his letters, Hank had talked about what a great anthropological bath the Army experience was—how encountering so many different kinds of people, so many different ways of thinking, had broadened him in a very important way. "You shouldn't act as though you're superior to people just because they don't speak English. They might teach you some things, you know? Why, they—"

"Aw, muffle your face in your mouchoir," Tish said.

A wounded silence. Kitty supposed world peace was a difficult concept indeed; she couldn't even get along with her sister at their kitchen table.

Again, Tish began laughing. "Just one more," she begged.

Louise put down her pen. "What."

"This one's the best," Tish said. "This one means 'accordion.' 'Lik lik bockiss'—'bockiss' means little box—'Lik lik bockiss you push him he cry you pull him he cry.'" She looked at them, tears from laughter bright in her eyes.

"That is funny," Louise said, but she wasn't smiling. She was writing to Michael, who had heard he would soon be transferred to an active combat zone, and there was nothing funny about that.

Tish started to read more, but Louise told her, with uncharacteristic sharpness, "Be quiet!"

Kitty touched Tish's hand. She would listen. Her sister whispered in Kitty's ear, "If you need a bath, they tell you, 'Skin belong you be stink.'"

"All right, but better not say any more, now," Kitty whispered back.

"There isn't any more!" Tish said, triumphantly.

Kitty stared into space while her sisters scribbled away. Those natives and the Scottish and the English and the Americans and the Indians and the Italians and Nazis and Japs, too. A representative from every country at a round table, just like King Arthur's. *Now, boys, let's see if we can't come up with a better solution.*

She turned back to her V-mail form and wrote Julian that she missed him, that she'd write him tomorrow night to tell him what had happened with her application, signed *Love,* and began another V-mail to Hank, about her peace plan. She'd tell him her concerns about Tommy, and she'd ask what Hank had been like as a little boy. Yes. She would like to know that. She'd asked Julian once what he was like as a little boy, and he'd answered, "Shorter."

She'd tell Hank that the sky today was a Fra Angelico blue. Then he would see that she knew something about art, anyway.

"I'm telling Michael to put a little pressure on Julian to pop the question, too," Louise said.

"Oh!" Kitty said. "Okay."

Gosh. She'd forgotten all about that.

KITTY CAME BACK TO BED FROM THE BATHROOM, where she'd splashed cold water over her chest. She'd gotten a little carried away; she was dripping clear down to her toes. But who cared? It was so hot, and now the breeze from the attic fan might finally soothe her into sleep. She wanted to get enough rest so that she wouldn't fall asleep at Mass tomorrow and get a sharp poke in the ribs from her mother. Or worse. Once, seeing that Kitty had drifted off, her mother had reached over and pinched her thigh so hard Kitty had cried out and embarrassed them all. ("Well, you dope, your head was all to the side, and your hat was falling off," Louise had told her when Kitty wondered aloud how her mother, sitting so far away from her, had noticed that her eyes were closed. "If you're going to sleep," Louise said, "sit up straight. And keep your mouth closed!") Yes, you'd better pay attention during Mass if you were a Heaney. Sometimes there was a surprise quiz during Sunday dinner about the content of the priest's sermon. Though lately those sermons had all been pretty much the same: how to make sense of war, how to cope with the ongoing bad news, how prayer and faith were more important now than ever.

Kitty did pray; everyone in her family got down on their knees each night beside their beds and bowed their heads. But from the time Kitty was a little girl, she had found it hard to do this. She wasn't so good at concentrating. She'd start out all right, saying the familiar words to the Our Father or Hail Mary or improvising a bit as the Protestants did, asking God to protect those she loved, asking Him to help her be a better person. But then her mind would drift to the sound her sister's nose was making, to the hardness of the floor beneath her, to a memory of her and Julian driving down the road together, or laughing hard, or kissing in the moonlight. Worse than that, she might think of what movie she wanted to see next, or how she craved a chocolate bar, or how cute that blouse was that someone at work had worn and how much it must have cost.

If Kitty was the worst in their family at prayer, Tommy seemed best—every time Kitty saw him rise from his knees, he was nearly glowing. He seemed to find genuine peace and inspiration from this oldest of rituals. Kitty wanted to ask him sometimes how he did it, if he really felt the way he looked. But she didn't want to reveal how hard a task prayer was for her.

Oh, but surely even Father Fleishmann wasn't perfect at praying, especially these days! Sometimes Kitty wished he would throw up his hands and say, "I can't make any sense of this, all the evil in the world. There are no words I can say that will console those of you who have lost a child or a husband or a brother or a sweetheart. Let's just be quiet together for a while, and then go and have coffee and doughnuts."

"Hey?"

Tish. At the foot of the bed and as wide awake as she, apparently.

"What?" Kitty whispered, lifting her nightgown away from her chest. Tiny rivulets of water were running into her armpits; it felt swell.

"Do you love Julian?"

Kitty bristled. "What a question! Of course I do!"

Next to her, Louise mumbled, "What time is it?"

Kitty squinted at the clock. "Almost four."

"I'm so hot I could die," Louise said.

"I'm so hot I am dead," Tish said.

Kitty snorted. "Then you wouldn't feel hot."

Tish yawned loudly, elaborately. "I don't think you love Julian, Kitty. I think you love Hank."

"What?"

"Aw, keep your socks on. It's just that you never know what to say to Julian. It's kind of ridiculous. And you never seem to have trouble writing to Mr. Dreamboat. Your pen just flies across the page when you're writing to him. And you talk about Hank all the time, too, and you hardly ever talk about Julian anymore."

Kitty waited in vain for Louise to defend her. Then she said, "I talk about Hank because he talks to me. I haven't heard that much from Julian, so there's not that much to say about him. It doesn't mean I don't love him. I love him, and someday I'm going to marry him, and we're going to have four kids, and we're going to live in Oak Park and have a maid and a collie and we'll each have our own car, and every year we'll go abroad." She took a breath. "If it's still there."

Tish said, "Look, I don't care. So don't go off on me. But it seems as though you never have talked about Julian much. Even when you were with him. I mean, you guys did stuff together, but you didn't really talk about him. Usually if a girl loves a guy, she talks about him all the time."

"That's actually true," Louise said.

"I love Julian!" Kitty said. "Jeez!"

"But *what* do you love about him?" Tish asked.

Kitty said angrily, "You can't just list things like that! That's not what love is."

"Well, what is it, then?" Tish asked. "Seems like you should be able to list some things. I mean, if you love someone, you—"

"In case you hadn't noticed," Kitty said, "Julian is very good-looking."

"Yeah?" Tish said. "What else?"

Kitty scoffed. "There is too much to tell, and anyway, it's none of your business if I love Julian. *What* I love about him, I mean."

"Louise could say a million things she loves about Michael, couldn't you, Louise?"

Louise sighed. "Oh, Tish, the things you can list about a person are only . . . So what? All that 'the way he smiles at kids, the way he always offers you a bite first, how he gets so wrapped up in the movies, the things he knows about—'"

"See?" Tish interrupted triumphantly. "See all that stuff she just spouted out?"

"All that *stuff* is not so important," Louise said. "I think the most important thing about loving someone is not even the way you feel about him, but the way he makes you feel about yourself. And I'm sure Julian and Kitty . . . I'm sure if Kitty says she loves Julian, she means it."

The room grew silent, but Kitty could feel Louise's thoughts moving toward her. *Hey, wait a minute. Is it true? You do talk an awful lot about that Hank guy. You seem to have gotten to know him awfully well. You seem to tell him a lot of things, to ask him a lot of questions. You seem to really care what he thinks. Do you love Julian anymore? Did you ever, really?*

Kitty wanted to smack her sisters hard, both of them. What did *they* know? She swallowed drily. What *did* they know?

AFTER MASS, MARGARET TOLD HER DAUGHTERS to get busy on Sunday dinner; she'd be back soon, she was going to see Mrs. O'Conner. Louise asked to come along, but Margaret told her it would be better if she didn't. "This needs to be woman-to-woman," she said.

"I'm a woman!"

"Yes," Margaret said, "but I mean *old* woman to *old* woman." And then, after a beat, when no one rushed in to say that Margaret was not really old, she made the pronouncement herself.

By the time their mother got home, the chicken had finished roasting, Louise was mashing the potatoes, and Tish was setting the dining room table. Kitty, having finished preparing the green beans and the rolls, was playing double solitaire on the kitchen table with Binks. Frank was in the basement with Billy and Tommy, helping them work on the go-cart they were building from orange crates and scrap lumber.

"Binks," Margaret said. "Go down to the basement and get me some of those pickled beets."

"We already have—" Louise began, but Margaret looked sharply at her, then told Binks, "Go on now, and tell your father and the boys to wash up for dinner."

After Binks had left the room, Margaret sat down heavily at the table. "Bad news," she said. "Katherine is very, very ill. It's . . . Well, it's female trouble. She's very bad." She looked at Louise. "Do you want my advice?"

Louise hesitated, then said yes.

"I think you should tell Michael. Apparently she has a few weeks. Not much more."

"Does she know?" Louise asked.

"Doctor didn't tell her. But yes. I think she does know."

Louise nodded, her eyes filling. "Did you talk to Mr. O'Conner?"

"I did."

"Does he want me to tell Michael?"

Margaret sighed. "The poor man's beside himself. He doesn't know what to do. If Michael knows, he'll worry. If he doesn't know, he might regret that he wasn't able to say some things he might want to say, if only in a letter. I told him I was going to advise you to let Michael know, and he said thank you." She lifted her shoulders. "I suppose that means he agrees that you should."

"I'll tell Michael tonight when I write him. But . . . don't you think his father should tell him, too?"

"I think his father will, now. I think when she . . . I only hope they'll let the boy come home for the funeral."

"The funeral! Shouldn't he come home to see her now?"

"According to Mr. O'Conner, they'll not let him come home for an illness, only for a death. And depending on how things go over there . . . Well, I only hope they let him come for the funeral."

Louise's face was a mix of emotions, and Kitty, too, felt the pull of opposing feelings. Michael might be coming home! But it was because his mother was dying. And after his mother's funeral, he would go right back—Louise would have to say good-bye to him all over again. Kitty stacked the playing cards into a neat pile. Then she messed them up so that she could straighten them out again.

"ALL RIGHTY TIDY, THAT'S ABOUT IT," the woman at Douglas Aircraft who had read over Kitty's application said. Her name was Doris Morris ("I know, I know," she had said, upon introducing herself. "I shouldn't have married Dick Morris. I should have married my other boyfriend. His name was Hal Morris." Then she had laughed uproariously at her own joke, though Kitty figured she'd told it a few times before.) "Report at eight A.M. next Monday," Doris had said. "We'll have your identification button ready for you. You wear it on your left side, right over your heart." She'd smiled. "Welcome aboard."

Kitty had bitten her lip and shaken Doris's hand. She could hardly keep from shouting out; she'd been hired the very same day she'd applied! She'd called in sick to work, had gone instead to the factory and filled out an application, taken some tests, gotten fingerprinted, and she'd gotten the job! She hadn't gotten the swing shift—they liked to give that shift to working mothers—but she'd been hired right away! Oh, they'd call the insurance company where she worked for references, but Kitty should assume all was fine and report to work next Monday. Sixty cents an hour! At first, Doris had said she should wear a Jeepsuit coverall and have her hair tied back—no loose hair on the job. Then she'd said, Oh, what the heck, might as well tell the truth, most women didn't like the coveralls and just wore slacks and a top. But! When the cold weather came (and here Doris had looked meaningfully over her glasses), no tight sweaters. They'd had some problems with women wearing tight sweaters. Kitty had smiled, recalling Bob Hope on the radio with Judy Garland. Judy had said, "Bob, why are men so crazy about sweater girls?" And Bob had answered, "I don't know, Judy; that's a mystery I'd like to unravel."

Doris had told Kitty to bring the tools listed on the mimeographed sheet she'd been given, in her very own toolbox. She might not be able to buy everything, what with the metal shortage, but she should try her best. What she couldn't find, she could borrow from another worker. Bring a lunch to eat in the cafeteria or go out to lunch—a lot of workers liked to grab a hot dog at the place across the street. And one last thing, very important. "You know you're going to get your hands dirty, right?" Doris had asked. Kitty had nodded. "I don't mean a smudge on your pretty little pinkie that you quick wash off. I mean *dirty.*" Kitty had said yes, she knew. "Did you ever see a man's hands after he worked on his car?" Doris had asked. "I mean that kind of dirty."

Kitty had nodded gravely. Oh. *That* dirty. Golly! Julian loved to work on his car, and it took some powerful soap and sometimes a couple of days to get his hands clean. Would her hands really look like that? For one brief moment she'd hesitated about taking the job, then chastised herself. Who cared about rough hands when she would be so directly working on something that would help win the war? You could say all you wanted about the home front and how every job contributed in some way. Every ad in every magazine tried to claim some link to victory: Eat our beets to keep your health—that will help win the war! Buy our badminton racket and get enough exercise—you'll return to work refreshed, and that will help win the war! What was next? Brush your hair every night with our hairbrush to spur our boys on to victory?

But here was something real. Something direct. Kitty's hands would now be putting parts onto a plane that would be used in active warfare. In that respect, she would very nearly be fighting right alongside someone who was on a bombing mission, for he would not be able to get overseas without her. In her mind's eye, Kitty saw a handsome young man coming into her cargo plane. And though she knew it was foolish, she couldn't help it; she saw him look around and nod with approval at how well the plane had been put together, saw him looking at her part.

What part she would be responsible for, she hadn't yet learned, but her imaginary soldier was admiring it nonetheless.

Already, Kitty knew how she would do her job, whatever it was. No matter how difficult her particular assignment might be, she would stay focused and ever mindful of the importance of what she was doing. Her work would be perfect; she would not complain of fatigue; she would willingly work overtime if called upon to do so. And not for the money. The whole time she labored, she would be sending her thoughts and her prayers for the safe homecoming of every boy who rode in one of her planes. Men had to die; she knew this all too well, but she would pray that no man who'd ridden in her plane would die.

Though she had practically run out of the factory, now she walked slowly toward the streetcar. Because damping her elation at being hired was Tommy's question, come suddenly back to her. If war was a sin, was she now part of it?

"YOU'LL RUIN YOUR HANDS!" Margaret said.

"That's no place for a respectable young woman to work," Kitty's father said. "I'll not have my daughter being thought of as a . . . as a . . . It's not respectable, and you'll not do it!"

"It's not your decision," Kitty said. "It's mine. And I've decided to work there. And that's all."

"Eleanor Roosevelt thinks women should work in factories," Tommy said, and Kitty wanted to hug him.

"Who told you that?" Margaret asked.

"Everybody knows that. And besides, it was in one of your *Ladies' Home Journals.*"

To this Margaret said nothing. The *Ladies' Home Journal* was a publication she very much admired and often quoted from; and apart from the Virgin Mary, Eleanor Roosevelt was her most exalted heroine. Margaret set her mouth and cut her pot roast into smaller and smaller pieces. Frank pushed himself away from the table.

"Hey, Pop," Billy said. "Can I have your pot roast?"

Frank passed his plate down to his son. "Share with the rest of the family," he said.

Kitty felt terrible. She wished her father would get angry. Turning down pot roast that was probably at least eight points and over fifty cents a pound! She should have waited until after dinner, but then she'd have interfered with her father's radio and newspaper time.

"When are you to begin?" he asked her.

"Next Monday." Kitty drew lines in her gravy with her fork. "I need to buy some tools before then."

"I'm going out," Frank said, and the family sat still as he passed by them on his way to the front door. It closed quietly behind him.

"Sure he's on his way to O'Mallory's, and that's the last we'll see of him tonight," Margaret said.

"I'm *sorry*," Kitty said. "But I—"

"I'll hear no more about it now," Margaret said. "And there'll be no going out for any of you girls. You live in my house, you live by my rules. You sit and do your letters after dinner, and then it's off to bed with all of you."

"Cripes, *I* didn't do anything," Tish said.

"I didn't say you did. Now I'm leaving, and I want you girls to take care of the boys."

"Where are you going?" Binks asked. "Ma? Where are you going?"

"I'm taking myself to the pub, too. And that's the end of it."

She went out the door. Tish raised her eyebrows and looked over at Kitty. "Nice work, sis."

AT TEN O'CLOCK, THE BOYS were in bed and the girls had just finished writing their letters when their parents came home. Margaret took off her scarf and hung up her sweater and, without a word, headed upstairs. Frank came into the kitchen and stared at his daughters. He wasn't weaving, but it seemed as though he were ready to. From where he stood, Kitty could smell the whiskey. Frank didn't drink often, two or three times a year at best, but when he did drink, he made the most of it, as did his wife. Margaret could handle her liquor; Frank could not. Later tonight, he'd be kneeling at the porcelain altar, as Julian would say. For now, though, Frank's face was wearily benevolent, and he spoke softly, kindly.

"Kitty, darlin'."

"Yes, Pop?"

He waved for her to follow him, and this upset his balance. He bumped into the doorjamb. "Pardon me," he told it.

"Are you all right, Pop?" Tish asked. She didn't seem to know whether to be amused or alarmed.

"Never finer, grand altogether!"

"Let's go to bed, Tish," Louise said. She wouldn't look at her father. It didn't matter how rare his times of such overindulgence, she didn't approve of it.

"Sweet dreams!" he said and then, to Kitty, "Come down to the basement with me."

In his small workroom, rich with the scent of wood shavings, Frank pulled the string to turn on the light. There was the half-finished go-cart for Billy and Tommy. Kitty ran her hands along the sides, where the lumber had been sanded smooth as silk; Frank always did exceptionally fine work. ROLLING THUNDER had been stenciled along the side and was half painted; Billy's idea, no doubt.

"Now then," Frank said, crouching down next to his meticulously organized toolbox. "You'll be needing this, and this. Oh, here's a good one, you'll be the envy of the workforce with this." Beside him, he was amassing a shiny collection of mysterious things. He held up something Kitty recognized: a screwdriver. "D'you know what I first used this for?" he asked.

"No."

"Your crib that we carried home from the store, your pregnant mother and I, 'twas still in the box. What a sight, her big as a house and toting her end of that load down the sidewalk for the entire block, proud as a peacock. And woe to the men who offered to help—she'd have no part of anyone interfering with her caring for her child, born or not. And didn't I have a devil of a time getting it together! I was swearing at the directions so much your mother finally took them away from me and burned them."

Kitty laughed. "Did she?"

"As God is my witness." He wagged his finger at her. "Women are highly emotional and strictly unreasonable when they're in the family way; you'll see when your time comes. Or rather your husband will! No arguing with an expectant woman; there's only one answer for her, and that's 'Yes, dear.'

"So anyway, she burned the directions, and I congratulated her on her good sense, and then I sat staring at the parts for half the night, and then finally I put the thing together. I still don't know if I ever did it right, but it held up for all of you kids, anyway." He moved from crouching to sit on the floor, his back against the tool bench. "I remember when your mother and I brought you home from the hospital, both of us scared to death, and lay you in that crib. I couldn't stop crying, and I didn't want your mother to see. But she didn't mind; she was crying even more; we were both so happy.

"You were a wonderful baby, so you were. We used to brag about you to everyone, how pretty you were, how you never cried. No one believed us, but it was true—you almost never cried. In the morning, you would wake up and just lie there cooing to yourself, waiting patiently for someone to come in. Your mother would fuss at you sometimes, such a tiny thing and we weren't sure you were getting enough to eat, but you just didn't cry. On weekend mornings, I would come and get you myself and bring you to your mother. But first I'd sneak over to the rocker just to hold you a wee bit. I'd never felt anything like that, the lightness of a baby. The sweetness. The top of your head smelled like a field of fresh-mown clover." He shook his head, remembering. "Ah,

Kitty. I wanted the world for you then, and I still do. Your mother and I both. I hope you know that."

"I do know that, Pop." Her voice was thick.

Frank patted the concrete floor for her to sit beside him. When Kitty hesitated, he closed the toolbox so she could sit on it; then he began to laugh.

"What?" Kitty said.

"You! Telling me you're going to work in a dirty factory and then you're too dainty to sit on your father's clean swept floor! You of the ruffles and the lace and the painted fingernails. I've never seen anyone stare at clothes in a magazine the way you do; I've often told your mother you ought to wear a bib for the drooling. And now it's off to work looking like Joe Blow. There's no explaining it. But then you know the expression, don't you?"

Kitty nodded.

"Tell it to me."

"'There are only three kinds of Irishmen who can't understand women,'" Kitty began, and she and her father finished the old saying together. "'Young men, old men, and men of middle age.'"

"Well! I'm glad to see we agree on that point, at least," her father said. "Now help a knackered old man off the floor and up the stairs, and we'll dream our way to tomorrow."

On WEDNESDAY EVENING, THE SISTERS went together to the Kelly Club, as the servicemen's center was now called. Louise volunteered to serve coffee at the canteen—she was feeling too bad about Michael's mother to dance—but Kitty and Tish took to the floor.

Kitty danced first with a sailor named Elwood, a redheaded, freckle-faced young man straight off the farm, headed for the Pacific. When he talked about catching the train to the West Coast that night, his voice cracked and his palms began to sweat. "It must be hard," she told him, "going so far from home."

"Yeah, but I got no kick," he said. "I'm willing to do my part."

"But . . . working on a farm, weren't you classified essential labor?" she asked.

"I got four brothers; they'll help out my parents."

"So you enlisted?"

He nodded. "Seemed like a good idea at the time. You eat good in the Navy." He looked down into her face. "You sure are pretty. I never danced with such a pretty girl before."

"Thank you," she said and pressed her cheek to his. His ears stuck out so far they were almost like visors; Kitty could see the glow of light coming through them. "And you are a very fine-looking fellow."

He laughed. "No, I ain't. But thank you for saying so." "Yours" ended with a musical flair, and he dipped her dramatically. The dancers around them smiled and applauded.

Next the band started up with "Beat Me Daddy, Eight to the Bar." Elwood said, "I ain't handsome, but I can swing. How about it, toots?" He moved his eyebrows up and down.

Kitty laughed, then went on to dance every dance with him. On the fast songs, he showed off; during the slow ones, he talked softly into her ear. He had a cow he'd raised from birth, named Goldie. He had a chicken named Red; she came when he called her, too. He had a few good dogs and too many cats to count—barn cats, real good mousers. He had a girl he liked a lot, had liked her for a long time, but he hadn't told her until the night before he left for basic. Her name was Mary, and she had blond hair clear down to her knees, looked like corn silk. She was going to write to him, and he hoped that when he got home she'd marry him and they'd live on his family's farm. He didn't know of a place prettier than that farm. If you watched the sun come up over the fields, it could make you feel like busting out crying. Once he did bust out crying, he confided, but he was just a little boy then. He was about to see the world, that was one of the reasons he'd joined the Navy, but he knew he'd never see any place better than home; he just knew it. He couldn't hardly swim, though, wasn't that funny, that a guy who couldn't swim would join the Navy? Yes, that was funny, Kitty told him, but she didn't think it was.

When it was time to leave, Kitty and Louise waited impatiently for Tish, who was taking far too long to say good night to a young lieutenant. "I told you, I can't give you my address!" she said, laughing. "It's against the rules!" He whispered something in her ear, and she said, "Oh! Okay. They live at 411 Pine." She'd given them the Lawsons' address, their next-door neighbors.

With this, Kitty marched up and grabbed her sister's elbow. "We have to go, nice meeting you," Kitty told the soldier and began walking quickly away.

"Wowsa. What's *your* name?" he called after her.

"That man is stinking drunk!" Louise told Tish, and she said, "I know. But did you see the cleft in his chin?"

After they were home and dressed for bed, the sisters gathered around the kitchen table to write their letters. It was hard, sometimes, to remember that they hadn't always done this, that the practice was relatively new. It was a lesser equivalent to what one of Tish's penpals had said in a letter to her: that he and his buddies felt they'd always been fighting this war, that their life before seemed somehow to have fallen away, this life now was the only life they knew.

The kitchen still smelled of that night's dinner of tuna loaf, which all of them, even Margaret, had found revolting. The compensation had been that she'd made a real yellow cake with chocolate frosting for dessert—a small one but a real one. Wednesdays and Fridays were meatless days in the Heaney house, as they were in many households across America now. Wednesdays and Fridays were also the nights Frank tried to schedule meetings of one kind or another. He had failed to find anything to do tonight, however, and had suffered through dinner with the rest of them. "Oh, it truly *is* awful, isn't it?" Margaret had said and then admonished her family to eat it anyway. Billy had asked why they couldn't just have cold tuna sandwiches. "This makes my *eyes* water," he'd said.

"Believe me, next time we will have sandwiches," Margaret had said. "But you've got to try new things; that's the only way you know if something's good. Imagine if Ruth Wakefield had thrown away those Toll House cookies—they were an accident, you know! Don't worry, you won't see me making this recipe again; I've given it the black X. I wouldn't feed it to a Nazi." She'd stared miserably at another bite on her fork, put it in her mouth, and spoken around it. "Although if I did, we'd probably win the war a lot faster."

Now the front door opened and slammed shut, and into the kitchen came Margaret, the bun at the back of her neck slid off to the side, her cheeks flushed.

"What happened to you?" Tish said. "Were you the victim again at the Red Cross meeting?"

"'Tisn't the meeting I'm coming from," Margaret said and sat at the table with her daughters. She was humming, and she had an odd light in her eyes.

Louise looked up from her pages. "You said you were going to a Red Cross meeting!"

"I'm well aware of what I said, but that's not where I went." She got up to open the bread box. "Where's the rest of that cake?"

"Billy and Pop ate it," Kitty said. "Where have you been?" She and her sisters looked at one another. Why was their mother behaving in this mysterious way?

Margaret turned to her daughters and spoke quietly. "Now, don't be telling your father, but Maureen O'Reilly and I went to a USO dance."

"What?" Tish said. "Where?"

"The Catholic Center on South Wabash. I wanted to see what those dances were all about, and I did see. You girls can keep on going, it's perfectly innocent and nothing I'd ever forbid you from doing. Oh, that narrow-eyed water snake Mernie Gunderson and her talk about the immorality there, how she won't let *her* daughter go to the dances and how I'd better go and have a look if I don't believe her! All that goes on is some lonesome soldier boys barely old enough to shave dance with some pretty girls and forget about their troubles for a while. It's lovely."

"Well, I told you," Tish said, but it was all she could do to keep from wiping her brow. Good thing their mother hadn't gone to the Kelly Club, where the latest fad was the infamous dance taught to American boys by French sailors. It was called the Kiss-on-the-Carpet, and you took turns going around a circle with a little rug, choosing a partner and then kneeling down on the rug to kiss. Some "dance"! None of the sisters had taken part in that yet, but Tish kept talking about how much fun it would be, and how it wouldn't hurt to try it, it wouldn't hurt to just *try* it.

"Did you dance?" Louise asked Margaret.

"Did I! And may I say more than one young man pronounced me light on my feet and good-looking to boot!" Her face grew sober, and she said again, "Don't be telling your father; he wouldn't understand."

From the parlor came Frank's voice: "And who would I be to deny the pleasure of your company to our fine boys?" He came into the kitchen and regarded his wife. "So long as all you did was dance! In fact, may I have the honor?" Margaret smiled but waved him away.

"Ah, come on, aul' doll. Don't break a man's heart." He held out his arms, Margaret walked into them, and they waltzed out of the kitchen.

Louise shook her head, smiling. Then she said, "Michael and I will be just like that. We will be."

The sisters said nothing. They knew it was true.

AT BREAKFAST ON THE MONDAY MORNING she was to start her new job, Kitty couldn't eat much and Tommy wouldn't eat at all.

"Here now, son," Frank said. "Don't you know an egg is good as gold these days? Only yesterday I read in the paper about a minister in France charges an egg to marry people! He won't take money, only an egg. They get only one a month over there. Think how he'd feel, seeing you let yours go to waste."

"It doesn't have to go to waste," Tommy said. "I'll give it to someone. I'm just not hungry, Pop. Do you want it?"

"Give it to one of your brothers," Frank said, and then, anticipating the brawl, he said, "Give it to little Binks over there, wasting away to nothing."

"What about me?" Billy said. "I'm wasting away to nothing, too!"

"If you're going to fight about it, I'll take it," Tish said. "I need more protein for my hair."

"Is that where my mayonnaise is going?" Margaret asked. "I noticed a lot of mayonnaise missing. Did you take it to put on your hair again?"

"I have to go to work," Tish said and ran out the back door. Inspired by Kitty's new job, Tish had begun volunteering at the hospital. She was the juice girl, pushing around the cart and offering patients their choice of beverage. She'd come home the first day resolved to be a nurse; on the second day, she'd said maybe not—she'd seen a bedpan.

Margaret put the backs of her fingers to Tommy's forehead. "Do you feel sick?"

He shrugged. "Not really."

"Why don't you eat something? You'll feel better if you do."

He got up from the table. "I will. I'm just not hungry now. I'll eat a big lunch."

"All right then," Margaret told him, lightly, and watched him go outside. But worry was in her face when she told Frank, "He's not himself."

"The boy's not hungry, that's all," Frank said. "He'll make up for it later. I'm off now; don't expect me home too early. It's not only the mail that's gotten heavier, it's the time I spend. Used to be I'd exchange a few pleasantries here and there. Now it's a woman waiting for me on the porch half the places I deliver to, standing there and wringing her hands: 'Is a letter there for me today? Are you sure? Oh, Mr. Heaney, do you think he's all right?' Sometimes they're so disappointed they start to cry, and nobody to comfort them but yours truly. It's getting so I dread seeing them, for I've run out of things to say."

"It doesn't matter what you say," Margaret said. "Just say something. Say you're sure he's fine, that the mail is slow."

"It is really slow, even V-mail," Louise said. "That I can vouch for." She was anxious about hearing from Michael; every day now was weighted with concern over how he'd take the news about his mother. Louise was stopping by every evening after work to see Mrs. O'Conner; no apparent worsening yet, but no improvement, either. Their visits were bittersweet; Mrs. O'Conner told Louise stories about Michael as a little boy, as though she were entrusting her memories of him to his wife-to-be. Thus far, Louise's favorite story had been the one in which nine-year-old Michael had labored long at the counter of a fancy women's dress shop, trying to find something he could buy his mother after he'd learned he could not afford the tweed suit in the window. The saleswoman had practically been in tears, she'd later told Mrs. O'Conner. Young Michael had been so earnest in his desire to buy the suit, then so devastated to learn he could not afford it. But how resolute he'd become, and what care he took in choosing a belt! And all this for the occasion of nothing—it was not his mother's birthday, or Mother's Day, or Christmas. Rather, it was that Michael had filled his cigar box with money he'd made doing odd jobs, and he wanted to spend it, and it would never occur to him to buy something for himself.

Kitty contrasted this story to one she knew about ten-year-old Julian, who gave his mother a birthday gift of a paperback book of riddles and a candy bar from which he'd taken one discreet bite. Still, even at that age, there was something irresistible about Julian. His love of life was contagious—he wanted everyone to have as good a time as he did. And if he was insensitive at times, well, just tell him what you wanted and he'd do it for you, no hard feelings, and was there anything else you wanted?

Kitty forced down another bite of toast and then pushed her plate away. She was too excited to eat. It felt odd to be going off to work in slacks, but she liked it. It felt as if she were going to a picnic, or to ride horses with Julian. "Well, here I go," she said, and her parents said nothing. Frank hid behind his paper, and Margaret noisily stacked dishes in the sink. Still disapproving. Well, they'd come around. Kitty slid her purse over her shoulder—it was heavier with her lunch packed inside. Then she grabbed her toolbox, heavier still, and headed for the streetcar.

As she walked down the block, she felt her neighbors' eyes on her. Florie Dorrisburger, out watering her garden in her robe, shouted, "Good for you!" and flashed her a victory sign. Everyone else who saw her said nothing. She knew that women all over were working at men's jobs now—they were cabdrivers, elevator operators, bellhops, trolley drivers, even long-distance truck drivers. Was she such an oddity, leaving her office job to work in a factory? Or was she being oversensitive, reading things into an innocuous silence?

Oh, but if the truth be told, she herself was ambivalent about her decision. Last night, she had tossed and turned, thinking about how she'd no longer be dressed in pretty clothes—and those new V-necked ruffled blouses worn with massive beads, weren't they just the cat's meow! But she'd not buy such a blouse now, and she'd no longer go to the drugstore for lunch with her office girlfriends; and she would indeed ruin her hands.

When Kitty boarded the streetcar, she saw a number of other women wearing slacks. She had seen them before, of course, but now she saw them in a different way, and she felt reassured by them. She found a seat and stared out the window during the long ride, wondering exactly what she'd be doing. She imagined telling her sisters about her job, tossing off technical terms—and then patiently explaining them—while she washed the grime off her hands. Maybe she'd get muscular like that woman on the poster. Though if she did, she wouldn't be rolling up her sleeves that way. In fact, maybe she'd request a job that required no heavy lifting. Then Kitty felt ashamed and resolved again to do whatever she was asked without complaint. If she got muscles, she'd find a blouse that would work well with them. No more sheer sleeves, that was for sure.

When at last Kitty reached the stop near the factory, a number of women got off the car with her. One of them, a robust girl with dark, curly hair and ruddy cheeks, seemed unsure of herself. Kitty moved to walk beside her. "This your first day, too?" she asked, and the woman nodded shyly.

"I've only just moved here," she said.

English! Kitty asked the woman where she was from.

"Just south of London," she said. "I've been in America for five years now, but I've been living in New York—I'd only just come to visit my sister when the war broke out in Europe, and of course I've not been home since. Last month, I married the best man in world, Don Ramsey, just before he shipped out. He sent me here to Chicago to live with his parents for the duration. Then we'll get a little place of our own, and truly, I can't wait. It's not that I don't like his parents, they're lovely, but a girl needs a little more privacy than sleeping in the dining room allows! I really should have stayed with my sister, but Don felt—" She laughed. "Listen to me go on. My name is Laura. Laura Ramsey." She blushed, saying this, and looked at her wedding band.

Kitty felt a familiar surge of longing. Oh, that Julian. If he'd done what he was supposed to do, she could have introduced herself as Kitty

Stanton, also married to a man in the service, and she and Laura could talk about . . . Well, they could talk about whatever wives talked about.

As it was, Kitty introduced herself and asked Laura if she'd like to have lunch together. "I would," Laura said. "But I brought my own." She held up her purse. Kitty held up her own. And then together the women walked down the hall to the small room where they were to have their orientation.

"MY DADDY, HE WAS ASKED to grow peanuts for the war effort," Hattie Johnson said. She was a tall, light-skinned Negro, another one of the new girls starting today. She, Laura, Kitty, and another new girl named Lala Denet, from a small town in southern Illinois, were having lunch together outside. Lala was a curly-haired blonde who, at four feet eleven, was as short as Hattie was tall. She said her real name was Helen, but when she was born, her two-year-old brother couldn't pronounce Helen, so he called her Lala, and it stuck. She was married to an Army man stationed in Hawaii; he did something there with radio equipment. After he shipped out, Lala had decided to come to Chicago to get a defense job and had rented a small apartment that an older couple had made out of attic space in their large home in Oak Park. They charged very little rent—said it was their way of helping out with the war effort. Lala said they had fixed the place up real cute, but holy moley, there was enough chintz in there to drive you nuts, and Mrs. Dooley really needed to make some friends her own age.

Hattie had come up north from her daddy's farm in Mississippi. "When they asked him 'bout growing peanuts," Hattie continued, "Daddy said hell, he'd grow elephants if it would help! We're all of us kids helping in the war: one brother, he serves food to the officers on a Navy ship. 'Nother one is in North Africa somewhere, driving a truck. Third one's on one of those islands, he drives a truck, too. Me, I left Miz Jamison's house and came up here to Chicago to get me a *good* job. That old lady was fit to be tied, shaking her fist in my face, telling me I didn't appreciate how good I had it there, what a nice salary she paid me, though it wasn't but a dollar twenty-five a week. She said she treated me good, too, but that wasn't true, either; she treated her little poodle dog better than she treated me. I miss my folks, but I like it here much better than home."

"Where do you live?" Laura asked.

"Oh, I share a place on the South Side, six of us in a one-bedroom apartment. It's pretty crowded! But half of us work nights, and half days, so that helps."

"Still," Lala said, putting down her sandwich (she didn't eat the crusts, Kitty noticed), "it must be nice to live with people your own age, ones who have the same interests as you."

"Oh, yes," Hattie said. "We share patterns to make our dresses, cook our dinners together, talk our heads off. We've got the place fixed up pretty cute, too. When we go to USO dances, we really have fun. Only thing we have to be careful of is: don't compete for your roommate's man. I met me a Tuskegee flier at a dance a few weeks ago, and I told every one of those girls, 'Hands off!' "

Kitty knew of the Negro USO dances. All soldiers were welcome at all USO centers, but the Negroes seemed to prefer their own. "What's your flier's name?" she asked.

Hattie looked down, smiling. "Will. Will Duncan. And I was gone the minute I laid eyes on him." She looked up at the other girls. "Honest I was."

"I was gone the minute I heard Ricky's voice," Lala said. "You should hear that man's voice. And he's easy on the eyes, too. He could be in the movies, I swear. I fell like a stone."

"Me, too," Laura said. "They say there is no such thing as love at first sight, but there is. Did you feel that way about your Julian, Kitty?"

"Oh, sure." Kitty looked at her watch. "I guess we'd better go back."

Lala looked up at the sky. "It's going to rain, anyway. I'd better get in before I shrink even more—I used to be six feet tall. Race you all!"

They ran back toward the factory, laughing and shrieking and bumping into one another. How wonderful, Kitty thought. New friends already! What fun it was going to be to work here!

The women reached the doorway just as the rain began. The drops fell furiously, hitting the dusty ground like tiny bombs. They all stood at the doorway for a moment, watching, then started back to the orientation room. A man leaning against the wall spoke around the toothpick in his mouth. "Back from recess, girls?" he asked, then said angrily, "This ain't no playground. You're going to learn that in a hurry." The women looked at one another and burst out laughing.

"Go ahead and laugh now," the man called after them. "You won't be laughing long!"

"Come on, Gunderson," another man said. "Lay off."

"Lay off? I'm going to lay *on*," the man said. "How about that pretty one, looks just like Rita Hayworth, I think I'll lay on her. If she's lucky."

Kitty had a thought to turn around and say something. But she followed the other women's example and acted like she hadn't heard a thing.

"OH, NO. OH, NO!" KITTY SAID.

"Hush!" Tish told her, buried in a letter from Donald Erickson, her pen pal from Madison, Wisconsin. It was the sisters' standard practice now to read to themselves any letters they'd gotten that day, then share selected parts with one another before they began their own correspondence.

"Oh, *no*," Kitty said again, though more softly. "Louise?"

"What." But her sister didn't look up.

"Something terrible happened."

Now both sisters looked up.

"I mixed the letters up," Kitty said.

Louise frowned. "What are you talking about?"

"I mixed the letters to Julian and Hank up."

"You mean you sent Julian Hank's letter?" Tish asked. "And vice versa?"

Miserably, Kitty nodded.

Tish sighed. "I *told* you to *always* write the address first!"

"Oh, it's not so bad," Louise said. "You don't seem to get all that intimate with Julian." Her eyes narrowed. "Unless . . . What did you tell that Hank?"

"I don't really remember," Kitty said, though she did remember saying that it had been a Fra Angelico sky that day, which now mortified her. Also, she remembered she'd asked Hank to tell her what he'd been like as a boy, something she'd also asked Julian. But maybe Julian wouldn't remember, Julian wasn't so good at remembering things like that. Oh, poor

Julian, suffering away in the middle of the Pacific Ocean while she complained all the time about how hard it was to write to him. Shame on her! From now on, she'd read a book if she had to, so she could quote from it. She'd tell him what she'd done at work. She'd watch people on the street, and then tell him funny things she'd seen. She, like Louise, would talk about all the things they'd do when he came home and recall, in a very romantic way, things they'd done together. Why had it been so hard for her to write Julian? Because she was lazy, that was why.

"Well, if you don't even know what you wrote to Hank, what are you so excited about?" Louise asked. She scratched her arm agitatedly. "Jeez."

"I told you she liked Hank better," Tish said. "Didn't I say so, a *long* time ago, didn't I tell you?"

"First of all, it wasn't so long ago," Kitty said. "And, no, I don't like him better."

"Poor Julian," Tish said, sighing. Then she sat up straighter and blinked. "Gosh, but really. Poor Julian!"

Louise snatched away the letter that was in Kitty's hand. "It's from Hank," she said and began reading aloud. Kitty had a thought to grab the letter back, but the truth was, she wanted another opinion. Even from Tish, whom she also wanted to choke.

"*Dear Kitty,*" Louise read.

"*I believe there's been an error of some sort. I have received a letter addressed to me, but the salutation is to 'Julian.' I would like to say I am a man of such outstanding character that I stopped reading right there, but alas—*"

"Alas?" Tish said. "*Alas?*"

"Quiet!" Kitty said. "He doesn't mean it like that!"

"Like what?" Tish asked.

"It's not . . . It's just sort of tongue-in-cheek!"

"Be quiet and listen," Louise said.

"Alas, I shall, most eagerly," Tish said.

Louise looked at her. "That doesn't even make sense. If you say 'alas,' you're not doing it eagerly."

"I know that!"

"No you don't," Kitty said.

"Do you want help fixing this problem?" Louise asked, and Kitty nodded.

"Then . . ." Louise raised her eyebrows.

Tish folded her hands on the table. All right. She was done, now.

"I would like to say I am a man of such character—"

"Out*standing* character," Tish said, and then, when Louise looked daggers at her, "Sorry! But say it all! Just in the interest of accuracy!"

"of such outstanding character that I stopped reading right there, but alas, I did not. I read the letter through, and I hereby send both it and my most sincere apology back to you. May I assume that Julian got a letter intended for me? If so, I certainly can't complain if he read it, but will hope that he, too, will make an effort to have the right man receive the right missive. I await, rather anxiously, I confess, for same."

"What's he talking about missiles for?" Tish asked.

"Missive," Louise said.

"What's that?"

"It means 'letter.'"

Tish sat back in her chair, exasperated. "Well, then, why doesn't he just call it a letter? I don't like this guy. He's a big show-off."

"He's just a good writer," Louise said. "He was using alliteration."

"For what?" Tish asked. "It's a letter! What, is he trying to get a good grade or something? Oh, poor Julian, being jilted for such a creep."

Kitty opened her mouth angrily to speak, then shut it. And then, suddenly, something occurred to her. "Tish? Do you have feelings for Julian?"

"He's your *boy*friend!" she answered.

"I know," Kitty said. "But do you?" Image after image was popping up in her brain: Tish hanging on Julian's arm and begging for a ride in his car; Tish lighting his cigarette; Tish pointing out how the two of them looked alike, her hand lingering on top of his blond head. Once, driving away from the house with Julian, Kitty had looked back and seen Tish standing at the bedroom window, watching them go. Kitty had smiled and waved gaily at her, but Tish hadn't waved back. She hadn't been smiling, either.

Louise was rereading Hank's letter and shaking her head. "Boy. It's going to be interesting to see what Julian writes back."

Tish bent her face to the letter she was holding. "Listen to this," she said. "This guy in combat? He put on a clown hat, instead of his helmet. He said it made him look nuts and the Nazis are afraid of crazy people, so he thought he wouldn't get shot at. But he did. He got shot in the shoulder."

Louise spoke softly, staring into space. "He'll come home then. He'll get to come home."

"Is Mrs. O'Conner the same?" Kitty asked. She knew her sister was thinking of Michael coming home.

"She was worse. I was going to tell you guys about it later. She can't . . . She doesn't talk anymore. Mostly she sleeps. Gosh, she's gotten so thin. I don't see how she can go on much longer. And poor Michael, having no idea." She read from his letter: *"I'm going to bring you breakfast in bed every morning. You always said that was a dream of yours, and darling, I'm going to make it come true. Two eggs, bacon, and toast every day but Sunday, when I'm going to bring you waffles and a real rose. Guess you have to teach me how to make waffles first, though."* Louise smiled sadly and put the letter down. "He wrote this before he heard," she said. "I wonder what he'll say after he hears."

"'Tis enough, now," Margaret said at dinner the next evening. "You've got to eat more, Tommy."

"I did," he said. "I ate as much as I could!"

"Eat more," Margaret said. "You may not like it, but—"

"I like it, Ma. I do, it's real good. I'm just full." But he picked up his fork.

"May I join the Marines?" Tish asked.

A shocked silence. Then, "No, you may not join the Marines," Frank said.

"You free up the men to fight when you do!"

"Wonderful," Frank said. "No."

"You train at a college, and if you're an officer candidate, you get to go to Smith or Mount Holyoke!"

Frank raised his eyebrows, made a noise deep in his throat, and chewed, chewed, chewed.

"The base pay for officers is up to two hundred and fifty dollars a month!"

"Really?" Kitty asked.

"All right," Frank said, putting down his napkin and pushing himself from the table. "I'll say this once and once only. None of my girls will join any branch of the service. 'Tis bad enough, Kitty doing a man's job at a factory." He held up his hand to silence Tish. "And don't be asking me can you do that, either, for the answer is another resounding no, spelled capital 'N,' capital 'O.'"

"I don't want to work in a factory, I want to be a Marine."

"You're not even old enough," Kitty told her.

"I will be in January!"

"And by that time, you'll be suitably employed at Carson's cosmetic counter, just as you planned," Frank said. "You're lucky you're being given the opportunity. Your job now is fine for the summer, but come fall, you'll take that paying position. We all must do our part for the family."

"Pop, may I just ask you one more thing?"

He sighed. "If I say no, you'll only ask me why not."

"You'd be proud of your sons if they enlisted, wouldn't you?"

"With God's help, they won't have to. But yes, I'd be proud indeed."

"So why—"

"It's a man's place to fight the war. And that's all. Now pass me the beets and let's talk about something else." He pulled his chair back up to the table. "Who's got a scintillating nugget to inspire conversation?"

Silence.

"A pithy idea from one of my gifted offspring!" Frank said.

Silence but for the slurping sound of Binks drinking his milk.

"Some uplifting anecdote! A heartwarming story about a boy and his dog!"

"Are we getting a dog?" Binks asked. "Oh, boy! Are we getting a dog, Pop?"

"No, son."

Margaret cleared her throat. "Well, here's something I'd like to talk about. I'm getting awfully tired of Imogene Samuelson needing a pat on the girdle every time she bothers to come to a Red Cross meeting. And her the treasurer!"

"Ah!" Frank said. "Girdles! There's a captivating subject if ever I heard one. Now, who do you think came up with that idea?"

"Not a woman, I can assure you," Margaret said.

"Absolutely right!" Frank said. "'Twas a French designer, and he—"

"May I be excused?" Tommy asked, and Margaret nodded, then watched him go outside. The last few evenings, he had taken to sitting

on the front steps after dinner, quietly watching the boys in the neighborhood play stickball in the street, rather than joining them. "I'm asking Dr. Brandon to come over, and look at him tomorrow," Margaret
said. "He's not eating enough and he—"

"The lad's all right," Frank said. "He's just going through a reverse
growth spurt. Sure, Kitty did the same thing at almost the same age.
And weren't you worried to death then, too, nothing for it but Dr. Mayfield had to come right over, and then it was nothing. Nothing at all. Do
you remember?"

"No."

Kitty recalled Dr. Mayfield putting his cold stethoscope to her chest,
how embarrassed she'd been at him seeing her new little breasts sprout-
ing there. "I remember," she said.

"There you are," Frank said. "And now, Margaret, may I have some
more of your fine . . . ?"

"Cabbage Delmonico," Margaret said and smiled primly in spite of
herself. But then she said, "Still, Tommy's so quiet, Frank, and—"

"Margaret! The boy is fine! He's always been quiet. He's sensitive,
our own family philosopher. He's worried, that's all. He takes everything too much to heart. Don't let him hear the radio anymore. Next
Sunday, we'll go on a family outing. We'll take him somewhere and get
his mind off things."

"Hey, Pop," Billy said. "Did you hear about that boy who enlisted in
the Army Air Force when he was fourteen?"

"No, I didn't."

"He went on twenty-one combat missions over North Africa and
Italy and won four citations, and then he retired, at sixteen. Now he's
working at an airplane plant until he's old enough to enlist again!"

"That's not true," Frank said.

"It is!" Billy said. "Anthony cut it out of the *Chicago Daily News.*
June sixteenth. He showed me the article; he saved it."

Frank laughed. "You don't say. I'm sorry I missed it." He laughed
again and shook his head. "There's a young man I'd like to meet!"

"How did he enlist when he was underage?" Louise asked.

"False ID," Tish said. "I hear about it all the time. Guys change the dates on their birth certificates. Hey, Pop, did you hear about the USO shows in North Africa, where some of the girls went onto the battlefield with the boys? One even fired a mortar shell at the enemy."

"Both Greer Garson and Bette Davis were basket cases just from doing bond drives," Margaret said. "And Rita Hayworth, she broke down, too. Show business isn't all it seems."

"Well, they're not strong," Tish said. "They've gotten soft from all their pampering. I'm strong. If I—"

Frank spoke with his mouth full. "*No.*"

KITTY SAT OUT ON THE FRONT PORCH steps in the heat of the late July evening. The family had gone to a novena together, then come back to hear FDR deliver another fireside chat. It was always soothing to imagine him sitting there in his cardigan with his cigarette holder, to hear him speak calmly and with great assurance about events that were so very frightening. He had a way of making you feel as though he were in the room right with you, reaching over to put a steadying hand on your shoulder. People all over the country wrote to him as though he were their friend: "Take lemon for your cold, I keep telling you!" one man had reportedly written him. "If you could just send us thirty-five dollars," wrote another. Margaret always said that, next to the rosary, FDR was the best tonic for the times.

Kitty liked Mrs. Roosevelt even better. She was so intelligent—and so honest! Her monthly column for the *Ladies' Home Journal* was called "If You Ask Me," and in it she had vowed to answer whatever question she was asked—about anything. Sometimes the questions were about etiquette. Sometimes they were about relationships. Once she was asked about her taste in music. (She preferred classical, but only because this was the music she'd been raised with; it was most familiar to her.) This month, a woman had sent her a letter asking if soldiers from the midwestern states, which were normally Republican, were sent into combat zones before soldiers from Democratic states. Mrs. Roosevelt began her response by saying, "I have never heard anything so idiotic as your question."

Tonight, the president had announced that, with the invasion of the

Allies into Sicily, the first crack in the Axis had come. Hitler had abandoned the Italians in Sicily just as he had in Tunisia—more than 250,000 Axis troops were captured there. The Russian front was advancing and the Pacific front, too, with its Liberators flying from Midway to continue bombing the Japanese on Wake Island. Louise felt sure Michael had been part of the Sicilian invasion, for he'd been transferred to Tunisia from England. Kitty thought Julian would be involved somehow with the push of the Japanese from the Aleutians to New Guinea. Both women were worried for their men; neither spoke much about it. It was their job to, as the song said, "accentuate the positive." Little tolerance was given to women who behaved hysterically, to those who wrung their hands and wept over a lack of letters or complained about their lonely Saturday nights, or the way their babies were known to their fathers only by wallet-worn photos.

The president had explained how long military operations took—a little over a year since they planned the North African campaign, six months since they'd planned the one for Sicily. "We cannot just pick up the telephone and order a new campaign to start the next week," he'd said. Thousands of ships and planes guarded the sea-lanes and carried men and equipment to the point of attack. Here at home were the railroads that carried men to the ports of embarkation, and factories that turned out the necessary materials. (At this, Frank smiled at Kitty, and she smiled back—she *was* proud.)

Roosevelt made them feel better about rationing: gas for a single bombing mission was equal to 375 A-ration tickets—enough gas to drive one's car five times across the continent. The initial assault force on Sicily involved 3,000 ships that carried 160,000 men together with 14,000 vehicles, 600 tanks, and 1,800 guns. And this initial force was followed every day by thousands of reinforcements. Kitty thought of one blond-headed young man squeezed onto the deck of a ship, talking to another soldier as they stared out at the water. With so many men, so much equipment, did they feel safer? Or were they nervously awed at the sight of it all, wary of what such vast numbers of weapons portended? You could see different attitudes reflected in the letters the sisters got—cockiness, boredom, loneliness, but never did the men really complain. They made inquiries about the well-being of their loved ones and disregarded their own. They seemed to share a certain pragmatic philosophy: if your number was up, you'd get it; if it wasn't, you wouldn't. Tish had read aloud from a letter written by a soldier saying that he'd once gotten the creeps bad, he felt sure he was going to get killed that night. He told her he'd started to shake, even his teeth were chattering. His buddy in the foxhole with him had told him to think of some dame and he'd feel better. So the guy had done it, and he'd stopped shaking, just like that. He said he'd thought of Tish in her blue strapless dress with all the sparkles across the top (Kitty knew the dress; Tish had borrowed it from a friend and brought it home in triumph), and he had thought of how her shoulders were so smooth and white and had smelled so good, and he had stopped shaking. *So thanks, kid,* he'd written. *Thanks for being so beautiful.*

The president had praised the great increase in merchant shipping, saying that "tonight we are able to terminate the rationing of coffee." Frank stood and cheered so loudly the family almost didn't hear that in a short time more sugar would also be available.

What stuck most with Kitty from FDR's speech tonight was what he said about the home front: "No one can draw a blue pencil down the middle of the page and call one side the fighting front and the other side the home front. For the two of them are inexorably tied together." Kitty understood this with her head and her heart and her hands. But what she wished for on this hot summer night was an instant return to normalcy.

It was stifling, still up in the eighties and humid, the air so close it felt like hands around her throat. She sat alone, trying to cool herself with a pleated fan she'd made out of newspaper, her skirt hiked indecently over her knees, her blouse opened two buttons down. The fireflies were out, and they lit on and off, on and off, regular as a heartbeat. She watched them, weary and mesmerized, and each time they lit up there seemed to come another scene of a more innocent summer, scenes from her childhood: Pop churning strawberries into ice cream, his white shirtsleeves rolled up past his elbows and his forehead beaded with sweat. Cabbage roses grown so large and fragrant you could smell them a block away. Woozy the cat stuck up in a tree, Kitty's brothers at the base forlornly calling her. The plunk of the first blueberry into the silver bucket. The thrilling leap of grasshoppers in high grass baked warm and sweet-smelling by the sun. The plunge beneath the surface of the cool green water of the lake on North Avenue Beach. Disembodied voices from people's darkened front porches, offering greetings as the family walked home from a movie. The Fourth of July, babies asleep on their laid-out blankets while above them fireworks spread across the sky like giant chrysanthemums. Margaret's canning steaming up the kitchen windows, her apron gaping at the bosom and her hair escaped from her bun in wild, wet tendrils. The scent of outside captured in sheets pulled up to Kitty's chin by her parents before they kissed her good night. Kids standing out in the yard and calling, *"Ohhhhhhhh, Kiiiiitty!"* for her to come out and play kick the can. The musical concerts played by bands under ivy-covered gazebos, the goat cart they used to own pulled by the unimaginatively named Nanny. Once Nanny ate a pair of Margaret's underpants right off the line, and they'd all laughed, even, finally, Margaret. All of the family lying out in the backyard and wishing on stars. And what had she wished for then? A best friend who was not her sister. Free candy. The retirement of Mrs. Hornbuckle, a teacher as mean as her name suggested, before it was Kitty's turn to have her. All wishes so very different from what she'd wish now.

Kitty looked up and down the block. Nobody out. Everyone in, undoubtedly thinking about what FDR had told them this evening, including the fact that there was no telling when this would all be over. She looked up into the heavens and wished on a star for the safe return of Julian and Michael. And Hank. Then she went inside to write her letters.

Kitty sat at the kitchen table with her sisters and nervously opened the letter from Julian that had finally come that day. She read to herself quickly, biting at her lip.

Say, kid,

I think you goofed up here. I got a letter addressed to me, but you meant it for some guy named Hank. Who's that? Seems like you know him pretty well, but I don't remember anybody by that name. This isn't Henry Small, is it? Doesn't sound like Henry. You asked him what he was like as a little boy. I remember you asked me that once, too.

I hope you got the job you wanted. I guess life goes on back there, huh? Here, it's kind of hard to describe, which is why I hardly ever try. But I'll give it a shot. You know those movies we used to watch where they showed islands? Palm trees blowing in the breeze, the big moon and the gentle waves, Bing Crosby and Dorothy Lamour? These islands aren't like that. They're not like that at all. We've got coconuts aboveground and rats and ants below. And is it wet! The rain and humidity on these islands is awful—everything molds. We've got insects all over the place, and a lot of guys get sick with malaria and other diseases—fungus all over their feet. So far, I've escaped that. Hey, did I tell you that some of the guys here started a victory garden? Some guy's mom sent seeds from home. Who knows how long we'll be here to tend it, but it gives us something to do.

Sure wish I could fire my bean-shooter at old Schicklgruber himself and turn out his lights. That would move this thing right along. Then I'd come home, put you in my barouche, and you wouldn't see us for dust— I'd like to drive you all the way to San Francisco, it sure is a nice place.

Keep on writing me. You know what they say, we like our letters real cheerful and real often. Funny to say you feel bored when you're fighting a war, but when I'm not scared out of my wits, I'm awful bored and the letters do help. Some guys carry them around and reread them so often they fall apart. One guy got a crayon scribble from his kid he's never even seen, and when it disintegrated the guy cried—didn't even care that we all saw. We move around quite a bit, but the mail always finds us eventually. How are your sisters. Maybe you could tell them to write me, too. Some guys get fourteen, fifteen letters a week.

Love,

Julian

"What'd he say?" Louise asked.

Kitty handed her the letter.

Louise read it, then handed it back.

"Well?" Kitty asked.

"Seems like he's trying hard to write more."

"Let me see." Tish took the letter from Kitty, read it quickly, and sat up straighter in her chair. "I'll write him; I'll send him ten pages!"

Kitty looked coolly over at her. "Will you."

"He asked me to!"

No arguing with that. Kitty began her own letter: *Dear Julian, I sure was glad to hear from you.* She paused, holding her pen up over her paper. Then she changed the period to a comma and added, *sweetheart.* She stole a look at Tish. Julian was *her* boyfriend, not Tish's. Let Tish go ahead and write to him, she couldn't call him sweetheart.

It seems like years since you left, she wrote. *You're right, things are going along as usual at home. The only unusual thing is that I'm reading a book. Can you believe it?*

Kitty read what she'd written, then read it again. What to say about the book? What would he care about the book? In truth, what did she care about the book?

She blew all the air out of her cheeks and began to jiggle her heel. Back again to this awful inability to say something. What was *real cheerful?* She looked at her sisters, their heads bent over their letters, writing swiftly, smoothly. Sometimes Louise would smile or Tish would giggle, and when that happened, Kitty's frustration mounted.

Never mind something cheerful. Maybe she needed to try something daring, something that might spur Julian into some kind of action, some kind of admission. Maybe the trouble was that, in her heart of hearts, she didn't know what her relationship with Julian really was. Oh, she knew she was his girl, but always it came back to her wondering: what did that *mean?* They'd never been great talkers, not like Louise and Michael, who could sit out on the porch swing and talk for hours. Kitty and Julian weren't like that. Truth be told, she'd mostly been dazzled by his good looks: the gold flecks in his green eyes, the sweep of his blond hair, his strong, lean body. Once when they went on a picnic out in the country and were lying together on a blanket, Julian had picked up her bare foot and kissed the instep. She'd shivered at the almost indecent intimacy—and longed for more. But what had they ever talked about? What did she really know about Julian, or he about her? Well, here was an opportunity for them to learn something about each other. Somebody had to go first to try to make this relationship more romantic—it was what they both wanted, and men were no good at this kind of thing. Julian's way of saying he wanted to be intimate with her was to say, "Hey, kid, let's go swap saliva." He needed an example set for him.

Her mouth set determinedly, Kitty wrote that she loved Julian like peaches and that she hoped he loved her, too, that she dreamed of the day they'd be married. She knew what their Hotpoint kitchen would look like, with its Mixmaster and electric dishwasher and white ruffled curtains and cheerful decals everywhere. Their bedroom would have matching pale gold quilted satin spreads and blond nightstands with lamps with ruffled shades. She knew just how she'd feel when she heard his key in the lock, how she'd melt a bit inside. She wrote that she wanted to go to sleep with him and wake up with him. Take that, Julian Stanton.

She reread the letter, addressed it, and sealed it shut. She saw Julian in the bathroom, shaving his handsome face; herself in the kitchen, cooking unrationed bacon, her hair tied back with a length of blue satin ribbon.

Next she wrote to Hank, and again asked him, *What were you like as a little boy?* It would be interesting to know. There was nothing wrong with asking him that; it was something she might ask anyone. Then, as long as she was getting things straightened out, she told him that he must not misinterpret her writing to him, to remember that she was all but engaged, that her relationship with him was only a friendship, and she knew he would have no trouble finding a girlfriend worthy of him, for he was one swell fellow. Really. Exclamation point. There. She couldn't be any clearer than that about her intentions toward him. She addressed the envelope and sealed it. Then she held it in her hand a long moment before she dropped it into the pile of letters in the center of the table.

Kitty leaned back in her chair and thought of all the mail on all those planes, going to all those places—England, Italy, the myriad islands in the Pacific, the Panama Canal, the Aleutian Islands, New Guinea, Iceland, India . . . Dangerously, she let herself wonder how many of the letters would be sent back to those who had written them. Despite the mighty efforts to keep up morale, the staggering number of casualties could not be ignored. Replacements were constantly being sent to companies that had lost great numbers of their men— sometimes fifty percent or more. An entire National Guard regiment from a tiny town in Iowa had been wiped out.

Just last week, a church friend of Margaret's had shared with her the letter her only son had written to be given to his parents in the event of his death. Kitty had overheard Margaret telling Frank about this, her voice shaking. "Imagine, Frank, that young man writing a letter knowing that, if his parents received it, he'd be gone. He told them about his airplane—'ship,' they call it—he told them it was beautiful and he was so proud his name was painted on it. He said he wanted them to go on with their lives and be happy, to remember that he was not in any pain and that he had joined the service willingly. Give away his clothes to the relatives, he said, but he wanted his father to have his camera. And he"—here Margaret had begun softly crying—"he thanked them for being good parents, and said he hoped that he was a good son, he had tried to be. Ah, Frank, not even twenty years old."

Frank had spoken gently. "It's the cost of war, Margaret. You must not dwell on such things."

"And I try not to. But I have these dreams, Frank, once I dreamed they were all coming to the house, all the boys who have died. Here they came, up the front steps of the porch—tall and short, dark- and fair-complected, all dirty-faced and, oh, God love them, so weary but grinning, just passing through the house, coming in the front door, going out the back, seemed like thousands and thousands of them. One of them took an apple from the bowl on the table, and then he looked at me with such gratitude. Oh, I don't know. I just don't know. We can build the Brooklyn Bridge, but we're not as intelligent as dogs, whose tails wag automatically in recognition of their species."

"Sure, dogs fight, too," Frank had said. "It's animal nature, and people are animals who dress up in clothes. God gave us free will, and this is what happens. All we can do is—"

"But, Frank, if you'd only seen them in that dream. All so young. And all of them gone now, and with them the promise of all they might have given the world. Who knows what they might have been able—"

"Margaret," Frank had said. "You just can't think that way."

"But I do think that way!" she'd said. And then she'd asked, "Wasn't there ever a time that you believed there could be lasting peace?"

Frank had been quiet for a long moment. Then he'd said, "There was one time. You remember when we had the blackout in Chicago?"

"August twelfth, 1942," Margaret had said. "I'll never forget it. Even the lights at Holy Family, the ones at the altar of the Virgin, were out."

"Well," Frank had said, "I looked up into the sky that night and it was just jammed with stars, they were packed in tight all across the horizon, I never knew there were so *many*! Of course I knew they had always been there, that the lights of the city just prevented us from seeing them, but somehow, on that night, it seemed the stars had come together from distant places, had been called to heaven's town square from all over the universe, and they were pushing and shoving and craning their necks to have a look at us foolish mortals, all of us craning our necks to have a look at them. And I took off my silly OCD helmet and I felt the night wind in my hair, and I felt a great humility, Margaret, 'twas a very full feeling. And I felt as well a great sense of promise. For all that we might be, if only we'd let ourselves."

"And then . . . ?"

"Ah, Margaret," he'd said. "We're so far away from those stars."

Kitty capped her pen and stacked up her writing paper. She feared her father was right. And her mother was right, as well. So many had died in this war already, and no end in sight. And now the wounded had begun coming home in great numbers, too. At the factory where she worked, there was a young man who'd lost an arm and one who was paraplegic. They were the "healthy" wounded. Kitty had heard of others who had come home and wouldn't leave their houses for some sense of shame they felt. She honestly wondered sometimes which fate was worse, death or standing behind a curtain and looking out at the street at all the things you felt you could no longer have.

"Who wants tea?" she asked, in a voice so small her sisters didn't hear her.

"STUFFED BEEF HEART LAST NIGHT!" Frank said. "Tonight, boiled tongue! Mother of God, Margaret, can't we at least have some pork-u-pines?" He meant the little meatballs made mostly from rice but with bits of pork sausage and ground beef in them.

"Sure, you complained enough when I made them, too." Margaret dabbed at her mouth with her napkin.

"Now they would be welcome as the Second Coming!"

Margaret lay her napkin down and stood. "Here's what, Frank Heaney. I hereby resign from the position of cook. I've taken on other work now, too, and it's gotten too hard for me to do everything myself. *You* cook for the duration. *You* shop at the butcher and the bakery and the grocer, and *you* juggle the points and the stamps, and *you* stand in the lines, and *you* come up with the menus. I'm sure I'll enjoy the vacation. And now, if you'll excuse me." She pushed her chair under the table, went into the parlor, and turned the radio on loudly.

The family sat still, looking down into their plates. And then Frank cleared his throat and said, "Well. I'll be right back."

No one could hear the brief conversation over the sound of Kate Smith, but their father returned to the table after only a minute or so. "Good news from the front," he said. "We'll have the fine services of your mother in the kitchen after all. And you're none of you to complain!"

"*I* didn't say anything," Binks said.

"Just a general reminder," Frank said. "Pass me the tongue, please." He tucked his napkin into the top of his shirt and very quietly sighed.

KITTY LAY MOANING IN THE BATHTUB. She was ready to quit work. Lala had quit after lunch on the first day after their orientation. Laura had lasted several weeks before she went to work at Marshall Field's. Hattie said that, hard as the work was, it was the most money she'd ever made and she was staying no matter what. They ate lunch together every day, comparing notes on the abuse they'd taken.

The work was claustrophobic and mind-numbingly dull. Most often, Kitty attached fixtures and assemblies to a tail fuselage. When she was lucky, she got to sit on a wooden toolbox and work near the hatch, where she could see out of the plane; otherwise, she knelt down low or stood on a stool and reached up high to work on what felt like the inside of a gigantic barrel. But that was better than being shoved into tiny places to work, like the nose or the tail of the plane, or the circular belly turret. Sometimes she worked with her knees bent up against her chest, her shoulders hunched so far forward her chin was right there to meet them. But no matter where she worked, at the end of the day every part of her—her neck, her legs, her arms, her shoulders, her back, her hands—ached. If she banged her head, which happened often, that hurt, too. She'd seen one girl get her nose broken when she dropped a wrench onto her upturned face, and Kitty lived in fear of that happening to her.

Tired as she was on the way home, she rarely got a seat on the streetcar. It was because she wore pants; if a girl wearing a skirt got on a streetcar where Kitty was standing, a man would invariably get up for her. It infuriated Kitty. Sometimes she wanted to sit on the lap of the girl with the skirt (who no doubt had been sitting all day in a comfortable office like the one Kitty used to work in) and say, "Listen, sister, I'm the one who needs this!"

The first day she'd worked on a plane, Kitty had slept from the time she got home until the next morning—she wouldn't come downstairs for supper, and finally Margaret had told Frank and her sisters to stop trying to make her get up; she'd give her a big breakfast the next morning. And indeed she had: Kitty's bowl had been piled high with oatmeal and raisins. Frank had been concerned when he saw her that morning and had asked if she was in pain. "Oh, no," she'd said. "Just a bit stiff. I'll get used to it!"

She'd gotten used to it all right—she'd gotten used to being in pain. Every day she came home hurting and exhausted. Kitty was proud of the work she was doing, but it was so much harder than she had anticipated. The men she worked with swore and spit and oftentimes smelled—and frankly, so did many of the women. The men made rude remarks about her and the other women, calling them "victory girls," the term for women free with their favors to almost any soldier. She'd thought all the workers would be consumed with patriotic fever, and many were; but some were shamelessly lazy, literally sleeping on the job. The noise was awful, so loud that sometimes when Kitty came out of the factory, she couldn't hear quite right—for a few hours, it was as though her head were stuffed with cotton. And the dirt! She simply couldn't get what was left of her nails clean. And it wasn't just her hands that got soiled; she got dirt up her nose and in her ears, around her neck and, unbelievably, between her toes. After she bathed, she had to scrub a ring of black from the tub and rinse down the drain the shiny metal shavings that had come out of her hair.

She'd made a mistake. Her father had been right; this was no job for her. So what if she could toss around terms like "command deck" or "top gun turret" or "A- and N-bolts" or "cotter keys." She preferred terminology like "sweetheart neckline" and "baby-doll ankle straps" and "chenille-dotted rayon nets." So what if she could use a ratchet wrench and a drill? Weren't the jobs you learned to keep a household running just as valuable? *Any* job these days was helping the boys. Truly. There was no shame in doing another kind of work. Sure, she'd have to go back to making less money, but what difference did that make? Sooner or later (quite a bit later, it appeared), she'd be marrying Julian, and then she'd have all the money she needed. In fact, it was better for her future to take care of herself for Julian; he'd never want to have anything to do with a girl who didn't take care of herself. He'd told her to take the job, but he wasn't at all aware of the toll it took. It didn't matter how often she used Hines Honey and Almond cream for "war workers' hands." Why, if Julian saw how rough—

A knock on the door, and here came Billy's urgent voice. "Kitty? Are you almost done?" Another knock, louder. "Kitty?"

"I'm coming out!" she said and lowered herself into the warm water one last time. She pulled the plug, stood, and wrapped a towel around herself. It would be so nice to be married and have just two people using the bathroom. Just she and Julian, and if one of them was in there, even for a long while, why the wait would still only be . . . Kitty froze. Then she quickly dried off, dressed in her nightgown, cleaned the tub, let Billy in the bathroom, and ran to her room.

"HEY?" KITTY WHISPERED BREATHLESSLY TO LOUISE, after she had settled in the bed beside her.

"What?" Louise answered sleepily.

"Have you thought about what you're going to do about using the bathroom when you're married?"

"What do you mean?"

"You know, number two."

Louise laughed.

"I'm serious," Kitty said. "You don't want him to come in right after. It would change his whole image of you."

Again, Louise laughed.

"Shhhh!" Kitty said. "Don't wake up Tish!"

"I am awake," Tish said. "And as usual I know more than you guys. I know exactly what to do about that situation."

"What, then?" Louise asked. "What do you do?"

"If both of you have to go, always let him go first," Tish said, with tired authority. "If it's an emergency and you can't wait, then make sure the window's open and flush *right away.* When you come out, close the door and distract him. For ten minutes."

"Oh," Kitty said. "That's good advice, actually."

A moment of quiet and then Louise said, "What about gas?"

"Well," Tish said. "You just *don't.*"

"But what if it slips?"

"Make sure you have a dog to blame," Tish said. "Seriously. It's worth getting one for that reason alone."

"But I don't *like* dogs," Kitty said. Oh, everything was too hard. She punched her pillow and closed her eyes. "Good night."

Louise said, "Do you guys ever think about how Hitler has affected the whole world? That just one man did all this? I mean, what if he had been a good man, instead?" Neither of the sisters answered. Kitty sighed. Everything really was too hard.

"DEAR PERKY LITTLE PUSS," TISH READ and giggled. The sisters were comparing salutations.

"*My darling,*" Louise said quietly.

"*Dear Miss Heaney, who has freed Diogenes to lay down his lantern at last,*" Kitty read.

"Huh?" Tish said. "What does that mean?"

"I'm not sure," Kitty said.

"Diogenes was a Greek philosopher," Louise said. "He spent his whole life wandering around with a lantern, looking for a honest man."

"So what does that have to do with anything?" Tish asked. And then, to Kitty, she said, "Read the whole letter."

When Kitty hesitated, Tish said, "It's only from Hank!" She sat back in her chair and crossed her arms and narrowed her eyes. "Or do you have something to hide?"

"No, I don't have anything to hide!" Kitty said. "He just says he got my letter, and he talks about his commanding officer, things like that. That's all. It's nothing."

"Then why don't you read it to us?" Louise asked.

They would not stop until she did. "His commanding officer is named Carl Peters," Kitty said, then read:

"*He has handsome features but is hung badly inside himself, if you understand what I mean, one of those poor souls who seems as though his head should be twisted gently and pulled, like a cork in a bottle, in order to free his real body from that clumsy, sagging, bent, and apologetic mass of flesh. Lest you think me unkind for saying these things, this last is by his own admission and quite literally in his own words. Furthermore, lest you feel sorry for him, you should know that, in addition to his skill at self-deprecation, he has as well a deliciously wicked, often ironic sense of humor in describing others. He calls me Durante for my inability to crack wise, for example. But he is never cruel; rather, his jabs feel like true affection.*

"I have noticed as well that Captain Peters has a keen sense of balance—in the psychological sense, I mean. His mood is even; he does not give himself over to despair or to elation. He surely must feel terrible fear from time to time, as all of us do, but he knows how to keep his mind clear and make good decisions quickly. He is a born leader, quite popular with both men and women; I suspect there is much I might learn from him where women are concerned, in fact. And as you seem so keen on my finding another woman besides yourself, I shall study him from afar and take note of his habits, much as I would the mud-crested winkadink. I hope you are smiling; of course there is no such bird! Or if there is, I know nothing of it.

"You ask what I was like as a young boy. Too serious, I should say, most succinctly. And as enraptured of the toad as of any young girl—I found the world rich with delights and had difficulty prioritizing. Whom should I pursue, the amphibian or the redhead? In some respects, the problem persists. Or did persist, until I met you."

Louise gasped, and Kitty held up her hand. "Just wait."

"But there, I am back at doing what you say you do not want me to do. Still, as a student of Nature for all these years, there lingers in me a suspicion that my affections might not be so unwelcome after all. True? Tell me true, Kitty."

Kitty looked up and spoke quickly. "Of course, I already did tell him. Last time I wrote him, I told him in no uncertain terms."

"How does he sign the letter?" Tish asked suspiciously, and Kitty read the last few lines.

"I am off for a night flight now and shall look for you in the heavens. If you would be so good as to send me a picture, I would not have to be so dangerously distracted in my work. Your friend and nothing but! Mr. Cunningham."

Kitty folded the letter. "So," she said. She felt something strange inside, an agitated kind of sorrow.

"Are you going to send him a picture?" Tish asked.

"No."

"Oh, go on and do it. You've told him you're just friends."

Kitty studied her sister's face. No guile. She meant it.

"Listen to what my guy wrote," Tish said. And she began to read excitedly from the soldier who'd sent her four pages in a wild, loopy script, describing the visit they'd had from Marlene Dietrich, who'd stretched out on a piano to sing her sultry song. Kitty tried to listen but couldn't. In her mind, she saw a young Hank watching a frog, a shock of his black hair falling on his forehead. He sat quietly and patiently on the banks of an otherwise deserted riverbank, unmindful of his wonderful good looks, focused instead on the world before him, and beyond.

IN AUGUST, MRS. O'CONNER DIED, and Michael was home within thirty hours. At the funeral home, Kitty stood alone in the corner, discreetly fanning herself. She was watching Louise hold Michael's hand and speak with the people who had come to pay their respects. It was so strange seeing Louise and Michael together again. The circumstances were sad, of course, and maddening, too, if you could be so crass as to put such a term to it. Kitty supposed she was crass, because mostly what occupied her mind was what it must be like for Louise to have so little time with the man she loved and then be spending it this way.

Michael had grown much thinner, and there was a look in his eye Kitty had never seen before. A gentle distance. A weariness out of sync with his age and formerly easy and upbeat disposition. You couldn't quite reach him. Some of this, Kitty thought, was grief for his mother, for what had been, for him, a sudden death. But there was something else, too.

He'd be going back tomorrow. So little time for him to be home and with Louise. Margaret had invited him and his father to dinner, but Michael's father was going to stay with his sister in Wisconsin that night, and Michael and Louise had asked for the evening alone so that they could go for a meal and to a movie, just like old times. Who could blame them? But oh, what wrenching sweetness would now be attached to this simple thing.

Kitty saw Louise whisper something to Michael. Then she let go of him and went off toward the ladies' room. Michael looked around the room, a sorrow he'd been holding at bay now apparent in his face. But then he spotted Kitty, smiled, and walked over to her.

"Hey, good-looking."

"Michael, I'm so sorry," Kitty said.

He nodded. "Thanks."

"Gosh, who'd have thought . . ."

"I know." He studied the carpet, then looked up at her. "Kitty? I want you to make sure my fiancée takes good care of herself."

"I will."

"God, I miss her."

"She misses you, too."

"Don't let her worry about me so much. And help her feel better about everything—Dad said Mom was in an awful lot of pain. It's better she didn't linger any longer."

"Yes." Kitty didn't know what else to say. How could you say you were glad someone's mother had died? She thought of Margaret lying in a coffin, of herself weeping over her own dead mother. Then she thought of Margaret sitting up in the coffin and saying, "Enough now, we'll get our drama from the motion pictures, thank you very much." That was exactly what she'd say.

"Hear from Julian much?" Michael asked.

"Oh, sure."

"I get a lot of letters from him," Michael said, smiling. "Still the same old Julian."

"Yes," Kitty said. Was he? She didn't even know.

"I suppose he *is* tired of the wardrobe by now," Michael said.

"And no gang to boss around," Kitty said. "Now it's him taking orders."

"Definitely not his style," Michael said and then saw Louise. He raised his hand to signal that he'd be right over, and gave Kitty a quick hug. "Good seeing you, Kat. Drop me a line sometime. And tell Julian that when it's all over the four of us are going to have one hell of a party."

"I will."

"And please . . . take care of her until I come home. Promise?"

"I promise."

Kitty watched him walk away. Billy had talked about how smart Michael looked in his uniform, and he did. Oh, how she missed men, their height and low voices, the firmness of their touch! Well, Julian, she meant, of course. How she missed Julian.

IT WAS VERY LATE WHEN LOUISE came up to bed. The light outside the window was pinkish gray; the birds had begun to call. Kitty was awake but said nothing. The idea of letting her sister believe she had some semblance of privacy was right, for soon she heard the soft sounds of Louise crying. Sometimes nothing but tears would do. Kitty wanted to turn over, her hip ached from being in that position too long, but she kept still, and would, for as long as it took.

EARLY ON MONDAY MORNING, MARGARET SHOOK Kitty's shoulder. "Have you seen Billy?"

Kitty opened her eyes and blinked once, twice. "What?"

"Have you seen Billy? Wake up, all of you; Billy's missing!"

Louise sat up and yawned. "Ma, calm down. I'm sure he's somewhere nearby. He's probably out playing."

"Don't tell me to calm down!" Margaret held out a note with a trembling hand. "I found this on his bed! He's gone and enlisted! '*I'm off to win the war*,' he says. '*Don't worry, I'll write soon.*'"

"He can't enlist!" Tish said. "He's too young!"

"Yes, and who gave him the idea of how easy it is to lie about his age? All of you so loose with your talk, and now look what you've done!"

Tish began to cry.

"Wait," Kitty said. "Wait a minute, Ma. Are the other boys here?"

"No," Margaret said. "They and your father are out looking for him."

Tish wiped her eyes and reached for the clothes she'd left on the floor. "I'll go and look."

"Wait for me," Kitty told her, and Louise said, "I'll come, too."

"You girls have to go to work," Margaret said. And then, when it became clear that none of them would do any such thing, she said, "Don't all of you go together. Go in different directions. And come back to the house every hour on the hour in case he shows up. I'll wait here. Oh, the licking I'm going to give him. Right out in the front yard, in front of everyone!" Then she began to cry, saying, "If he'd only come back, I'd forgive him, God love him. He just wants to make his father proud. Oh, where did he go? Why must we live in such a big city?"

"I'm sure they won't take him right away," Kitty said. "We'll find him." But she wasn't so sure. She had heard from one of the men at the USO dances that he had been taken the very afternoon he'd signed up. And she also knew the usual procedure was that the men got their paperwork done one day, then headed off for basic training camp the next. There was so very little time.

"MAY I HAVE MORE OATMEAL, PLEASE?" Tommy asked. Margaret mindlessly passed him the bowl. It was two weeks after Billy had disappeared. Tommy had begun eating again—with a vengeance—and that was the only good news the Heaney family had enjoyed. There was little conversation; mostly mealtimes consisted of the clinking of silverware against the dishes.

"May I be excused?" Tommy asked.

"Yes, go," Margaret said irritably. And then, "Where is that father of yours?"

Every morning, Frank went early to the post office to check through the mail before their carrier set out, looking for some word from Billy. So far, nothing.

Kitty pushed away from the table without excusing herself. Who cared now about such formalities? She went to the bathroom and found the door locked. "Tommy?"

"Yes?"

"Are you almost done? I have to get in there, honey. I've got to go to work."

"Okay." Kitty heard the toilet flush, and then Tommy opened the door. He looked up at her and smiled. Kitty stepped into the bathroom, stopped, and came back out into the hall. "Tommy?"

Nothing. She called louder and then heard his thin reply. She went down the hall and into the boys' bedroom. It wasn't a place she liked to go very often, for despite Margaret's insistence on cleanliness, Billy was a slob—messes seemed to follow him wherever he went. But now, in his absence, the room was clean—the bed made, all the toys and books and papers put away, the model cars and airplanes neatly lined up on the shelf. It was awful.

Tommy lay on the bed, his back to Kitty. She sat beside him and touched his shoulder. "Are you sick, honey?"

"I don't know. I don't think so."

"But . . . Didn't you just throw up in the bathroom?"

"Yes. Sorry."

She smiled. "Oh, Tommy, you don't have to apologize! Turn over, let me see you."

He turned toward her, embarrassed. Despite having begun to eat again, he didn't look well. He had circles under his eyes, and even his freckles seemed pale.

"Did you just eat too much? Is that it? Got a little too full?"

He nodded.

"Are you trying to eat more to make Ma feel better?"

"I guess so."

"Well, that's nice, but just take it easy, okay? Just eat normally, and that will be fine. Okay?"

"Kitty?"

"Yes?"

"Will Billy get killed in the war?"

"Oh, sweetheart, no. If he hasn't been found out already, he's off in some training camp—he hasn't gone overseas yet. We're going to find him and bring him home. Don't worry. You worry so much, and you've got to stop! I know everybody's upset about Billy, but believe me, we'll find him."

Tommy stared at her. "Do you promise?"

"I promise!" she said, with a hearty conviction she didn't feel at all. Who knew where Billy was or what had happened to him? All the efforts Frank had made to find him through the armed services had thus far failed.

She leaned in closer to Tommy's face. "You know what? I have something up my sleeve that I'm going to tell Pop as soon as he gets home. And I'll bet you we find him right away after that. One thing I really know for sure, Tommy, is that Billy is fine. I just know it." Oddly, she did feel sure of that.

"What about Julian, and Michael?"

"Them, too."

"But every day guys get killed. More and more."

"I know. It's awful. But Julian and Michael and Billy won't."

"How do you know, though?"

"You have to have faith. Okay?"

"Okay." He sat up, and Kitty rubbed his back. She could feel his rib cage, his knobby vertebrae.

"I want you not to think about these things so much, Tommy. You're making yourself sick. I'll tell you what. I'll worry for you. Whenever you start to feel bad, you think to yourself, *Hey, I don't have to do this! Kitty's worrying for me!* Okay? Can you do that? I'll worry for you."

"What's your plan?"

"My plan?"

"Yes, you said you had something up your sleeve. About Billy."

"Oh!" she said. "That's absolutely right. But it's top secret. I have to go to work now. I'll see you at dinner."

Kitty sped down the hall to get into the bathroom before it became occupied again. But she was too late. She knocked on the door and heard Tish's "One second."

Kitty sighed and slid to the floor. One second. More like one hour. "Hurry up!" she yelled. "I have to get to work."

"So does everybody," Tish yelled back.

"I have to go the farthest!" Kitty yelled. To this Tish said nothing.

Kitty crossed one ankle over the other and tried to relax. Nothing would make Tish linger more than telling her not to. Kitty looked down the hall toward the boys' room. She felt bad telling Tommy she had a plan about Billy when she didn't. Only suddenly, she did have an idea. She got up and ran down the stairs, calling for her mother.

A FEW DAYS LATER, MARGARET STOOD on the porch with the rest of the family, watching Billy come down the block. She was crying, her hands over her mouth, and her hands were trembling. She'd come outside without taking her apron off, something she'd never done before.

When Billy at last stood before them, Margaret embraced him, though she'd said the first thing she was going to do when she laid eyes on him was beat him senseless. But how could she? It was a Sunday morning, the church bells were ringing, a coffeecake in the oven was scenting the house with cinnamon, and the missing son had returned unharmed to stand before her with his crooked smile and his bright blue eyes.

Kitty's own eyes filled with tears as she watched her mother hold Billy close to her, swaying and sobbing. Then, abruptly, Margaret stepped back from him and pointed to the front door. "Inside. I might as well tell you, you're going to get the licking of your life."

Billy grinned.

Margaret grabbed his ear. She wasn't kidding.

The rest of the family waited uneasily on the porch. Binks pressed his nose to the window and cupped his hands around his eyes. "She's still got him by the ear," he said, adding, "That really hurts. Now she's . . . Wait. Billy dropped his duffel bag. Now she's coming out of the kitchen with that big wooden spoon and she's . . . Uh-oh. She made him turn around and now . . . Oh, boy, she's giving it to him now."

This they knew. Billy's howls made it to the front porch and beyond. But they were more like howls of joy, Kitty thought.

She sat on the top front step in the morning sun. She was overjoyed to have her brother home, but she was a little miffed that she hadn't been recognized enough for her sleuthing abilities. Billy had used his friend Anthony's birth certificate to enlist. "Of course!" Frank had said, smacking his forehead. But do you think he thanked his daughter? Do you think he acknowledged her excellent reasoning ability? No. He got on the telephone, and now, three days later, here his son was, back from his Louisiana boot camp. And in spite of Frank's worry and his anger, Kitty could see that her father admired his son's derring-do. Well, let him calm down, her father. She needed his full attention to tell him the next bit of great news: she was quitting the airplane factory. She was going to sell gloves at Carson's, Tish had told her about an opening. Tomorrow she would let the factory know, via telephone. And then she would once again dress prettily for work. And grow her fingernails and keep them painted. And browse in department stores after a lunch she'd had with girlfriends who all smelled like perfume. And be treated as the lady she was.

"Ow!" Billy cried one last time, and then there was Margaret at the door, her face flushed, her apron askew, exuberantly waving them all in to have sour cream coffeecake made from Gert Nelson's excellent recipe. It had taken a blue ribbon at the state fair three times, and if you ever forgot that, don't worry, Gert would remind you. No matter; the cake was so good, it was worth it to have to offer congratulations over and over again.

AT SUPPER (ROAST BEEF!), BILLY REGALED THE FAMILY with the story of his adventure. Apparently the punishment phase was over, and now everyone had moved on to adulation. Well, not Kitty. She knew what behavior should be admired and what behavior should not be.

"There was this really crabby sergeant?" Billy said. "And one guy, he did something wrong and the sergeant kicked him and made him do fifty push-ups. It was a terrible place. We had to take fifteen-mile hikes. Our clothes that they gave us didn't even fit. We had to get up real early and then lights-out at nine. If you got up after that to go to the bathroom or something, you had to walk on tiptoes. They made me practically bald, you should have seen me when they first cut my hair. You had to clean everything so much it was ridiculous. We even had to wash windows!"

" 'Tis a wonder you survived," Margaret said wryly.

"Don't I know it," Billy said.

"I SEE," FRANK SAID. He was sitting in his chair in the parlor, and Kitty stood before him, waiting for him to congratulate her on coming to her senses. "Well, if you think that's the right thing to do . . ."

"What do you mean?" Kitty said. "You didn't even want me to take that job!"

Frank sucked at his pipe. " 'Tis true."

"You said it wasn't right for a woman to work in a factory."

"I did."

"So . . . ?"

"Well, you took the job anyway, didn't you? And now you want to quit. I don't like to think of any of us in this family as being quitters, including Billy; sure he'll enlist when it's time, should the war still be on. If you believe it's right to leave the factory, you must do it. Never be afraid of doing the thing you know in your heart is right, even if others don't agree. Just be sure that your decision sits well with your conscience. If you leave that job, make sure you can look yourself—and your country—in the eye."

"Pop," Kitty said. "It's hard. I don't even want to tell you some of the things that go on in that place."

"I'm sure you're not quitting because your fingernails get broken."

Kitty stared at the floor. That certainly was a part of it.

Frank's voice grew gentle. "I think all the time about our boys, Kitty. Sometimes I imagine them in their foxholes, all those young men in all those foreign places from which they might never return. I wonder what they talk about before they go into battle—or if they talk at all. I wonder how many of them look up at the stars and try to realize what their young lives have meant, and if they don't come home, what their deaths will mean. I know they realize one thing more than any other: there's no turning back. They've got to carry their mission through." He tapped his pipe against the ashtray. "But the person with a bleeding finger doesn't hurt less for the person next to him with the bleeding arm. You do what you have to do, Kitty. There'll be no blame coming from me."

IN THE MORNING, KITTY ROSE before anyone else and made her way downstairs. She telephoned the factory and spoke quietly into the mouthpiece, identifying herself. Then she stood tall to say, "I'm sorry to have to tell you this, but I . . ."

"Yes?" The woman on the other end of the line was impatient-sounding. No doubt she'd worked all night shift and was tired, ready to go home.

"I . . . might be a little late this morning."

"Well, get here as soon as you can," the woman said. "And don't think you won't be docked, either." She hung up.

Someone from the party line picked up his phone. "Hello? *Hello?*"

Kitty hung up.

So, then, off to work. Jeez, how much was a person supposed to sacrifice, anyway? How did you decide when it was enough? When she was little, Frank had told her something she'd never forgotten: If you win something, it feels good. If you help someone else win something, it feels even better, because it lasts longer, it might even last all your life. Uh-huh, she'd said at the time, not believing him for a second. And just the other day, a woman at work who was selling war bonds had said, "People say you should give till it hurts. I say you should give till it stops hurting. Know what I mean?"

"I do," Kitty said. But here was something Kitty meant: she was going to buy herself a pretty dress now and then, even if she hardly ever got to wear it. A girl had to live.

"I DON'T FEEL LIKE GOING TO A DANCE any more than the man in the moon." Kitty sat at the edge of the bed, rubbing her feet. She'd taken a shower in cold water, hoping the unpleasant jolt would wake her up, but it was no good: she was still thoroughly beat, and now she was freezing, too. She understood the need for oil to be conserved at home so that it could go toward fuel for the boys. But because she had taken a cold shower in the middle of November to wake up and do her part as a morale booster at a USO dance (in addition to doing her part as a defense worker!), she was sitting inside her own house shivering, unable to get warm. When the temperature was kept at sixty-five degrees, keeping warm at any time was hard to do. But now!

Besides that, she was working harder than ever in the factory; there was a mania to get things done and get them done even more quickly than before. The Italian surrender had helped throw everyone into high gear. Hitler was reportedly depressed and staring silently into his soup; Himmler had set up a special SS team to destroy evidence of the mass murder of Jews; new offensives had been launched in the Pacific. Everyone was galvanized, but there was a price to be paid: she and Hattie were often so tired at lunch they hardly spoke. When Hattie's birthday had come last week and Kitty had given her false fingernails as a joke, neither of them had laughed. Instead, Hattie had started crying, and then Kitty had, too. They'd both been embarrassed. Ruined hands did not in any way compare with the ultimate, horrifying sacrifices the men were making, Kitty knew that, and she felt guilty for complaining. Still, at such times she also remembered her father's words about the hurt finger not hurting less because of someone else's more seriously injured arm. She'd offered a hankie to Hattie and told her to come on, she'd buy her a Coke. Hattie had said fine, she'd buy one for Kitty.

"Don't go to the dance, then," Tish said, pinching her cheeks to raise some color. "Louise is coming; she can 'chaperone.'"

"I'm not so sure I should go, either," Louise said. "After what happened last time."

Louise had danced with a young man from Boise who made Fred Astaire look like an amateur. Also, his looks reminded her of Michael, and when he'd held her close during "You'd Be So Nice to Come Home To," she'd closed her eyes and imagined that it was indeed Michael holding her. Then, to her horror—for the girls were there above all else to cheer up the soldiers—she'd started crying. When the boy had pulled back from her and asked her what was wrong, she'd confessed that she'd been pretending he was Michael. He'd told her that was all right, he'd been pretending she was his wife. He had a young wife and a little son, only six weeks old when he left. And then Louise had begun to cry harder, thinking of how that baby might never know his father. The man had told her not to worry, he wasn't scared, all his life he'd been a very lucky fellow. "Tell you what," he'd told her. "When I get home I'll send you a sign. Four four-leaf clovers—I'm always finding them everywhere I go. And then you'll know that the lucky man you danced with got home safe and sound." Louise had disobeyed the rules and given him her address. It didn't seem to be so much of a risk—the men in his unit were taking the train out the next morning.

"Oh, let's both go," Kitty told Louise. "I'll dance; you do something else. Why don't you help the guys make records to send home?"

"That's dangerous," Louise said. "You never know when a guy's going to send a record to a girl who sent him a Dear John letter. That's even worse than the guys who are telling their parents they're coming home amputees. I don't see how anyone could do that, send a guy who's fighting a war a Dear John letter. What kind of person would be so cruel? At least wait until he gets home! I'll come to the club. I'll just serve coffee again."

Kitty didn't want to go to the Kelly Club, but she didn't want to stay at home, either—what was there to do at home but go to bed early? She'd had enough of that. Despite her fatigue, she was young, she wanted to do things. And she wanted a man to look at her *that way*. Surely all women did. There were rumors that flew around at the factory about married women who were apparently having relations with men there as well as outside the factory. One such woman, a thirtyish redhead named Dellrene, had admitted openly that she wasn't going to deny herself. She'd told Kitty, "What he don't know won't hurt him. I got needs. And don't tell me he ain't helping himself to whatever he can find. When he comes home, we'll be with each other. For now . . ." She'd shrugged. "It's war, honey."

Another reason to go to the dance was that, so far as Kitty was concerned, Tish needed two chaperones. She was always on the verge of getting in trouble; she was a terrible flirt. She was doing very well at her job, and any money she didn't give to the family went toward clothes or the fabric to make them. She loved showing off her Charmode dress-up frock, with its figure-molding drapery, and her whirl skirt in fine rayon crepe, and her pleated dress with an elongated bodice and lowered waistline. Kitty had a few new things as well, her favorite being a classic line dress with a shirred bodice and jeweled buttons, but it didn't feel the same to dress up when your fingers were callused, your face too thin, your hair dry from overshampooing.

"*Girls?*" their mother called, and in her voice was such panic that all three of them raced down the stairs.

There's a fire! Kitty thought, and she sniffed at the air and worried about where the rest of her family was. Why hadn't she gotten dressed faster? Now she'd have to go outside barefoot and in her robe.

But there was no fire. Instead, there was Tommy, lying white-faced in his mother's arms, his eyes closed, something dark caked at the corners of his mouth.

. . .

AFTER THEIR PARENTS AND THEIR BROTHERS left Tommy's hospital bedside, the sisters took their turns and pulled their chairs up closer to him. He had been tentatively diagnosed with a digestive disorder, and though the doctor thought he would be fine, he would not be coming home for a while. True to his nature, he'd complained about nothing. He lay still with his hair wetly combed—Margaret's doing—and with Frank's wristwatch huge on his arm. A transfusion was running, and squeamish Tish pointedly turned her back to the bottle of blood. "Did you meet any cute girls in here yet?" she asked.

Tommy smiled. "No."

"Well, keep your eyes open," Tish said. "I think there might be cute girls running around here."

"Can you bring them in to meet me?" Tommy asked, and then Tish had to stop smiling. "I was just kidding, hon," she said.

Tommy said gravely, "Me, too, sis," and Tish laughed.

"Want me to bring you some ice cream tomorrow?" Kitty asked him.

"That's okay, I'm not so hungry."

"When you come home, then," Kitty said, and the words reverberated inside her head. *When you come home.* It was funny; with all that was going on with the war overseas, these domestic trials seemed outrageous, a kind of bitter insult. Michael's mother dying. Tommy seriously ill. But nothing in nature stopped in deference to anything else. In apology for it. For the sake of some kind of balance. Kitty thought of a film she once saw where an antelope ran from a lion. Its head was high, its dark eyes wide in panic. Then it was down, being eaten alive. That antelope, on that day. Nearby, a mix of other animals drank from a great pond, watchful, wary, but mostly just thirsty. Was human nature so different from animal nature? Or nature nature? How did one find sense in anything? How did one find comfort?

Kitty leaned over to kiss Tommy's forehead. He still smelled like a little boy sometimes. He smelled of pencils and lunch meat and clean sweat. "I love you," she told him. There. That was how to find comfort.

Louise leaned over and spoke quietly to her little brother. "I'm going to tell Michael to send a letter just for you," she told him. "Would you like that?"

He nodded happily.

"Want one from Julian, too?" Kitty asked.

"Yes."

"Want one from a whole *bunch* of guys?" Tish asked. "And one of them is a really good artist who draws really funny pictures?" Kitty knew the Army flier Tish meant. He was stationed in England, and he'd sent a drawing of Churchill smoking a cigar the size of himself.

"Yes," Tommy said and yawned, and the sisters gathered up their coats and purses. Their parents would come in one more time, and then the family would go home, minus one.

On Monday, Hattie met Kitty for lunch at the corner table of the employee cafeteria. There was something different about Hattie, something wrong. She wouldn't look directly at Kitty, and in place of her usual chattiness, there was a heavy silence. She sat staring at her lunch bag, refusing to meet Kitty's eyes. Kitty touched her hand. "Hattie? Is everything all right?"

Finally, "I have to tell you something," Hattie said.

Kitty stopped unwrapping the waxed paper from around her sandwich. "Did Will . . . ?"

Hattie nodded. Two tears slid down her face, and she hastily wiped them off.

Kitty reached across the table for Hattie's hand. "Oh, Hattie. I'm so sorry. When did you find out?"

"His mama wrote me. I got the letter Saturday. It's funny; I knew, soon as I saw the envelope. We'd been writing, she and I. But I knew this was going to be the letter telling me that he got killed." Hattie looked at the employees all around her, talking, laughing, smoking. At the table next to them was Arlene Burns, whose son was a Navy flier and had just been written up in the paper. Sitting with her was Luddie Stevenson, who'd returned from Guadalcanal completely deaf in one ear and was always cocking his head like a puppy to hear you better, and Tiny Hermon, who was mildly retarded and anything but tiny. You could always count on Tiny to help you lift things.

"Sure took a while to find out," Hattie said. "There I was, getting up every morning thinking I was one day closer to being back with him.

Writing him every night. I used to get all dressed up to write him, isn't that silly? Used to put a dress on, and my lipstick, my high-heeled shoes. Just like a date. I put his picture next to me, turned on the radio, and wrote him everything I could think of." She smiled and shook her head. "He was one handsome man, old Will Duncan. I wish you'd met him."

"I do, too," Kitty said. Her throat hurt. She wanted to go home.

"And he wrote me such nice letters. Romantic, but also just *nice*. He'd say things 'bout how he missed oranges, that little spray when he first dug in to peel them, that scent. Said he missed the sounds of his neighborhood, the little kids skipping rope, old Mrs. Dooley leaning out her window in her nightgown and yelling for her cat, sounding for all the world *like* a cat the way she yowled, but he missed it. I fell in love with him from those letters, it's how I got to really know him. I remember thinking, Well, who wants a war, but how else would I have ever gotten these precious words? I thought after the war was over, we'd all get together. You and Julian and me and Will. It was a surprise I was saving for all of us. I had a big dinner planned, I was going to play music and serve dinner, and we'd eat and we'd dance. . . . I wish I'd told Will about it. I had the whole menu planned, I'd asked him once what his favorite foods were, and he gave me this big long list—Lord! But I was going to make every single thing he told me, from catfish to hot dogs to strawberry shortcake to buttered noodles, and I was going to invite you and Julian, and we were going to celebrate the end of the war and the beginning of . . .

"Well, I didn't really know, see. I didn't know for sure. I think me and Will were perfect together, and I guess I just thought we'd get married. We'd have the kids and the house and . . ." She looked at Kitty. "You do that, dream in your mind 'bout all you and Julian going to do after the war? Do you see everything just so clear?"

Kitty nodded. "All the time."

Hattie stared into her lap. "I knew the house we'd live in like it was a real thing out there, just waiting for us, the door cracked open. I knew how it would feel when we were lying in bed together every morning." She looked up sharply at Kitty, and her voice turned hard. "I wish I'd done more with him. I wish I had done everything. Those people that tell you to wait? They're wrong. Because now I'll never know what . . . I'll never know."

Kitty wanted to tell Hattie that she had been better off not doing more. That there would be another man for her, in time. That then she would be glad she had waited. But what she said was "I know." Then she asked, "So . . . are you going to stay here?"

Hattie nodded and opened her lunch bag. "I'm going to stay here. Least until a better idea comes along. I'm going to build me a plane kill a bunch of Nazis dead." She pulled out a sandwich and an apple and stared at them. "I don't guess I'm so hungry. Would you like my lunch?"

"You need to eat, Hattie," Kitty told her gently.

"I know you're right." Hattie took a bite of her apple. "It's good," she said. "You know, I just feel so bad about how good it is." She dropped the apple, put her hands to her face, and began to cry, and Kitty moved her chair to shield her friend from the stares of their co-workers. She put her arm around Hattie's shoulders and rocked her. Rocked them both.

THAT NIGHT, ON THE WAY HOME FROM WORK, Kitty miraculously found a seat on the streetcar. She stared out the window, noticing all the fringed flags in all the windows that were decorated with blue stars, one for each person from that house who was in the service. One flag had three stars, and Kitty imagined what it would be like to have all her brothers gone. She looked especially for gold stars tonight, gold stars for those buried at home or at sea or in foreign soil, those men who'd waved jauntily from departing trains and jitterbugged at USO clubs, those who would never again hear the sounds of their neighbors, or kiss their girlfriends, or pet their dogs, or father children, or breathe in the scent of an orange. Gold stars for those men barely old enough to shave, who had written wills specifying the disposition of their few things. *I want Dad to have my camera.* A soldier she'd once danced with had told her that you never hear the sound of the shell that kills you. She hoped that was true.

AT LAST, TOMMY CAME HOME, still weak and needing time to recuperate. Margaret made soups and stews and casseroles and compotes and a little pan of apple crisp, for it was Tommy's favorite. Frank made puppets from socks and put on a show every night. The sisters brought Tommy comics and crayons, books from the library, small bags of candy. They sat on his bed and read him letters from the boys. Billy made Tommy a slingshot and dropped in several times a day to make sure he was perfecting his aim. And Binks often sat by the side of Tommy's bed, folding newspapers into hats and boats and singing songs to his brother in his nasally little voice.

After a few days, Dr. Brandon made a house call to check on Tommy's progress. The rest of the family followed him upstairs and squeezed into Tommy's doorway. Frank, his arms crossed and his posture ramrod straight, watched the doctor's every move, occasionally grunting his approval. Margaret peered over his shoulder, Binks and Billy silently punched each other for obscuring the view, and the sisters held stock-still behind all the rest, as though their standing at attention would guarantee a good report on their pale-faced brother.

The doctor sat on the edge of Tommy's bed and pressed and prodded at his abdomen. He listened to Tommy's heart and had Tommy open his mouth wide and stick out his tongue. He lifted his pajama top in back and listened to Tommy's lungs, his eyes on the ceiling. He told Tommy to cough, and he did, rather dramatically, which caused a worried look to pass between Margaret and Frank. The doctor had Tommy stand and then sit down and then stand again. Then he tucked him back into bed and told Tommy he was doing very well. He turned to the rest of the family and raised his bushy eyebrows. "Shall we all go downstairs?"

When the family had assembled in the living room, Dr. Brandon said, "If you don't all stop taking such good care of him, he's going to have to go back into the hospital."

"What do you mean?" Frank asked, halfway between anger and fear.

"I mean, you've got to let him rest! Now here, listen to me. I want you to give Tommy a little bell. If he needs something, he's to ring it. You may poke your head in on him every three or four hours, but do *not* wake him up. The boy's exhausted!"

Binks began to blink back tears. "Tommy's not better?"

The doctor turned to him and softened his voice. "Now, son, I didn't say he's not getting better. And I know you all only mean to help him. But what he needs most of all is to rest. So here's an idea: why don't you each pay him a visit at a certain time every day? But listen to me now, only one at a time! *One!*"

"I'll go first thing in the morning," Frank said.

"Can I go with you?" Binks asked, and Frank said that would be a fine idea.

"I want to see him in the morning, too," Louise said, "before I have to go to work."

"That's my time," Kitty said.

Exasperated, the doctor put on his hat and his coat. "You work out a schedule," he said. "But I want that boy to get some rest! Now, can I rely on you to give it to him?"

All of them were silent, nodding. And then Margaret asked would the doctor like a loaf of the lovely rye bread she'd made that morning. And Binks asked but could he just go up now and say good night to Tommy.

"IT'S SHORT; SHALL I GO FIRST?" Louise asked, after dinner. No one answered. And so she began reading from the letter that had come from Michael.

"Dearest Louise,

"I'm so beat I'll resort to V-mail for tonight, and even at that I may fall asleep over the page. Today tested us all to the limit; one fellow broke down. And yet despite all the hardships, there is something to love in this man's Army. We are all on one side, united in this fight against evil, and of course that brings with it a certain camaraderie. But what I'm talking about is more mundane than that, more day-to-day. In basic training, there was a kind of stripping away of ego that now serves us well—there can be no stars in battle, there can only be a team. We aren't competing in that desperate and backhanded way that men do when they're trying to climb the corporate ladder. Black, brown, white, red, and yellow men fight together. When you need something, there is someone who will do his best to get it to you. There are no phony standards to live up to. Strange as everything about this war is, it is still the realest thing I've ever known. Except for my love for you, my darling. Except for that. Here's a kiss. And as always, my heart."

Louise smiled and folded up the letter. "Your turn," she told Kitty.

Kitty had not heard from Hank Cunningham in well over two weeks, and she feared the worst. But she did have a longer-than-usual letter from Julian, and she shared it with her sisters as well as her father, who had come into the kitchen looking for matches for his pipe.

"Hello, Kat.

"Well, hi de ho, from a brand-new island in the same old Pacific.

"Guess what I'm going trick-or-treating as. A U.S. Marine!

"Yipe, I'm cooking on the front burner now. Did I ever tell you about Too-Too Padama? He's a Philippine who works in the motor pool. We call him Too-Too because he's this real excitable guy and that's the way he talks: 'I'm too too hungry!' 'It's raining too too much!' Anyway, old Too-Too got tired of wearing the same stinking clothes all the time, so he made a washing machine using a big barrel and two wooden paddles. It's powered by a one-lung gasoline motor. I traded him all my hoarded-up smokes to get my laundry done. Then I spent all afternoon with my nose buried in my collar.

Detergent: my new favorite perfume. I am now once again the best-dressed man around.

"*Last night we saw Abbott and Costello in* Pardon My Sarong *and* Ship Ahoy *with Eleanor Powell and Red Skelton. Pretty good. It's strange when the lights come up and you're not there. I know you're not there of course, but in the darkness, you sort of are.*

"*Wowser, you sure have learned a lot in that factory. I'm impressed. You asked if I've learned a lot in the Army. Oh sure. I've become an ace fly killer. Flies take off backward, did you know that? So if you want to kill them, you aim from behind them a couple of inches and you get them every time. I'll bet I've killed more flies than any man in my division. Just waiting for my medal. Maybe it'll be a big round silver medal featuring a compound eye.*

"*This all is more difficult than I can say. I can't write to you about what we do, other than to tell you we go from zero to a hundred miles an hour, not much in between. I'll have a lot of stories when I get back, but for now I just have to talk about safe things. The guys say the censors all have a case of scissoritis. Beats malaria, I guess. Say hi to the family, and send me some more cookies anytime.*

"*Love, Julian.*"

"Cookies! What cookies?" Frank asked.

"Gingersnaps," Tish said. It had been Tommy's idea to send Julian cookies, and Tish was the one who had made them. But she had let Kitty send the accompanying note as though she were the one who had made them. This was because Kitty had let Tish wear her only pair of nylon stockings.

"Any left?" Frank asked hopefully.

"Sorry," Tish said.

Frank grunted. He was hungry tonight, for Margaret had served them baked-bean sandwiches for dinner—the butcher had had no meat that day. "Be grateful you've dinner at all," Frank told Billy, who'd stared dismally at his plate. They had all cheered up a bit when Margaret told them that meat loaf was slated for tomorrow, the Good Lord and Emmet the butcher willing.

When her father left the kitchen, Kitty read Julian's postscript:

"One more thing. I just want to say that I'm not a guy who's jazzed up about any kind of romantic writing, Kitty. Some guys are regular Shakespeares—whether they're chinning on paper or in person, the words just flow. I don't care two whoops up a rain barrel about that kind of thing. To me, it's just showing off. Still waters run deep, you know. I care very much for you. That's the crop, duchess. I guess it counts for something."

"There you go," Louise said, and she said it proudly, as though she were the one who had written it, or the one who had encouraged Julian to.

"That's *it*?" Tish said.

Kitty looked levelly at her, and Tish turned away.

On a dark Saturday morning in early December, while snow clouds gathered outside, Margaret told Louise, "All right, now, sit sideways, take in a deep breath, and stick out your chest!" She had decided to take photographs of her daughters to send to the men for Christmas. Right after breakfast, she told them to get dressed up, fix their hair, put on some lipstick. Louise was first. "Come on now, push it out," Margaret said.

"Ma," Louise said, embarrassed.

"You and Michael are practically married," Margaret said. "Show him your stuff, 'twill cheer him up. Go on now, take a nice deep breath. All the girls do."

"How do *you* know?" Tish asked.

"Quiet, and let me focus properly," Margaret said. And then to Louise, "Turn to the side and breathe in, darlin'. There's no shame in it. Just yesterday I saw photos that Tootie Bensen took of her daughter, and wasn't she trying to look like a pinup queen, pushing out her bosoms and holding her hair up and winking to boot. And her daughter can't compare with any of mine. Go on now, take a deeeeeep breath." And then when Louise sighed and did just that, Margaret pulled the camera down from her eye. "Well, maybe not that deep," she said. Louise readjusted herself, and the flashbulb brightened the kitchen.

"You look pretty, Louise," Binks said. He was kneeling on a chair, working a button of yellow dye into the lumpy white margarine.

"What about me?" Tish asked. She'd piled her hair on top of her head in a Grable upsweep.

Binks looked over at her and shrugged. "You look okay, I guess. I like when your hair is in braids."

"When you're older, you'll like this better," Tish told him, and he didn't bother to look up from the bowl to say no, he would not. He liked to see the exact moment when the white turned all yellow.

Outside, the mailman opened the box to put letters in, and Kitty went running to retrieve them.

"Five!" Tish said, when Kitty passed them out. Kitty had gotten one from Hank, finally. It was such a relief to know that he was all right. Louise had received only a package with an unknown return address. The name Miller had been carefully printed, followed by an address in Boise. "I can't imagine what this is," she said, and then, remembering the man she'd danced with from Idaho, she said, "Oh, I'll bet it's from Tom, that boy I danced with who promised to send me four-leaf clovers when he got home. I wonder why he's back already." She unwrapped the package and found an envelope along with a smaller box. She opened the box first and smiled. Inside, pinned carefully to paper, were four four-leaf clovers. "He's okay!" she said. But then she read the note, first to herself, then to her sisters.

"*Dear Miss Heaney,*

"*My son, Tom Miller, was killed in action on November 4. Among his personal effects was this box with your name and address on it. I thought you might like to have it. I assume you were a friend—Tommy had a gift for making friends wherever he went. As such, you will like to know that his wife and son are coping as well as can be expected. We surely will miss him, and I would like to thank you for any part you may have played in his all too brief but very happy life.*

"*Sincerely, Velma Miller.*"

Louise looked up, tears in her eyes.

"Say a prayer?" Tish whispered, and the sisters bowed their heads.

After a moment, Margaret asked briskly, "Who's next?"

"I'll go," Tish said solemnly. She sat on a chair and turned sideways. Then she inhaled and stuck her chest out mightily.

"Face me," Margaret said.

"But you said—"

"That was to Louise. You're just a girl. Now turn around and smile prettily."

"But you said to cheer up—"

"There's cheering up one way, and there's cheering up another," Margaret said. "You look lovely. Any man would be happy to see that smile."

"Fine," Tish said. But just before Margaret took the picture, she shifted her shoulders and winked.

HANK WROTE AGAIN OF THE FUTILITY of war. Kitty didn't read aloud those parts to her sisters; the one time she'd tried, they'd gotten angry. But in this letter, he said that when war was seen at close range, it was so brutal and idiotic. It seemed impossible that men with hearts and brains were capable of it. Such devastation of cities, so many innocent lives lost. It seemed to him that if just a small part of the effort put into war could be put into peace, they'd be so much better off. When the war was over, he said. When this most catastrophic of wars was finally over, surely the world would have learned the need to never make war again. Then he went on to say something that made Kitty gasp, and this she did share with her sisters. "Hank Cunningham is coming home on leave!"

"*Here?*" Tish asked.

"Well, he's going home to San Francisco," Kitty said. "But he's coming to Chicago first. He'll be here the Saturday after next—all day!"

Silence.

"I guess he deserves a furlough!" Kitty said. "He's flown twenty-five missions! Jeez! You'd think a person would be honored to be with a soldier like that!"

"Well, *I'd* like to meet him," Louise said. "I'd like to very much."

"I didn't say I didn't," Tish said.

"Who asked you?" Kitty muttered.

What news! Soon Hank would be back in Chicago, stepping off a train in Union Station. It made her stomach hurt, but in a good way, like the way it hurt before you got into the car on the Ferris wheel. She thought for a moment about how she might not recognize him, then realized that she would have no trouble at all. She'd not forgotten anything about him.

Kitty sat still, trying to pay attention to the letters Tish read aloud, but she heard only bits and pieces: stories of German prisoners sitting on the ground and taking off their shirts to suntan, those same prisoners telling their American captors in perfect English that they had been told New York City had been bombed to smithereens and that the Japs had gotten all the Russians out of Siberia. She heard about enemy helmets attached to jeep radiators, blood-soaked Japanese flags being sent home, dogs accompanying pilots on commando raids, men huddling in the cold under blankets to write letters by candlelight and always, always dreaming of home. Sometimes Kitty wondered if *home* would become something in the men's minds that their families could never live up to, something that perhaps never even was. She supposed the idea of home had become as much religion to the boys as anything else, a thing to believe in, to turn to, to help keep them going. The responsibility was awesome; Kitty felt it behind her knees, in her breathing; it permeated her unconscious. Last night, she had dreamed Julian came into the house and asked expectantly, "Where is it?" His eyes were bright, he was smiling his famous Julian smile. He was in uniform, dirt in his hair and smeared across the bridge of his nose and caught in the creases of his pants.

"Where is what?" Kitty asked. She wanted to take his hand; she wanted him to hold her, to kiss her. He was home!

"*You* know," he said.

"I don't."

He went to the living room and sank down into a chair. "I'll have to go back, then." He turned away from her to look out the window. His knee began to bounce. "Julian?" she said, but he wouldn't look at her. He stared out the window, shaking his head slowly, and she stood before him, her hands twisted in her skirt, smiling and calling his name: "Julian? Julian? Julian?"

. . .

KITTY AWAKENED WITH A START, terrorized by yet another dream that she was already forgetting. Something about turning a corner and . . . what? Well, why try to remember, when it had frightened her so much? She would say a quick Hail Mary and drift back to sleep. She was sleeping at the bottom of the bed that night and had slid down, or up, so that her feet were pressing against the headboard. Luckily, neither of her sisters had awakened to slap or pinch her away.

She grabbed on to the mattress to pull herself back down and heard the rustling of paper. Money? Had someone been stuffing money under the mattress? Tish. Stuffing away her earnings, only Tish would do such a thing. Kitty slid her hand beneath the mattress and found not money but paper, a tablet. She pulled it out and tilted in toward the moonlight.

November 30, 1943

My darling Michael—

I am waiting to send this until I'm very sure. But if you do receive it, you'll know that what we feared has happened. Yet I find I'm not afraid at all. And I want to start writing to you about every aspect of this wonderful experience, since you're not here to share it with me.

First of all, know that I am happy. And I'm not worried about telling my family. No one need know for a while. I've not gained a pound, nor have I had any morning sickness. In fact, it's the way I feel so well that makes me wonder if I'm pregnant at all. But I have missed my "friend" for two months now. So something is going on.

Kitty swallowed so loudly she feared her sisters would hear her and awaken. But neither stirred, nor did they when she carefully put the tablet back under the mattress. She turned onto her back, folded her hands across her chest, and lay wide-eyed, thinking.

"GOING UP!" THE ELEVATOR OPERATOR SAID. Kitty and Louise squeezed into the overly full car. Someone's elbow knocked into the operator's little hat, perched like a monkey's at the side of her head. She adjusted it wearily; it was clear this happened many times a day. Kitty figured the operator felt it was worth it; after all, Dorothy Lamour had been discovered here working as an elevator operator. And even if you didn't get discovered, you still got to go to charm school—Field's sent all its operators there.

Kitty and her sister exited on level 7: lingerie, bridal wear, better dresses, junior deb department. Kitty didn't want to overdress for Hank, nothing so obvious as a new dress, but having nice new underwear always gave a girl a certain kind of confidence. She wanted a lacy slip, a well-fitting bra. To Louise she'd simply said she needed underpants; Louise had said she needed some, too, and Kitty had invited her along. She was glad Louise was coming, glad they'd have time to be alone. They'd have lunch at the Walnut Room; with her salary from the factory, Kitty could now easily afford to pay for both of them. And after they'd eaten and were lingering over dessert, Kitty would tell Louise what she had discovered.

The sisters separated in the lingerie department; Louise looked through underpants, and Kitty moved over to the lacy slips. My, but they were something. When she got married, she'd wear a slip like this every day. And she'd wear a beautiful nightgown every night. She wished she could look at them now, all the fancy negligees and peignoirs, but it wouldn't be right. You had to at least be engaged, it seemed to Kitty. What would a woman with no ring on her hand be doing, searching through such filmy, frankly suggestive things? Before whom would a single girl parade such an outfit? Still, a girl could look. A girl could be trying to find something for a friend's bridal shower. Maybe she'd find something to suggest to Louise.

All but licking her chops, Kitty moved to the rack with the gossamer, beribboned garments. Oh, it was heaven just to touch them. They came in all colors: white, black, blue, turquoise, pink, yellow. How must it feel to pull one over your head, button the little buttons (some had rhinestone buttons, some had pearl), and tie the pretty ribbons, knowing that they were meant to be undone by your husband. At this, Kitty's stomach flipped: to have a man undress you! How could you ever stand for it? How could you not simply die of embarrassment? What did you do while he undressed you? Stare at the ceiling? Say a prayer to Saint Thérèse, the Little Flower? Did you keep your eyes closed? If you smiled, did you look loose? If you didn't smile, did you look like an old crab? And what if the man fumbled, his big hands trying to undo all those dainty closures? Were you to help him? Oh, it was awful to contemplate the many ways things could go wrong. Kitty thought if she ever got a negligee, what she would most want to do was lock herself in the bathroom and stare at herself in the mirror, turning this way and that, trying out different expressions. As for men, she knew enough about them to know that they didn't need a negligee and peignoir; come out in a potato sack with your shoulders bare and your hair loose and perfumed, and there'd be a knock at the zippered door, as Julian would say. In fact, Kitty doubted that most men would ever really notice what you were wearing, no matter what the occasion. No, these delicate creations were more for—

"What are you doing?" Louise asked, and Kitty jumped.

"Nothing. Aren't these pretty?"

Louise tilted her head to one side, then the other. Finally, "Sure," she said, "if you go in for that kind of thing."

"So you don't like them?" Kitty felt insulted, as though she were standing in front of her sister wearing one of these gowns and Louise was looking her up and down with a critical little smile on her face.

Louise shrugged. "Well, sure, I like them. Who wouldn't? They're beautiful. But for that amount of money, you could get three regular nightgowns that would wear a lot better." She reached out to touch a turquoise-colored gown. "Gee, they do feel nice, though, don't they?"

Kitty pulled the gown off the rack. "I'm buying this for you."

"No!" Louise grabbed the hanger from Kitty, and Kitty grabbed it back from her.

"Let me!" Kitty said, laughing. "I can afford it." She could, and she really wanted to buy it for Louise. Kitty knew her own faults, her smallness of spirit or outright meanness, her jealousy and greed, her laziness and lack of spiritual devotion. But sometimes her heart opened and she was wildly generous, even saintlike, if she did she say so herself.

But, "Please, Kitty, *no!*" Louise said, and tears came into her eyes. Embarrassed, she turned to the wall.

"Louise?" Kitty returned the gown to the rack and put her arm around her sister. "Coots? What's the matter?"

"Oh, Kitty, I can't have anything like this. I . . . Listen, I have to tell you something." Louise wiped at her face, where the tears were now flowing freely.

One of the salesclerks, an older, well-dressed woman, her maroon leather sales book in hand, came over. "May I assist you with something?" She had a pencil tucked behind her ear, a pleasantly expectant look on her face. Kitty wished she could simply say, "Yes, we'll take the blue negligee and matching peignoir," and watch the woman write the purchase up, carefully fold the garments in tissue, add the carbon copy of the sales slip, and then put everything in the beautiful white shopping bag, complete with the silver *MF* with green detailing—Kitty loved those regal bags. But now the saleswoman saw Louise's tears, and she put her hand to her breast and peered over the top of her glasses at her. "Well, for heaven's sake. Are you all right?"

"She's fine," Kitty said. And then, to her sister, "Just relax, okay, honey? Let's go get some lunch." She took Louise's hand. "Don't worry, okay? Don't worry. Come with me. We're going to get some nice chicken pot pie. You won't believe how good it is." Over her shoulder, she said to the saleswoman, "She's just hungry. She gets that way."

AFTER THEY HAD ORDERED, Louise sat staring down at the table. Kitty waited, then waited some more. She knew her sister; Louise would talk when she was ready. Oh, what hard news for Louise to deliver, even to Kitty, to whom she'd always told everything. And despite the bravado Louise had shown in her letter to Michael, she must have been so frightened for weeks, she must have felt so ashamed. Kitty and her sisters had always looked down on girls who got pregnant out of wedlock, on those who had relations outside of marriage. But now everything was different. Yes, it was wrong, what had happened, but it had been Louise and Michael who had done that wrong. And so the impropriety was mitigated by love, by familiarity, by knowing that there was far more to this situation than just another girl in dutch. Kitty couldn't wait for Louise to confess, so that she could reassure and comfort her. She would remind her sister that in this, as in all things, Kitty would stand by her.

It was funny, how sometimes it took someone getting hurt to remind you of the depth of your feelings for them. Once, at Kiddieland, she'd seen then four-year-old Binks get injured on one of the rides—he'd banged into something and gotten a bloody nose. He couldn't get off until it was over, and Kitty had thought her heart would break, watching him go round and round with his hand up to his face, holding back tears, until the ride finally stopped.

Kitty wanted Louise to feel no pressure to talk—to know she could take all the time in the world. So she leaned back casually in her chair and looked around at the diners—mostly women, wearing wonderful suits and gloves and hats and heels—smiling, chatting, blowing cigarette smoke up into the air. The Walnut Room was such a grand place. Once a year, in December, the Heaney family came here to eat lunch and admire the gigantic Christmas tree. They saved all year for it, threw spare change into a big Mason jar kept in a high kitchen cupboard.

Some years, they didn't have enough for dessert; some years, they had enough for two apiece. But here Kitty was, making enough money all by herself to take herself and her sister out to lunch and not worry about the price of anything on the menu, including dessert. And it was her factory job that had given her this privilege.

Not that the job wasn't still difficult. In addition to the physical challenges, almost every day some annoying incident happened to her or to Hattie—or to both of them. A disparaging remark about the quality of their work. A pat on the behind. A torrent of terrible cursing used right next to them just to irk them. The injustice of working up until the last minute as they were supposed to, right next to another male worker who lay loafing or a woman worker patting her hair and putting on lipstick while staring into her compact mirror. Last Friday, Hattie had said she was really going to quit this time, until Kitty had talked her out of it—they did this, took turns talking each other out of quitting. Usually it was Kitty, sighing and saying she'd had enough. But this last time, someone had kept throwing the word "nigger" around, and Hattie had been so upset, she'd said she was going back to Mississippi to work as a maid. "Least there it's out in the open," Hattie had said. "Least there, I might not make much money, but I don't have to work myself to death, either." Kitty had insisted Hattie come out for a hamburger with her, to calm her down. They'd sat at a dime-store booth beneath posters warning them that spies were everywhere, reminding them to write to the boys, to buy war bonds, encouraging them to join the WAACs or at least to take their place in Civil Defense. It was hard to remember when these messages weren't everywhere, when their lives didn't revolve around the war.

After dinner, she and Hattie had gone to see *So Proudly We Hail*. Both of them had loved it. Oh, that Claudette Colbert, with her long eyelashes and bright smile, waking up in the morning with George Reeves. Never mind that their honeymoon suite was a ditch, what a love they shared! After one of the couple's romantic kisses, she and Hattie had looked over at each other in the dark, sighing. Kitty had come out of the theater resolved to be more like Claudette: gorgeous and cheerful and strong, even under extreme duress.

But that, too—how wonderful that Kitty was able to go to movies as often as she wanted, and to contribute to the household in a way she'd never been able to before. Her mother may have resented Kitty ruining her hands and working at a job Margaret would rather not have her daughters do, but she certainly appreciated the extra income—and regularly told Kitty so. It made for a feeling of pride, of power, and Kitty liked it.

Now Louise cleared her throat, and Kitty sat up straighter in her chair. "Okay," Louise said.

Kitty waited.

"I think I might—" A burst of laughter came from a corner table, and then their waitress came to the table to ask if there would be anything else.

"The check, please," Kitty said, and Louise sat silently waiting until Kitty paid it, then thanked her sister. "I would have put in some, you know," she said, and Kitty said, "I wanted to treat you."

"Let's go outside," Louise said. "I don't feel like I can talk here."

The sisters rode the elevator down in silence, listening to the operator musically list all the departments on each floor and then finally say, "Main floor, State Street to your left, Michigan Avenue to your right."

In the thick of the crowd on Michigan—girls like themselves excitedly shopping, families with their children, the ever-present soldiers and sailors—Louise linked arms with her sister. Then she said, "I think I might be pregnant."

Kitty swallowed. Now that Louise had come out and said it, she wasn't quite sure what to say back. She stopped walking and turned to look at her sister. "You are?" she managed.

Louise wasn't crying now. She even smiled. "I want to go to confession," she said. "Then I want to talk to you about what I should do next. Okay?"

"Yes. And Louise, I just want you to know . . . I just want to say . . ."

Louise threw her arms around her sister. "I know. Thank you, Kitty."

The girls began walking again, their arms linked. Kitty thought she might as well go to confession herself. It had been two weeks. She actually liked going. The way she pushed aside the burgundy velvet curtain and came out of the booth feeling so much lighter than she had going in. The way the air came more easily into her lungs, the immense relief she always felt. It was as though she had just escaped some terrible danger and needed to wipe her brow and say "Whew!"

Kitty always said her penance gratefully, knowing that, in exchange for this simple task, her soul was once again snowy white and not peppered with the black of sin. And then the careful walk home, trying so hard to keep that perfect state of grace. It never lasted long, but while it was there Kitty felt lit from the inside, held in the hand of something so much bigger than herself. It was at such times that she thought she might like to be a nun. But then she would remember all the reasons why she would *not* like to be a nun. For one thing, a veil and a black habit every single day!

The sisters walked slowly toward the downtown cathedral, admiring the Christmas displays they passed in the windows. It came to Kitty that now that Louise was pregnant, everything would be changed, irrevocably. And there was a sadness to it. Outweighing that, though, was a great sense of joy. The idea of a new life in the midst of all the deaths they were hearing about—well, it was swell. Already, Kitty's mind was crowded with ideas for how she'd buy her sister baby clothes, how she'd babysit on a Saturday afternoon, how, after the shock and disappointment had left their parents, they'd lift the baby high up in the air and laugh with it. It. A boy? A girl? Suddenly, Kitty couldn't wait to see.

Surely Louise and Michael could get married, somehow. Kitty had heard about German soldiers getting married while they were in war zones, far away from their sweethearts. An empty chair with a hat on it to represent the groom, a minister, and the bride, all dressed up so that her photo could be sent to her new husband. Well, if they could do it, so could Louise and Michael. And then after the war, they could get married all over again. And Kitty could be the maid of honor and wear a beautiful green dress, Julian loved her in green. And Julian would be the best man. Oh, Julian, home again, turning her around and around on the dance floor. Kissing her forehead, her neck, her mouth.

She and Louise were bareheaded, so they bobby-pinned hankies on their heads before they entered the cathedral. Very few people were in line for the confessionals; the sisters took their place behind one man. When he went in, he spoke so loudly they could hear almost every word. Kitty and Louise looked at each other and laughed; then Kitty sang songs in her head so that she wouldn't listen anymore. *It'll be so nice when my man comes home,* she "sang" in a jazzy, sultry way she'd never be able to do for real. *He was a famous trumpet man from out Chicago way,* she sang. *I'm dreaming of a white Christmas,* she started, but oh, that was much too sad. She moved to "Jukebox Saturday Night." Singing in her head worked fairly well to distract her from listening to the man's confession, but Kitty couldn't help but hear him admit that he'd gotten drunk six times, mostly because the man practically yelled that one. It made her wonder if the sixth time wasn't right now. When the man came out of the booth, the sisters looked pointedly away from him. Then Louise straightened her shoulders and went in, and when she came out, it was clear she'd been crying. She made her way to the altar rail, where she knelt and bowed her head, her hands clasped before her. Kitty wanted to reach into the confessional and throttle the priest. "Did you have to make her cry?" she wanted to say.

Kitty's turn. She took in a breath and entered the confessional. After her eyes adjusted to the darkness, she looked up at the crucifix hanging on the wall, and it came to her that if Jesus could speak, He'd say, "Never mind that priest, your sister is a good girl, and I love her." She wished that when she went to confession Jesus really would be there, for surely He would speak to her with great compassion and wisdom. The priests were all right, but Kitty could never help thinking about how they were really just men in there, wearing boxers and T-shirts beneath their black suits.

The sliding door opened, and Kitty jumped. Then she said softly,

"Bless me, Father, for I have sinned." And her toes curled inside her shoes as she began her recitation of wrongdoings.

After they had completed their penance, the sisters lit candles for Julian and for Michael, and an extra one for all the fighting men. "And their families, too?" Kitty whispered, and Louise whispered back, "I think we have to buy another candle for that much." Kitty put more coins in the slot, and together the sisters lit one more candle, their faces solemn and pleading. Then they walked slowly toward the streetcar that would take them home. Louise didn't speak until Kitty finally said, "You okay?"

Louise smiled. "Yes. It will be hard to tell Ma and Pop, but in a way I'm relieved to do it."

"Want me to help?" Though if the truth be told, Kitty had no idea how she would do that.

"No, thanks. I think I know what I want to say. But I'll be glad to have you around afterward. Gosh, I hope they don't . . . Well, anyway, I'll be glad to have you there. *Will* you be there, even if it takes a long time when I tell them?"

"'Course I'll be there," Kitty said. "I'll always be there."

"I know," Louise said, and her voice was small, like a little girl's.

The streetcar arrived, and after the girls boarded, Kitty said, "Guess what? Next time I go downtown, I'm buying you one of those nightgowns."

Louise shook her head. "Don't. They're too expensive, and I don't need one. But thanks."

"What color do you want?"

"I don't want one, Kitty! Honest, I really don't. I'd rather have pots and pans. Truly." She stared out the window. Snow was starting to fall.

"What color?" Kitty persisted.

"Butter yellow," Louise said. And then she turned to her sister and smiled. They rode the rest of the way in silence, each imagining what their parents would say when they heard the news.

. . .

AT HOME, THE SISTERS HUNG UP THEIR COATS. Then Louise nodded at Kitty, took in a deep breath, and headed for the kitchen to find Margaret. Their mother would get told first; Frank would be given the news after dinner—that way, Louise wouldn't be working against the irritation Frank always felt when he was hungry. And Margaret would have had time to calm down and might be able to help Louise with Frank.

Kitty found Binks sitting on the landing with his head in his hands, looking miserable. "What's wrong with you?" she asked.

"I hate the gum they have now," he said. "It's all grainy and you can't blow bubbles. Your tongue goes right through."

Kitty sat beside him. "Hmmm. Seems like a pretty long face for such a small problem."

Binks said nothing.

"Is anything else wrong?" Kitty asked.

Now he burst out with his real concern. "I took the dime for my victory stamp and bought gum instead! And it wasn't even good! And now I won't have a stamp for school next week!"

Kitty spoke gently. "I think it's okay for you to buy something for yourself sometimes, Binks. You don't have to spend all your money on victory stamps."

"I don't! A couple of weeks ago I went to the matinee!"

"Well, you spend *almost* all of it on stamps. It's okay if you skip once in a while."

"Our teacher said our boys need it to save their lives."

Suddenly, a great anger rose in Kitty. It was too much, all that was being thrust upon these children! First Tommy, now Binks. All well and good that they contribute to the war effort, that they be made aware of the fact that great events in history were occurring in the world. But didn't they deserve some protection? Young boys delivered newspapers with stories about entire regiments of American boys wiped out. *Life* magazine regularly showed gruesome photos of the war, including a Japanese officer beheading a blindfolded American flier. And how did children feel about the posters? One showed a sad cocker spaniel with his chin resting on the middy blouse of a sailor, a sailor who would never come home. Another showed a bombed-out American home and car, and proclaimed ominously, IT CAN HAPPEN HERE. Even the poster of Uncle Sam saying I WANT *YOU* must have been frightening to children, that white-bearded man with the lowered eyebrows and fierce expression on his face.

The children's programs on the radio offered no relief: the Captain Midnight oath exhorting young listeners "to save my country from the dire peril it faces or perish in the attempt." Superman, with his long-distance hearing and X-ray vision and supersonic flying speed, was now tracking down spies, as were the Green Hornet and Tom Mix. Hap Harrigan, Binks's favorite hero, was an eighteen-year-old flying ace who constantly dodged bullets.

When kids went to matinees, cartoons showed Bugs Bunny on a Pacific island selling Japanese soldiers ice cream bars with grenades hidden inside, or Donald Duck singing a song about flatulence directed right in "Der Fuehrer's Face." Minnie Mouse talked about housewives saving fats. There were newsreels shown of actual fighting in air, land, and sea battles. Binks had told Kitty about this and had said that sometimes when those images were shown, kids cried. "Not me, though," he'd hastily added. Even comic books had become war-oriented, featuring Captain Flight, V-Man, Pyroman.

Binks often lay on his stomach humming, drawing pictures of airplanes crashing, of cities burning. He had a "survival kit" in his closet consisting of a candle and a candy bar. At first, Kitty had thought it was kind of cute. But now she didn't. Now she wondered if Tommy's illness had less to do with any gastrointestinal problem and more to do with his constant worrying about the war. And here was little Binks, sitting devastated on the steps because he'd had the audacity to buy himself a few pieces of crummy bubble gum.

Despite her anger, Kitty spoke calmly to her brother. "You know what, Binks? You've helped a lot already, and you'll be helping more. But you get to have some fun, too, right? You get to have some things just for yourself. It's not taking away from our boys for you to do that some-times. They would want you to. Why, just before Julian got on the train, he said, 'Make sure that Binks has a lot of fun.'"

"He did? Really?"

Kitty looked her brother in the eye and nodded gravely. It was a lie she'd told, but for good reason. She hoped that kept it from being a sin or there went her soul, back in the hamper.

Binks offered her a piece of gum. "Want a piece? You can't blow bub-bles, but otherwise it's okay."

"You keep it," Kitty said.

From the kitchen came Margaret's voice. "Binks! I told you I need some help peeling vegetables. I'll never get this soup done in time for dinner." There was the sound of running water, the clanging of pots, and then Margaret said, "For the last time, I want you to come in here and peel these carrots!"

"Ma?" Kitty heard Louise say. "Hey? I'll do it."

"He can do it," Margaret said. "Marion Montgomery just tele-phoned to invite you girls to a come-as-you-are party. Tish has already gone, in her bathrobe no less, just out of the shower. That one never stops washing her hair. I tell her she'll ruin it, once a week is enough, but she listens as well as the rest of you. You and Kitty go to the party. I'll get the boys to help. *Binks!*"

"Ma," Louise said. "I need to talk to you."

A sudden silence. And then, "I know you do," Margaret said quietly.

Kitty wished she could see her mother's face. And Louise's. Instead, she took Binks's hand. "Come on," she said. "Let's go up to your bed-room, and I'll play cards with you."

"And that's another thing," Binks said. "Tommy's in there taking a nap, which he always is, and I can't even play in my own room! And it's too cold to go outside."

"Ah," Kitty said. "Well then, you'll just have to come to my room."

"Can I?" Binks said. It was a rare treat for the boys to be allowed in the sisters' room.

Kitty pulled her hand away from her brother's, saying, "You're all sticky. What have you been eating?"

"Molasses," Binks said. "Hey, sis? Can we jump on your bed again?"

"Shhhhh!" Kitty told him. Margaret would soon have enough to carry on about. But Kitty put her finger to her lips and nodded at her brother. She liked jumping on the bed, too.

WHEN LOUISE CAME UPSTAIRS, Kitty and Binks were coloring a picture of Santa Claus that Binks had drawn. Kitty told her little brother to go to his room and play cards with Tommy, who was up now, and with Billy, who moments ago had come banging in the front door yelling that he was starving to death.

After Binks left, Kitty turned expectantly to Louise.

Her sister shrugged.

"What did she say?" Kitty asked.

"She knew. Or at least she suspected. She said she'd noticed my chest was bigger, especially when she took that picture. And she said I hadn't complained of cramps, like I always do on the first day. And she said a pregnant woman just has a certain look, and I had it. Do I have it?"

"I didn't notice anything."

Louise went to the mirror and leaned in close to look at herself, then turned away. "Maybe you have to have been p.g. yourself to see it. I don't see a thing."

"Come here and let me look," Kitty said.

Louise came over to stand before her, and Kitty stared into her face. "Well . . . Maybe a little around the eyes," she said.

"A little what?"

"I don't know. A little pregnant. You have pregnant eyes."

Louise laughed, but then her face grew serious and she said, "Really?" There was wonder in her voice, a softness. And so Kitty told her yes, there was definitely a change. Then she asked what else their mother had said.

"She wanted to know who else I'd told. I said only you. Then she just sat still for a long time, and it was awful because her face was so sad. I told her I was sorry, and she just kind of waved her hand, as though she were saying, Oh, never mind with *that*. I told her I'd been to confession, and that seemed to help a little bit. She said I shouldn't tell Michael."

"Why not?" Kitty asked.

"Because he can't do anything about it right now. And it might worry or distract him. But I think I should tell him. I think he'd be glad. And anyway, I want him to share in this with me."

"I know you do."

Louise looked sharply at her. "How do you know?"

"I just . . . That's how I'd be. I'd want the man to share it with me, even if he was far away."

"Even if he was fighting a war?"

"Even then. And think how you can send him pictures that show you getting bigger."

Louise pulled up her sweater and looked at her stomach. "You can't tell anything yet." She sat on the edge of the bed. "Gosh. I'm pregnant! I'm so glad I went to confession."

Kitty sat beside her sister and put her arm around her. "Is Ma going to tell Pop or are you?"

"I am, right after dinner," Louise said, and now her voice betrayed her fear.

"What do you think it looks like now?" Kitty asked, wanting to distract her.

"I don't know. I guess it's a really really little *baby*." She put her hand over her stomach. "It's so . . ." She turned to her sister. "Oh, Kitty, just think. It's me and Michael, together. Inside me, all the time! I think it's wonderful, really. I know all the things that get said about women who aren't married and have babies, but I don't care. I'm glad I'm pregnant. If something happens to him, at least I'll have his child."

Kitty nodded. She didn't want to say anything about how hard it would be for Louise to raise a baby on her own, how unlikely it would be that she'd find a man who would take on a widow with a child.

KITTY AND TISH LAY ON THEIR BED, reading letters aloud to each other. Margaret had sent them and the boys to their rooms, saying that she would call them when they could come back down. Louise was in the parlor, talking to Frank, while Margaret washed the dishes—very quietly, Kitty imagined, so that she wouldn't miss a word. Tish was reading a V-mail from her newest pen pal, a Navy man named Curly Higgins, who'd seen her picture and asked if she'd write to him, too:

"I know the reputation us sailors have; people think we're all wolves, out to take advantage of every girl we meet. But I think the thing all us guys miss most is just simple female companionship, the friend part of it. It's swell to just walk alongside a woman down some city street, her carrying her purse and all. All dressed up. And I just like to talk to a woman, to hear her voice and see how she waves her hands and laughs. I like how women think, they have a nice way of looking at the world. I'm sure glad you agreed to write to me. I feel like the luckiest man on this ship, because next to my bed I've got a blonde, a brunette, and a redhead. Say, don't take that the wrong way. I just mean it's something to wake up and see those three smiles. Can't help but smile back myself! Please write back soon and keep me always in your prayers.

"He sounds sweet," Tish said. But then she put the letter down and said, "All right, that's enough of this. Tell me what's going on down there!"

"No," Kitty said. "It's not up to me to tell you. You'll know soon enough." She looked at the alarm clock beside their bed. "I predict you'll know in . . . seven minutes."

Tish crossed her arms over her chest. "I'm not a child anymore! You don't need to play those kinds of games with me."

"Read me your last letter," Kitty said.

Tish looked at her pile. "Didn't I read them all?"

"You had four. You read three."

"Oh! Right. But this last one is just a note from Julian."

"Really," Kitty said.

"Yeah, just a note, nothing new, nothing you don't know."

"Read it," Kitty said, and she made a great effort to keep her voice neutral.

Tish stared at her sister, deliberating, then unfolded Julian's letter. "He just talks about—"

"I want to hear the whole thing."

"It's my letter!" Tish said.

"He's my boyfriend!" Kitty answered. "And I want you to read it to me, every word."

"Fine!" Tish said and read:

"November fifteenth, 1943

"Surprise! Still here in the South Pacific

"Dear Tish,

"I think your idea about a pearl necklace for Kitty is fine. Munson's Jewelers downtown on Wabash is the place to get it—they know me and my family real well. Then if you could take it over to Field's and get it gift-wrapped—"

"Oh!" Kitty said.

Tish folded the letter back up and put it on the bottom of her pile. "Okay? Satisfied?"

"I didn't know!"

"Well, now you do." Tish looked at the clock. "Seven minutes are almost up. I'm going to the bathroom." She took her letters to her dresser drawer and dropped them in. Then she looked at herself in the mirror. "I might cut my hair," she said, more to herself than to Kitty.

Kitty lay on the bed after Tish left and put her fingers to her throat, imagining herself in her pearl necklace. She loved pearls. They looked wonderful with everything. Maybe he'd decide to buy earrings, too! Or a bracelet! Oh, and all she had sent Julian for Christmas was cigarettes and socks and food: sardines and pumpernickel and rye. Cookies and nuts. One of Margaret's famous fruitcakes. But that was the way it always was with Julian; he spent freely on everyone, and never really expected anything in return. He would be the kind to buy a bracelet and earrings along with a necklace and think nothing of it. He might even have told Tish to go ahead and do that later in his letter.

Kitty listened for the sound of the bathroom door closing, then went to the dresser. She cracked Tish's drawer just enough to slip out Julian's letter and read it quickly.

. . . and get it gift-wrapped real nice, I'd so much appreciate it. The lettuce I've enclosed ought to cover all this and then some—take any extra and buy yourself and all your friends an ice cream soda. Although I wonder if you do that anymore, go to the soda fountain and sit with your friends smack-dab in the middle of the counter like the queen bee. I like to think of you the way I saw you that day, all pretty in blue and surrounded by your many admirers. I always think of you as a kid in saddle shoes and bobby sox, your pullover with the sleeves pushed up just so. But I'll bet you've grown up a lot in the many months since I last saw you. I'll bet you're quite the hep kitten now, a real heartbreaker. Why don't you send me another picture? Zeeps, seems like just everything has changed so fast. I've changed a lot, too, though not in the nice way you have. I'm pretty low most of the time. Keep your letters coming, they help more than anything.

Julian

Kitty folded the letter up and stuck it back in the drawer. Then she went to lie on the bed. She didn't know how to feel. On the one hand, Julian was buying her pearls. On the other hand, he was sharing such intimate thoughts with Tish, telling her little sister more than he told her! And what was this about how pretty Tish looked, about him wanting another picture of her? When had she sent one before? And why did *her* letters cheer him up so much?

Suddenly there came the sounds of Frank yelling and then Margaret yelling and Louise crying. Kitty sat up and leaned forward, listening. The front door slammed shut so hard the house shook. This was followed by a terrible silence. Tish came into the room, her blue eyes wide. "Should we go down?"

Kitty nodded. The boys were already thundering down the stairs, Binks yelling, "Ma? Ma?" and Billy shouting in his new man's voice, "What the devil is going on down there?"

"We're supposed to stay here!" Tommy said. And then, "Hey? Wait for me!"

"IT'S ONLY THE BOYS I'M WORRIED ABOUT," Louise said. "I don't care about Pop."

It was nearly midnight, and the sisters were in bed, still wide awake and talking in whispers.

"I'll bet Pop's drunk as a skunk when he comes home," Tish said.

"Undoubtedly," Louise said. "And when someone behaves that way, why should I care what he thinks about me?"

But she did care, Kitty knew. She cared that her father had bellowed and slammed out of the house, she cared that Billy had flushed terribly on hearing the news about her pregnancy and that her younger brothers had sat silent and wide-eyed at the dining room table, their hands folded before them and staring straight ahead as though they were being reprimanded by the nuns. Margaret had admonished the boys as well as the sisters not to tell anyone else. "For now, this is strictly our family's business," she had said. "We will decide when and how others will be told." Louise cared that her mother's shoulders had slumped as she was saying this, that when she'd gotten up afterward, she'd moved slowly, nearly aimlessly.

"Pop will be all right," Kitty said. "Look how he acted when I took this factory job. He went out drinking that night, too—and so did Ma, don't forget! Now he's proud of me."

"He won't ever be proud of me for getting pregnant outside of marriage," Louise said. "You should have seen his face. How disgusted he was. How angry. He turned purple!"

"Well, it was a shock!" Kitty said. "He just needs some time."

"He needs a drink," Tish said, and her tone was pragmatic. Tish didn't often condemn people for their weaknesses. Her reaction to her sister's announcement had been unbridled joy, and when the sisters came upstairs, she had hugged Louise and said, "What are we going to name him?"

Louise's face had had red spots from her crying, but she'd smiled as she blew her nose. "How do you know it's a boy?" She'd pronounced "know" *doe.*

"Because it's what Michael would want," Tish had said.

"He likes little girls a lot," Louise had said.

"But he would want a boy first. Every man wants a boy first."

"Pop didn't!" Kitty had said. "Pop says he wanted all girls!"

"Oh, he just says that to you," Louise had said. "He lies, too."

Kitty had bristled. "What do you mean, 'too'?" But she'd known exactly what her sister meant. She'd wanted to defend her father, but she couldn't. The truth was, he shouldn't have gone off that way.

AT JUST PAST ONE IN THE MORNING, Kitty awakened to the sound of voices. She crept downstairs and saw Margaret standing before Frank at the front door. She was in her nightgown, her feet bare, her hair wild about her shoulders. ". . . for all the world to see," she was saying. "You're doing this far too often, Frank Heaney. I'll not have you going off and getting drunk every time a problem comes along!"

"Who says I'm drunk! An Irishman is never drunk so long as he can hold on to one blade of grass and not fall off the face of the earth!"

"Ah, Frank, would you stop," Margaret said.

Kitty hid in the shadows and watched her father go to the living room and fall heavily into his favorite battered brown wing chair. "My beautiful Louise," he said. "Ruined."

Margaret moved quickly over to Frank and, astonishingly, slapped his face.

He looked up at her, his hand to his cheek.

"Don't you ever say that about any of our children! They are every one of them fine human beings. And a credit to us as parents. Louise is not yours, she is her own. And her terrible crime was to show love to her fiancé, a man grieving for his mother and on his way back to a war he may never come home from. Is it the way I would have wanted things to go? No. 'Tis the cart before the horse, and we all know it. Will we all have to endure the stares and the comments from all those around us, *especially Louise,* who has never been unkind to anyone? Yes. But these are terrible times, everything all topsy-turvy, and I for one will hold Louise's baby with great happiness and pride. This child is here, asleep in his mother's womb, and he isn't going away. He's part of our family now, part of me and you as well as Michael and Louise, and we will love him and stand by him. Starting now and lasting forever. Do you understand me, Frank Heaney?"

He grunted and leaned back in the chair. Then he looked up at Margaret and smiled. "And how d'ye know it's a boy? Sure it could be a girl, a little bitty thing, pink-cheeked and beautiful like her mother. And her mother's mother." He pulled Margaret onto his lap and kissed her shoulder.

"Ejit," she said, but her voice was soft.

Kitty walked noiselessly back up the stairs and into her bedroom. She stood beside Louise, who was sleeping soundly at the foot of the bed. Her sister was curled up on her side, covered for once, the blankets pulled up to just under her nose. Kitty leaned down and kissed her sister's forehead, then climbed under the covers herself. She remembered helping her mother give newborn Louise a bottle, how her sister had clung so tightly to her finger with her tiny hand, how Kitty had felt a rising up of defiance against anyone or anything that might ever hurt Louise. It hurt *her* whenever she felt that kind of love; it was a solid ache, right at her center. But it was a good hurt; it helped make her strong. And it made her her best self.

A WEEK LATER, LOUISE ANNOUNCED to her family that she had been fired as a teacher's aide. After she'd shared the news of her pregnancy, the director had said they were sorry to lose her, she was one of the best they'd ever had, but surely she could understand. Most pregnant women quit anyway. And what kind of example would she be setting, being pregnant and not married? No, she would have to go.

"They can't do that!" Tish said, but of course they could, and they did.

"I don't care," Louise said, but clearly she did.

"There's a less narrow-minded child-care center at St. John's that's desperate for more workers," Margaret said. "I can't think of a more perfect place for you to be now." She acted as if this were a happy solution, but she buttered her bread so hard it tore. The only one allowed to criticize her children was herself.

"No!" <small>LOUISE SAID.</small>

"Yes," Kitty answered mildly. She had bought her sister the yellow negligee and peignoir. Word had gotten out about Louise—*Somebody talked!*—and many of the neighbors now offered a tight-lipped silence in place of a greeting. Louise wasn't safe from wagging tongues even in church: at coffee hour only yesterday, a group of women had talked in disapproving tones and kept looking over at Louise until Margaret burst into the middle of them, saying, "And how are my *friends* here at *church* on this fine Sunday?"

"Kitty, you have to take this back."

"Never. And I want you to try it on; I want to see you in it."

"No!"

"*I'll* try it on," Tish said, grabbing the bag. She ran into the closet and emerged moments later in the nearly transparent gowns. She looked wildly improper. Sexier than any starlet sticking her chest out on any movie magazine cover. *Holy Toledo,* Kitty thought, but what she said was "Take that off right now."

"Why?" Tish danced left and right.

"Because it does not belong to you and it will bring bad luck to the marriage."

Tish stopped moving. "It will?"

"It will," Kitty said solemnly and hoped that Louise wouldn't contradict her. And Louise didn't. Instead, she said, "Oh, all right. Give to me. I'll try it on."

Tish went into the closet again and came out with the gowns neatly folded. "Sorry," she said, handing them to her sister. Louise went into the closet.

"Oh my, they're so light," they heard her say. "They're like putting on meringue." Then she was quiet.

"Come out," Kitty said. "Let us see!"

"That's okay," Louise said.

Kitty yanked the closet door open, and there stood Louise with her hands clasped before her, her legs pressed tightly together. "Come out!" Kitty said.

"You can see practically *everything*," Louise whispered.

"That's the idea," Kitty whispered back, and she grabbed her sister's wrist and pulled her out into the room.

Tish wolf-whistled. And then, when Louise blushed and started back for the closet, Tish said, "No, you look so pretty. Hubba-hubba!"

Louise thought for a moment, then smiled. "Thanks. I guess I'll save this for after we're married." Now she laughed out loud. "Gee, I wish I'd had this for the honeymoon!"

"A SMIDGE TOO MUCH ROUGE," Tish said. She was sitting on the edge of the bathtub, watching Kitty get ready to go to the train station to meet Hank. Tish herself had been ready for half an hour; she and Louise were coming along. Kitty was glad for this, but she hoped her sisters would leave after a while; she wanted time alone with Hank. It was only polite. He was coming to see her, after all, not all of them.

"No it isn't too much rouge," Kitty said. The winter had made her pale. She wanted to look healthy. Well, she wanted to look pretty.

"It is!" Tish insisted. She came over to Kitty and rubbed away at one side of her sister's face. "Look now. See how much more natural that looks?"

Kitty regarded herself in the mirror. Darn it, Tish was right. In such matters, she was always right. Even before she had taken her job selling cosmetics at Carson's, she had been good at makeup. Kitty rubbed away at her other cheek, then tossed her black curls back. Her hair had come out wonderfully well. She'd used that Kreml shampoo that the John Robert Powers models used, and she'd made two perfect off-the-face rolls. She had on her new red Max Factor lipstick, a shade worn by Maureen O'Hara herself.

"What hat are you wearing?" Tish asked.

"The black one I just bought."

"I wanted that. My coat is black!"

"My suit is," Kitty said.

"You're wearing that black suit?"

"Yes." She tried to sound nonchalant. The suit was new, too. Kitty had decided she needed a new outfit, and not because of Hank. Now that the war was going better, a girl could splurge on herself occasionally without feeling guilty. Her other clothes were all just so old. She'd gone to Field's after work on Friday night and tried on a few things: a fuchsia wool daytime dress, a striped jersey blouse and a gray wool skirt with a pleat up the front, a black skirt with a soft white blouse and a red flannel weskit. The saleswoman, an older, highly knowledgeable woman named Violet Marshall, had recommended a black Lilly Daché felt hat to go with it. But then she had suggested Kitty try on—just for fun!—a stark black suit in a simple dressmaker style. But what style! The cut made her waist look even smaller and her chest more womanly. Kitty had stared at herself in the mirror, and Violet had put her finger to her chin and said, "Yes, that's exactly how I thought it would look." She'd suggested a Persian muff to go with it, as well as a Persian hat that sat low on the forehead and was decorated with red and green grosgrain bows. Next Violet had added a geranium-red ruffly-fringed scarf tied flirtatiously at the neck, and Kitty was a goner. "I'll take everything," she'd said, and Violet had said, "Well, of course you will."

"Isn't that suit awfully fancy just to meet a friend at the train?" Tish said.

Kitty shrugged. "We might go into the night."

"What do you mean, 'into the night'?"

"Why don't you go help Louise get ready? She probably needs help finding a good lipstick color. She always goes pink when she should go coral." Kitty leaned in to inspect her eyebrows.

"Louise is ready. I'm ready. You're the only one who's not ready. You're taking all doggone day to get ready."

"I'm done!" Kitty said. But she wasn't. She wanted to know how she looked from behind. She wanted to see how her skirt would move should they go dancing. She wanted to blow into her hands and check that her breath was minty, she wanted even to sniff under her arms to make sure she was "dainty," as the ads in the women's magazines suggested she should be. But she couldn't do all that in front of Tish. She didn't want either of her sisters to know how excited she was. Hank Cunningham III. A high little sound escaped her, and she turned it into a throat clearing.

"Nervous?" Tish asked, tauntingly.

"Of course not. Now, let's go." She started out of the bathroom.

"Kitty?" Tish said, pointing.

Her new purse. A balloon bag of black wool with a tortoiseshell fastener. Forgotten at the side of the sink. Kitty grabbed it and went downstairs for her coat.

"Invite the boy to dinner," Margaret called, as the girls were on the way out. "I'm making lamb pie with potato crust topping and a lemon sponge cake." Kitty pretended not to hear and went out to the porch, but Tish called back, "We will!"

Kitty stopped in her tracks. "*Tish!*"

"What?"

She stood there, thinking. Finally, she said, "Nothing. Hurry up or we'll miss the streetcar."

"You're the one who's dawdling!"

"THAT'S HIM," KITTY SAID, POINTING TO THE TALL, dark-haired man coming toward them. Golly, he was a handsome man, more so than she'd remembered. And he was staring directly at Kitty as though . . . well, as though she were his wife or something! Kitty didn't know where to look. She glanced at Hank, then away, back at Hank, then away. Her throat was tight; she doubted she could speak. But she had to speak! She had to introduce her sisters, and she had to think of things to say to keep the conversation rolling along. Although Tish was with them; she'd talk all the time, mostly about herself. And Louise was wonderful at drawing people out. Kitty wouldn't have to worry about talking much at first. But later, when she and Hank were alone, she'd have to guide the conversation. She'd have to keep things cheerful and light. She wanted him to think she was attractive—what fun it had been dressing up for a man she knew rather than for whatever random soldier she might dance with at the Kelly Club! But she'd have to be careful not to be too attractive to him, especially after she'd made such an effort to establish that they were just friends. She wouldn't be able to linger too long looking into his eyes. She shouldn't admire his strong profile. She'd have to be careful not to brush hands when they were walking or to dance too close. If they went dancing. If they were together that long. Who knew, his plans might have changed, soldiers' schedules were always changing, women would travel for days on overcrowded trains, sitting on suitcases in the aisles, just to meet their husbands for a few hours before they shipped out, only to find on arrival that they were already gone. Hank might just say hello and then say he was scheduled to depart on another train that was leaving in an hour. It would be a relief, actually. She and her sisters would have coffee with Hank, wish him the best, and then they could go shopping and to a matinee.

He was only a few feet away. Her heart beat so hard inside her. Her sisters were smiling, but Kitty felt paralyzed, her hands in fists she couldn't unclench. And now here he was before her, giving her a chaste little hug—oh, he smelled wonderful! Some spicy man's scent, and he was freshly shaven, how had he done that?

"Hello, Kitty," he said, and she said nothing for fear she would begin to cry. That was what she felt most overwhelmingly, the need to cry. But it was all right that she didn't speak, because Hank turned immediately to her sisters to introduce himself. And they were charmed on the spot, she could tell, even as she had been. There was just something about him.

She stood watching him, thinking that there were things she had to remember. She mustn't take Hank's arm, because a serviceman needed both arms free: one to salute any superior, one to smoke. But when he said, "How about we all of us take a tour of the town and then have lunch at the best place you know?" she took his arm immediately. And stood too close to him. And wished that by the end of the night she would have kissed him a thousand times.

. . .

"WHAT ELSE DO YOU WANT TO KNOW?" Hank asked Kitty.

Alone since after lunch, they were now sitting in the Black Hawk restaurant at the Congress Hotel, listening to the band play "G.I. Jive." It was late; Kitty was afraid to ask what the time was. She had had too much to drink—she'd wanted to try a martini with a twist, she liked the sound of it, but it had been much too strong for her. She was dizzy, but in a not entirely unpleasant way. Hank had told her all about how he'd learned to fly, how he'd been put in a simulated cockpit that spun rapidly about so he could practice defensive twists, turns, and dives. He had told her some of the things he'd learned about infantrymen, Kitty having told him that Julian and Michael were in the infantry. He said a lot of the men had pets: dogs, kittens, a Himalayan bear; he said one outfit in the Philippines had even adopted a little baby girl, but she'd been taken away from them after a month. He said that the infantry were the ones who were really fighting the war, that they had it the hardest. He told her about how their lives went from crushing boredom to bloody chaos, how when they fought it was sometimes for days at a time. They went without sleep, often with nothing more to eat than emergency K rations, which Hank described as really just big candy bars full of vitamins.

Kitty had tried to imagine herself doing that: staying awake for days on end, going without bathing for a month, wearing the same socks for weeks, pressing her face down into the dirt of a foxhole while bullets whizzed by overhead, or even more frightening, moving ever forward right into those bullets. It didn't seem possible that she could be sitting here in her pretty dress at a nice table with a white tablecloth while Julian was on the other side of the world, living in the way that Hank had described.

She stared down into her glass. Cleared her throat.

Hank spoke gently. "I've made you sad. I'm sorry."

"No, I wanted to know." She shrugged. "Gosh. The whole thing just seems so crazy."

"It is."

"But what else do you do when someone like Hitler comes along?"

"Well," Hank said. "That's a whole other discussion."

"You don't really believe in fighting. You were a conscientious objector."

"Right."

"When we first met, you told me you'd explain in a letter why you changed your mind and enlisted. But you never did."

"I didn't, did I?"

He stared at her intently, and she felt again the kind of thrill she'd been feeling all night, every time he looked directly at her. He lit a cigarette, and she admired his long lashes, his strong hands. He was so handsome. But there was something else about him. A kindness, and a guilelessness—she felt confident that he would never lie to her or anyone else about anything. And he so enjoyed her! He appreciated her observations, her questions, her jokes. And she knew he thought she was beautiful. She knew that.

Hank's face changed. He put out his cigarette and sat back in his chair. "Okay, I'll tell you why I enlisted. You know the guy I took care of in the hospital, the one who made me change my mind?"

Kitty nodded.

"That was my kid brother. Nineteen years old. He was injured in the Philippines, terrible burns. It was a wonder he survived at all, but he did, he survived and he came home and he was doing all right. He never complained, and I know the pain he suffered during his dressing changes was ungodly. He kept his spirits up, too; he knew he was going to look like . . . Well, he wasn't going to look like himself anymore. But he would joke about it, say he was going to wear a photo around his neck with a message: 'This is the real me.'

"We talked a lot about the war; he very much believed in it. He didn't see any other way to respond to Hitler's madness, and he felt his sacrifice was worth it. But then he ended up with an overwhelming infection, and he died. I was with him. I had seen people die, working in a hospital, but this was . . ." Hank shook his head. "This was different. And at that moment the war became very personal for me, and I couldn't sit on the sidelines anymore. I couldn't kill anyone, but I could help others do it for me. My enlisting was a cowardly thing, in that respect. But that's why I'm flying. My brother made the ultimate sacrifice, and I'm now making my own, for him." He shrugged, looked out at the dance floor, and said, "Aw, nuts. What do you say we dance? Let's just dance."

He took her hand, and they moved out to the dance floor. The band was playing a ballad. Hank pulled her to him, and Kitty closed her eyes and very gently put her lips to his neck and kept them there. He held her even closer. He didn't smell of cologne anymore. He smelled of his own sweet flesh, and Kitty felt an overwhelming urge to bite him. She giggled.

"What?" he said, and she said, "Nothing," and giggled again.

When the song ended, Kitty excused herself and went to the powder room. There, she sat in front of the mirror trying to sort out her feelings. How could she be so exhilarated? So full of desire? So sad and so happy? It was all mixed up! You heard such terrible things, and they made you want to grab on to everything beautiful and hold it that much harder, maybe that was it. Or maybe it had finally happened to her, the things she'd heard other girls talk about. She thought of Hank sitting at the table waiting for her return, and it was all she could do not to run back out and fling her arms around him. She wanted him in a way she'd never experienced want before. It wasn't physical attraction, though that was there, too. It was more a feeling that she had met her man. That one. The only one.

Oh, how could she be thinking such things when she'd learned so much about all that Julian was enduring? Was this what the Dear John girls went through, coming to the sad conclusion that they weren't in love with their fighting men after all, that in fact they were wildly in love with someone else? Hattie had told her about one woman who had written to a sailor, saying she was sorry but she'd met another "very nice" man. *I hope we can still be friends,* she'd told him, and had followed that deadly statement with something even worse—in a P.S., she'd asked for the photos she'd sent of herself to be returned. In a P.S.! Hattie had been aghast at the cruelty. But now here Kitty was, out on a date with another man and feeling head over heels about him. She had thought she loved Julian, but now she knew different. She had been attracted to Julian, but the two of them had never run deep, ever. Look at the difficulty she'd had writing to him. They couldn't talk to each other! What kind of a relationship could two people have when they couldn't really talk to each other?

"You going to sit there all night?" a woman standing behind her asked.

"Oh!" Kitty got up from the little white stool. "I'm sorry."

The woman, dressed in a long midnight-blue evening dress, sat down and began brushing her hair. "I don't know about you, but I'm beat!"

Kitty nodded. "Me, too." But she wasn't tired anymore.

She returned to the table and stared into her lap, nearly overwhelmed by her feelings. She wanted to grab Hank by the shoulders and tell him, but tell him what? He reached over to put his finger beneath her chin and gently turned her face to his. "My God, you are so lovely," he said. She didn't speak. Didn't move. "May I kiss you? Please?" And he put his lips so gently, so briefly, to hers. She began to cry then, and expected that Hank would ask her what was wrong. But he didn't. He said, "I know." And then he kissed her again and told her he was so glad, he felt the same way, they would work it all out, don't worry, everything would work out fine. He took her out onto the dance floor, and they moved slowly as the dark-haired singer in the white dress sang "I'll Be Seeing You." Together, she and Hank sang along: "'I'll be looking at the moon, but I'll be seeing you.'"

They left the club with their arms around each other, and their steps matched in stride and purpose. They rode the streetcar, and she kept her head on his shoulder, and she wanted to tell everyone who looked at them, "You think you know what I'm feeling, but it's so much more than that." When she kissed Hank for the last time, in the darkest shadows on her front porch, she began again to cry. "Don't," he said. "We have so much to be happy about."

"Please be careful," she said, and it came to her how different it felt saying it to him rather than to Julian. She had wanted Julian to be careful, too, of course, but her love for him was not like this. It never was. "Come back to me," she told Hank, and he pulled her to him and whispered in her ear, "Where else would I ever go now?"

Kitty let herself in the door quietly, fearful that one or both of her parents would be waiting up for her, but the house was still. She sat in her father's chair, thinking, and then she crept up the stairs to bed.

"OH, KITTY, WHAT DO YOU EXPECT?" Louise said. "You hadn't been with a man for so long, Hank is handsome and he's charming, but Kitty, he's not Julian, or—"

"But that's what I'm trying to tell you!" Kitty said. It was Sunday afternoon, and the sisters were up in their bedroom, talking in low voices. Because Tish had gone out with friends, Kitty and Louise had some semblance of privacy, though of course the house rang with the sounds of the rest of the family. "Something really important happened."

"I'll bet you were drunk, were you drunk?" Louise asked.

"No. I had a drink, but I wasn't drunk."

"Well, if you weren't drunk, you were affected. You drink about as well as Pop."

Kitty pounded the bed with her fist. "It wasn't that!"

Louise stared at her. "Jeez. You need some sleep. Why don't you take a nap?"

"Louise, I just want you to understand. I just want to talk to you about this!"

"I'm sorry," Louise said. "But I don't believe it was love. I think you had a nice evening with a nice guy and you just turned it all into some fantasy. You don't have a relationship after one night! You don't plan a future with a guy you've seen twice! Cripes, Kitty, don't you think you need to spend some time with a person before you can say you know him? Anybody can act like a dreamboat for a few hours!"

"Julian doesn't really care for me," Kitty said.

Louise sighed. "I'm not talking about Julian."

Kitty bit back the words she was about to say next. Instead, she said, "So . . . you don't think he really cares for me, either."

Louise looked into her sister's face and spoke gently. "I think Julian has been distant. I think he's changed. And . . . Well, I'll just tell you. I always did think that there was something off with the two of you. You weren't ever really serious with each other, either of you. It was like you decided to call what you had love, but it was more of a . . ." She shrugged. "I don't know. I don't know what it was."

"So why are you so resistant to the idea that I've found love with Hank?"

"Because I don't think that's love, either!" Louise said. "That's just a night on the town with a handsome fellow who's lonely and a pretty girl who's just as lonely as he is! Why do you think they don't let you give your address at the USO clubs? Because of these wartime infatuations that people call love! And then they get themselves in all kinds of trouble!"

Kitty went to the dresser and began roughly brushing her hair. She was exhausted. She wanted to cry. But mostly she was angry. She could hardly keep from saying to Louise, "You should know about getting in trouble, all right!" She brushed her hair harder.

Louise came and took the brush from her hand. Then she began gently brushing her sister's hair. Kitty stood still and let her. Louise would come around. She would.

"LAST NIGHT I DREAMED MY MOM *was alive again, and she'd come over here with all her pots and pans in a big trunk. She showed them to me and said she was going to cook me a big steak dinner, but that I shouldn't tell the other boys, because she didn't have enough for all of them.*"

"Ho," Tish said. "Michael would never do that."

Louise laughed. "You're right! Listen.

"*Well, I couldn't do that, of course, so I told her, Oh, just make hamburgers for all of us.*"

Louise was reading from Michael's latest letter. He was back in England, training again for the ever-coming European invasion, and Louise was happy that he was, for the time being anyway, not under direct fire.

The sisters sat in their warm robes around the kitchen table while outside the snow fell furiously. Binks had said it was going to reach the roof, and Kitty was beginning to think he was right. But soon it would be March, and then they would be one month closer to spring.

"*You said you wondered if Hitler's soldiers really believed in him,*" Louise read. "*Well, this story might help you. There was a German soldier who tried to surrender when we were in North Africa. His own men shot him. And then one of them shouted, 'Now you know Hitler.'*"

"I know another story," Tish said. "This guy met a German girl who had escaped the country, she and her family? She said in her school they showed a film of Nazi soldiers going into enemy territory. It was dark, and they were marching alongside deep water. One of them fell in, and with all that heavy equipment he was carrying, he couldn't get out. He didn't want to endanger the other soldiers by calling for help, so he put his face in the water and quietly drowned himself."

"They're monsters," Louise said. She put her hand to her belly, still relatively small, even though she was now seven months pregnant. Louise looked wonderful, even in her shapeless, faded, and mostly threadbare maternity clothes. The tentlike tops and elastic-paneled skirts had been donated from here, there, and everywhere. "No point in buying them new," their mother had said, but Kitty couldn't stand it and had bought a navy blue top for her sister with a crisp white bow, and Louise had wept, thanking her. "Gosh, I'm so emotional all the time!" she'd said. And indeed she was; she cried easily, and she laughed easily, too—the silliest joke from one of her brothers would have her howling, much to their delight, of course.

Louise's face glowed, her hair was thick and shiny, her fingernails were enviably long and even and strong. Kitty wished Michael could see her in person, rather than in the pictures she sent. And maybe he would soon. It seemed to Kitty that the war couldn't last much longer, even though Hank had cautioned her in his letters against optimism that might only lead to sorrow and frustration. But she couldn't help it. So much progress was being made! At Christmastime there had been a feeling, however briefly, of peace. (One man had written to Tish that on Christmas Eve, as he sat holed into his position, he heard the distant sounds of the Nazis singing Christmas carols.) Now the U.S. troops had landed and set up a beachhead at Anzio, and the Marshall Islands were being taken in the Pacific. There had even been escapes from concentration camps and revolts which, though quickly thwarted, showed that a fighting spirit lived on. Surely it would all end soon and the boys would come home. And then she and Hank could reveal the truth of their feelings to everyone.

Kitty had given up on trying to convince Louise that what she and Hank had was real. Instead, she kept up appearances by continuing to write to Julian. But Tish wrote him more enthusiastically, and he wrote back to her. Tish didn't read all the letters from Julian out loud any more than she shared all the letters she got from other guys. But Kitty could see what was happening. She could see how her sister's face lit up when a letter from Julian came for her. One night, as the girls lay in bed, Tish said, "Julian said if he got hurt he wouldn't blame Kitty for giving him the gate."

"What did you tell him?" Kitty asked.

"I told him not to worry, he'd be home soon and jigging to the juke."

"I wouldn't break up with him for being injured," Kitty said.

"You wouldn't?"

"Not for that."

The silence grew thick around them. And then Louise fell asleep, and then Tish, and then Kitty.

THE KELLY CLUB HAD BEEN DECORATED with paper hearts in honor of Valentine's Day. Only another thing for the Englishman Kitty was dancing with to criticize. He'd told her first about how spoiled the 10th Air Force in India was. "All they do is go to the palace for dinner and play cards," he'd said. "Ride elephants and go tiger hunting. There are servants waiting on them, and beautiful Indian princesses who put on shows for them. The officers live in a palace that used to belong to the prime minister. The enlisted men live in tents, but they're pitched in a grove of trees where there are lovely birds and flowers. The maharaja makes sure the men have plenty of records and movies, too. Oh, they've got it tough, all right!"

"Well," Kitty said, when she could get a word in. "That's certainly not the norm."

"Aw, you Yanks."

Kitty clenched her jaw tightly. What did he mean by a crack like that? Soon the song would end and she would be free from this awful man, with his terrible complexion and crooked teeth. Then she'd go over and serve food. She was tired of dancing. She wanted to serve food and listen to the trumpeter, who was almost as good as Harry James.

"You know, you American girls are much different from our women," the man said, and it was clear from the sound of his voice which girls he found superior.

"Oh?" Kitty asked wearily.

"You wear too much makeup, dreadful; and you're too forward. Plumper, too."

Kitty stepped out of the man's arms. "Any other complaints, buster?"

The man stared at her, surprised. Then he grew angry and said, "Plenty! You're always in a hurry here. You drive on the wrong side of the road. Your beer is served too cold, and it's too weak, and your food is too rich. Your skyscrapers aren't nearly so high as they look in pictures. And it's too *bright* here!"

"Thanks for the dance," Kitty said, and he said, "You're welcome!"

From across the room, Kitty saw a woman she knew from work. She moved gratefully toward her.

"How are you, Margie?" Kitty asked.

Margie held up her hand, showing off an engagement ring.

"Holy cow! When?"

"He sent it from Hawaii for Valentine's Day. Gosh, Kitty, I was so excited I almost fainted. I can't wait for him to come home so we can get married and move into our own house. I want five kids, just like in my family. What heaven it will be to quit this job and stay home!"

"Oh, I know," Kitty said, but privately she was beginning to wonder if she shared the dream that Margie and so many other women had after all. At Hank's suggestion, she had been reading some of the women correspondents' reports, Martha Gellhorn's especially; and she had wondered what it would be like to travel like that, to be so independent and free. Oh, not in a war zone, she wasn't that brave, but after the war was over. What would it be like to decide to go to Paris and just . . . *go!*

Kitty had grown used to her job: the challenge, the camaraderie, and especially the paycheck; and she didn't like the idea that, when the boys came home, she would have to quit. What would she do? Go back to an insurance office and sit all day? Or stand all day, selling gloves for a pittance to some overdressed dowager who looked down her nose at Kitty?

She had dreamed of the day when Hank came home, how they would resume their relationship and eventually get married, but now that it was a real possibility, she wondered about the rest of it. Did she really want to stay home with children? She knew Hank wanted her to;

his letters had made it clear that he valued more than anything the idea of raising a family.

Kitty had tried to imagine it: getting up in the morning, donning a housedress and low heels, brushing her hair and putting on a bit of lipstick, feeding Hank and the children breakfast, and then watching them go. And she remembered a time when Margaret had done exactly that, had sent what she had thought was all of her family off to work and to school, and then stood at the open door in her apron, her hand on her hip. She had turned around with a mighty sigh and seen Kitty, who had run back upstairs for a schoolbook, standing quietly on the stairs. "What's wrong?" Kitty had asked, and Margaret had quickly rearranged her features and said, "Nothing's wrong! What could be wrong?" Then she'd told Kitty to run quickly to catch up with her sisters. Don't be late to school! And button that top coat button! *And then what?* Kitty thought. Had Margaret gone back into the house and turned on the radio to keep her company while she washed the stuck-on oatmeal out of the cereal bowls? For the first time, imagining herself as a wife and a mother, Kitty thought, *Wait.*

Kitty loved her family, her little brothers, but she didn't gravitate toward children the way Louise or even Tish did. Oh, kids were cute, but the truth was that when they weren't in her family Kitty got bored with them. When she was a young girl, it had been Louise and Tish who were given to playing with their brothers, watching them for Margaret. Kitty liked jobs outside the house: going to the store for groceries, pulling weeds, returning library books stacked up high in the wagon.

This Christmas, when Pop had given Louise the crib he'd refurbished for the baby, she'd cooed over it as though it already held him. She'd put the crib in a corner of their bedroom, and Tish had put one of the girls' old dolls in it; every now and then she picked it up and patted it and talked baby talk to it. But Kitty had looked at the crib, admired the craftsmanship, and then thought, *Golly. Soon there'll be a baby in there and it'll be crying all the time.*

Kitty felt a tapping on her shoulder. She turned around to see a soldier half her size, smiling shyly and asking her to dance. To a slow one! She looked out at the crowd of couples nuzzling each other, women smiling up into men's faces. Then she looked into the face of a boy who seemed no older than Billy—she wanted to hold her hankie up to his nose and say, "Blow." Instead, she put a smile on her face and said she would love to dance.

On the floor, with his head pressed into her bosom, Kitty caught the eye of Tish, dancing with a handsome Marine. Tish lifted her shoulders at her sister: *Poor you, but what can you do?* Kitty pulled the boy closer and asked the top of his head where he was from.

"Hartford, Wisconsin," he said and cleared his throat to cover up the way his voice had cracked. "It's a real little town about two hours from here, did you ever hear of it?"

"No," Kitty told him.

"Well, that's okay, I didn't know about Chicago much, either, until the war. I'd never been here until the day before I took the train to basic. My folks came with me, and we 'bout busted the bank, doing up the town. We went to that big museum, and we had dinner at the Berghoff, and we spent the night at the Palmer House. My mom thought she'd died and went to heaven. After she fell asleep, Dad and me went and had ourselves a drink at the bar. Scotch whiskey out of a real nice glass. He told me he was awful proud I was joining—barely made it on account of my height. My dad couldn't be in the First World War because he's deaf in one ear. He would have made a hell of a fighter, though. Now he wants me to do it for him, go after those Nazis. Although we're German, and we still have a lot of relatives over there. It seems kind of funny, to think I'll be shooting at my own people. And them at me!" He looked up at her. Then he pushed his glasses higher on the bridge of his nose. "Wow! You sure are pretty."

"Thank you."

"Anybody ever tell you you look like Rita Hayworth?"

She smiled. "Yes. What's your name, soldier?"

"Walter. Walter Buchman. Listen, I was wondering. Would you . . ."

"Yes?"

"Well, I wanted to . . ."

Here it came, Kitty thought. A request for a little kiss outside, or off in some dark corner. That, or he would ask her to write him. "What is it?" she said.

"Would you like to have my gas coupons? It's a cinch I won't be needing them."

LATER THAT NIGHT, KITTY SAT at the kitchen table massaging lotion into her feet. She took a long drink of tea, leaned back in her chair, and groaned.

"What's your beef?" Tish asked.

"I'm tired! My feet hurt!"

"So do mine."

"Well, you don't work for hours in a factory before you go to a dance!"

"What are you talking about?" Tish said angrily. "I'm on my feet all day. I've got to sell like sixty—Carson's is understaffed and over-crowded with old bags who take half the day to decide between red lip-stick and red lipstick!"

From the parlor, over the sounds of a USO rebroadcast, came Mar-garet's voice. "If you girls wake up your brothers with your squabbling, I'll spank you like the children you're behaving like." And then from the radio came the voice of Kay Francis: "The Army flew us in a bomber from California to New York. And the pilot! Boy, he was the best-looking fellow I'd ever seen. I didn't know you could fly a plane with one hand, but you can. When we got to camp, we were pretty hungry. Martha Raye slipped up to the colonel and she said, 'Sir, where do we eat?' He said, 'You mess with the men.' 'I know that,' she said, 'but where do we eat?'"

The sisters laughed and sat silently for a while, listening. They heard about Mitzi Mayfair, who danced in pouring rain with a loose board that she had to keep an eye on. When one shoe came off, she kicked off the other shoe and continued dancing barefoot. The rain kept on, so hard that when Carole Landis tried to sing, it was like gargling. Finally, she stopped and just started talking to the boys. She said, "Gosh, I'm pretty nervous being up here all alone in front of a thousand men." In the background, from the men, ohs and ahs. "After all," she said, "how would you like to be all alone with a thousand girls?" Bedlam.

Kitty and Louise smiled, but Tish was still cranky. "You think you're the only one in the family who does anything, Kitty," she said, though quietly. *Let her be,* Louise's eyes told her. Kitty had already decided to ignore Tish—she was the youngest, and she was tired. They all were. Louise, working at the child-care center, probably had it harder than any of them, but she never complained.

Kitty picked up her big pile of letters—they often came in bunches like this—and counted them. "Cripes, eleven!" she said.

"You should be happy," Tish said. "I got only one!"

"From whom?" Kitty asked, knowing already what the answer was: someone other than Julian. Tish was always happy when she had a letter from him. And the more she tried to disguise it, the more obvious it was. Soon Kitty was going to have a talk with her. She'd already planned how she'd start this talk, saying wasn't it funny how you sometimes got to know someone best when you weren't with him, when your exchanges were confined to paper. Wasn't it funny how you could find you didn't know someone you'd spent a lot of time with and, conversely, come to see you felt very close to someone with whom you'd spent almost no time at all? That was what she'd say, and then she hoped Tish would open up with her feelings about Julian. And what appeared to be Julian's feelings for her. Kitty felt a small hurt, thinking that, but mostly she was glad. They were more suited to each other, just as Michael was suited to Louise, and she to Hank. There on top of the pile, his letter. And four more were from him! There was one from Julian, four from men she'd met at dances, and another with a name she didn't recognize, but surely that, too, was from someone she'd danced with, or served coffee to, or even met on a streetcar. She was going to stop agreeing to write to so many. Enough was enough. Surely she had done her part by now. There had to be a time when it was okay to say no. She leaned over to rub the balls of her feet again. "Next time we go to the Kelly Club, I'm working the library," Kitty said. Far fewer men went there than to the dances.

"That'll be the day," Tish said.

"Oh, and you read two books at a time," Kitty said. She waited for Louise to interfere; on these occasions she usually did. Their middle sister had been born a mother. Or a judge. But Louise was frowning, lost in a letter from Michael.

"What's the matter?" Kitty asked. "What did he say?"

Louise looked up, startled. Then she shrugged. "Not so much, really. But . . . Something's different."

"Read it," Tish said.

"He doesn't say anything, really, but there's something wrong. I can just feel it."

"Read it!" Kitty said.

"All right, all right." Louise leaned back in her chair, held the letter up and smiled. "I'm not going to read you the salutation. Or the end. Just the middle. Here's what he says.

"*I sure appreciate the sweater you sent, honey. Gosh, it's cold here at night. But at least I'll have another layer now. So many of our guys are sleeping outside on the ground, many with only one blanket, and some with none. No girls knitting for them. I guess some guys don't have much of anybody at home waiting for them. It's hard to imagine that, when I have so much. Sometimes it all seems like a dream—you, the baby. Like something I made up in my head to make me feel better. Sometimes it seems like too much. Oh, not in a bad way, but it was enough that I had you. Now I'm blessed with a baby on the way, and I just feel like I have to be so much more careful. So much is waiting for me at home now. Remember those races we used to run in elementary school, with an egg balanced on a tablespoon? Now I've got two eggs!*"

Louise looked up, tears in her eyes. "Ma was right. I shouldn't have told him."

"But in his last letter, he was really happy about it," Tish said.

"He was probably just tired when he wrote that," Kitty said.

"But listen to this," Louise said.

"*A guy told me a funny story the other day. When he was in North Africa, a shell exploded near him and knocked him way down a hill. He wasn't hurt, but he had the breath knocked out of him, and he couldn't move at all. Well, along come two guys who know him, walking past, and one pauses a little bit away from him and says, Ah jeez, Dooley got it. And the other guy walks up a little closer and bends down and says, 'Yup. Ain't he got a little baby daughter, too?' And then they just leave him there. And later he kind of comes to, and that night he goes over to where they're chowing down and they almost jump out of their skins. They still swear he willed himself back from the dead. Say, there's a trick I need to know.*"

Louise put the letter down. "That's it. Then he just tells me . . . Well, you know."

"He's okay," Kitty said. "What are you worried about? You know, those guys sometimes get a little rambling and—"

"Never mind." Louise yawned and rubbed at the back of her neck. "Yowsa, I'm *tired.*" But then she sat up and put her hand to the side of her belly. "Want to feel him kick?"

Kitty and Tish bumped heads, reaching over, but neither said a word. They held still, their faces rapt, and then said together, "I feel him!"

Louise yawned again. "I'm going to bed." She went into the parlor to say good night to their parents, then headed upstairs, saying, "Whoever's in the bathroom, hurry up. I'm peeing for two now!"

Kitty and Tish read their letters silently—it wasn't any good reading aloud unless they were all there. The letter from Julian was his usual impersonal message followed by *Love,* which Kitty now realized meant very little.

In the parlor, the radio went silent, and Margaret and Frank came into the kitchen to say good night. "You two turn in," Margaret told them.

"In a minute," Kitty said. Tired as she was, she wanted to take her time reading Hank's letters. He wrote about nature: the oxymoronic quality of flowers on a battlefield. The thin line of rose on the horizon at sunset. The way the boys stood still to hear birdsong and admired the beauty of various countrysides, even if they were neck-deep in mud.

He recounted conversations he'd overheard—some funny, some painfully sad. Most important, he continued to tell her about himself, both as a boy and as the man he was now. There were times she thought about making a scrapbook out of certain paragraphs he'd written. But she wanted to save all his letters intact. Someday they'd take them out and sit on the sofa with cups of tea and read them all again together. He liked Irish tea. He liked Boston cream pie. He liked french fries and bar-becue ribs. He hated radishes and liver.

It was strange. When she used to fantasize about living with Julian, she pictured scenes straight out of a magazine. But when she thought about living with Hank, she imagined them on a burgundy sofa she'd never seen anywhere, books lined up neatly behind them on floor-to-ceiling shelves, artifacts from their travels here and there: a painting from the Left Bank in Paris, a mask from Africa. They would travel, she was sure of it, even though they'd never really talked about it. But she was curious about so many of the places Hank had described; she wanted to see them for herself.

Kitty picked up the last letter, the one with the unknown name. She knew already what she'd find inside: *Dear Kitty* (or *Miss Heaney;* a lot of them liked to be a little formal when they first wrote). *I am the man from _____ whom you danced with at the Kelly Club. I hope you remember me, because I sure remember you.* They almost all started out with some version of that. But when Kitty opened the letter, what she read was *Kitty, it's Michael here, just writing to thank you for all those Christmas presents you sent.* All what Christmas presents? She'd sent only cigarettes. Her parents had sent him socks and hard candy and a salami and the heart-shield Catholic prayer book. They'd ordered it from a magazine ad that suggested you "Give your hero God's weapon." On the cover of the gold-plated steel front cover, they'd had engraved MAY THIS KEEP YOU SAFE FROM HARM.

Michael continued:

I hope I don't bore you, but I'm going to tell you about opening each one, what a delight it was, and also I'll write a little poem about each gift.

And then, suddenly,

Kitty, I have to tell you something and I don't want you to let anyone know.

She looked quickly over at Tish. Making the most of the one letter she was writing, she was busy illustrating it; she'd begun sending drawings the fellows found amusing, including one of her hiking her skirt up to well above her knees and winking. "Better not let Ma or Pop see that," Louise had said. And then, "Give me that." She'd regarded the drawing carefully, then handed it back to her sister, one eyebrow raised.

Kitty positioned the letter to make sure Tish couldn't see it, and read on:

I know you and Tish have been writing to a fair number of men, and I suppose every now and then one of them talks about the "jits." But just in case they haven't, let me explain it to you. It stands for "jitters," of course, and I'd guess every man gets them sooner or later. But I seem suddenly to have them all the time. I can't hold a fork without watching it shake in my hand.

I feel sure that I'm going to get it. I never thought that before, but now I just feel sure. I've dreamed about my death. I've seen exactly how it happens, a bullet right below my helmet on the right side, coming out of nowhere. I've seen myself lying on the ground, one leg bent up, my rifle not far from my hand. I'm sorry to write this to you, Kitty, sorry if it upsets you, but I just have to tell someone. I only hope the censors miss this. A buddy of mine said he knows that some censors just look at the beginning and the end, or that some letters slip by unread except to briefly scan for the names of places that would give away our location—there are so very many letters for them to go through!—and that is why I began this letter the way I did. I will end it the same way.

One reason for my telling you this is an odd one. I want someone to know I knew, and here will be the evidence. I don't know why that's so important to me. Maybe to reassure you all that I had time to get ready. I am getting ready, trying to think that if this is all I get of life, I'll make the best of it. I'll do my duty as honorably as I can, and I'll know that my sacrifice helped us win the war. We will win the war. But the main reason I'm writing is to ask you to promise you'll look after Louise in every way you can. I'm so worried about what will happen to her. Without the baby, she could have found another man, in time. It hurts me to think of her with someone else, but it's worse to think of her alone. And now with a baby it will be so much harder. You've told me more than once that you'd do anything for your sisters—and your brothers—and I hope that's true. I know your mom and pop will help, the whole family, but you're the one she really relies on outside of me. You know that, right? If you could just write me back saying you'll do that, it sure would help to ease my mind. Promise me in writing, Kitty. You don't need to send a whole letter or anything, I know how you girls stay up late writing letters each night. Just tell me yes and send it right away. I know exactly where I'm going to keep it.

And the socks! Well, I guess they're appreciated almost more than anything else. Here is my poem for them: Socks in a box are okay, I suggest. But socks that you knit are the very best. Well, I've gone on enough for one letter. Let me just sign off now with a hearty thanks for all you've done and will do. Regards to your family.

With love,
Michael

Kitty sat still, staring straight ahead. Then she quietly pulled out a V-mail form. On it she wrote, *Dear Michael, Someday we will share a laugh over this. But for now, I will only tell you yes. Of course yes. Take care of yourself. We all love you so. Kitty.*

She sealed the letter and put in the middle of the others she'd written.

"That was a fast one!" Tish said.

"Just a little note to some guy I danced with."

"Are you going to write to old Shorty?"

"Who?"

"That little guy you danced with tonight, the one who came up to your knees."

Kitty smiled. "He's not so dumb. He picks tall women so he can put his face . . . Well, you know." She picked up the letters. "Feel like a walk? I'm going out to mail these."

"Heck, no!" Tish said. "It's freezing out there, and I'm beat. I'm going to bed. But take mine, would you?"

Kitty put her galoshes on over her slippers, congratulating herself on her reverse psychology. If she had started to go out without inviting Tish to join her, her sister would have insisted on coming along.

Kitty put her coat on over her robe and slipped outside. The street was so quiet. Frost sparkled on the sidewalk and made her boots stick to the concrete. She looked up into the sky. Poor Michael. He needed a rest. When would he get one? She'd heard about a correspondent who, when he had encountered one dead man too many, would not pray but instead would repeat some pleasant sentence over and over in his mind: *I'm lying on the beach in California.* She hoped Michael was able to do that sometimes: absent himself from everything around him, at least in his mind. What would she say, Kitty wondered, if she needed a sentence like that? It came to her immediately: *I'm home. I'm home. I'm home.* She thought that if Michael had a sentence, that was his, too.

She thought about the first time he'd seen Louise. The sisters had gone bowling with a bunch of other girls, and there in the lane next to them was Michael, out with a bunch of guys. He had the curls and pink cheeks of a cherub, the girls agreed later. But otherwise he was all man, tall, broad-shouldered, and square-jawed. After he'd caught sight of Louise, he had never looked away except when it was his turn to bowl, and even then, it was clear his mind wasn't on the game. "Come *on*, O'Conner," his friends had kept saying. "Watch the *ball*, wouldja?" He'd been so shy, so hesitant, and yet so determined when he came over to introduce himself. And Louise, blushing and so uncharacteristically un- sure of herself. When she got home, she sat right down at the kitchen table and said, "Ma? I've met someone." She hadn't taken her coat off, or even her kerchief.

"Again?" Margaret had said. She'd been busy making dinner, only half listening.

"No," Louise had said. "Not 'again.' For the first time."

Margaret had stopped stirring and come over to plant a kiss on her daughter's forehead. That was all. That was enough.

At the mailbox, Kitty looked down at the letter in her hand. In a lit- tle while, it would be in Michael's hand. Such an amazing fact, that in the midst of a war, the mail came. That a man took time from trying to kill—and not be killed—to read a letter about how his son had learned that day to walk, how his girl lay in bed at night, longing for him. Kitty wished she could tuck herself inside an envelope every now and then and make the trip to one of the many places she and her sisters sent let- ters to. She imagined herself flying across some vast ocean and stepping out onto foreign soil, just an American girl come to stand before Amer- ican boys. It would be like a USO tour, only better. They wouldn't have to come to her; she would come to them, close up. All she wanted to do was wander around a camp smiling at those boys, an unspoken message in her eyes. And what was the message? Gratitude, most profoundly.

Kitty started to drop the letter into the mailbox, then pulled it back and kissed it. For one moment, she wondered about the propriety of such a thing. Then she laughed out loud, her breath making a puffy lit- tle cloud before her. What had they so often said in their household? If one Heaney girl loved you, the three of them did. And if you loved one Heaney girl, you loved them all.

When she climbed the porch steps, shivering, Kitty thought about the boys who slept outside in the cold. How did they do it? She sat on the top step and looked at her watch. How long she could last out here, a few steps from her own front door? Could she last fifteen minutes?

But they were lying on the ground, those boys. Kitty moved over to the corner of the porch and lay down, her knees hunched up close to her chest. It hurt her hip to lie this way, her shoulder. It made her dizzy to be without a pillow.

So hard to imagine, in any true sense, how the boys at the front lived. They were filthy dirty and without any semblance of routine or familiar surroundings. They were so far away—physically, yes, but even more important, psychologically—from all the things in their life that once meant stability, that meant home. No family or old friends. No beds or chairs or kitchen tables or toothbrush stowed neatly in its holder. No walls! Instead, the men awakened in a new place, sometimes every day, and lived by instinct, like animals.

Maybe, though, they were too tired to feel bad for themselves, too tired to feel much of anything. Kitty had read about the crushing kind of fatigue those soldiers endured, and still they went on, because they had to. Last August, in Sicily, the men of the 1st Division were on the front lines for twenty-eight days, walking and fighting all that time. Twenty-eight days! The moon went through its phases, Kitty went to the factory and browsed at the Fair store and saw movies at the Paradise, with its immense staircase and statues and fountains and ceiling full of stars. She went to Fritzl's restaurant and, stuffed, pushed away a plate with good-tasting, hot food still on it. She laughed and talked and slept late on Saturday and fingered the fine fabrics of the dresses she could now afford to buy. In twenty-eight days, birthdays were celebrated and weddings were performed. Women came to term and delivered and went home with their new babies, and all the while the men were walking and fighting, walking and fighting. No more talk about what they were going to do to those sons of bitches when they finally got over there. Now they were there. Now they were in it, and Kitty couldn't help but think that most all of those boys, those clench-fisted, wide-eyed boys talking so boldly about teaching those Nazis a lesson, now wanted only to come home. Especially the young ones, those who were learning to shave at the same time they were learning how to eviscerate the enemy.

When they lay down at night, what kind of sorrow overtook those men? Or maybe sorrow was a luxury they couldn't afford. And anyway, maybe when you were that tired, you didn't think about anything before sleep. You were probably just grateful that you could sleep at all. Kitty made a pillow of her arm, to keep her face from pressing against the cold floorboards.

So maybe it was something like this, only with the presence of extreme danger. Did fear make you warmer? She closed her eyes, imagining that all around her were unseen enemies, and that although she needed to sleep, she also needed to stay alert. She imagined a whistling in the air, a mortar shell coming in, how she'd have to get out of the way and run. She rolled over and over as quickly as she could in her coat and galoshes and then jumped to her feet, holding an imaginary automatic rifle.

The front door opened, and there stood Frank, squinting at her, clutching his bathrobe tightly around his throat.

"For the love of Mike, what are you doing out here?"

"Nothing," Kitty said.

"Sure I thought Bushman the gorilla had escaped from the Lincoln Park Zoo!"

"Sorry, Pop."

He looked around the porch, pushing down on his hair, which stood right up again. "Are you all alone out here, then?"

"Yes."

"Well, come inside. 'Tis late! What were you *doing* out here?"

"I mailed some letters." Kitty walked past him, refraining from hugging him, which was what she wanted to do. She felt as though she'd been far away, to a terrible place, and now here she was walking into her own house, safe. The thought of her bed and her sisters upstairs made her feel like weeping.

"I'm going to have a glass of milk and a wee bit of jelly roll," Frank said. "Will you join me?" He spoke quietly, for after dinner Margaret had given the family explicit instructions not to touch that jelly roll; she wanted to serve it again the next night.

"I will," Kitty said. She took off her coat and galoshes and went into the kitchen.

"We'll both be tired in the morning," Frank said. "And in a fair amount of trouble with the crossed-arms missus!"

Kitty said she knew. Somehow, she was honored. She sat down at the table.

Frank poured them each a glass of milk and cut them not ungenerous slices of jelly roll. He clinked his glass with hers. "Here's to my wife and great love of my life," he said. And then, leaning in conspiratorially, "May they never meet!"

Kitty's eyes filled with tears.

"I'm only joking!" Frank said.

"I know, Pop," Kitty said. "I just was thinking about our boys. I just feel so sorry for them."

Frank nodded. "All of us do. And always it's a struggle not to give in to that sadness. But you know why we mustn't, don't you?"

Kitty shrugged.

Frank put his hand on her shoulder. "Here now, look me in the eye."

Reluctantly, she did.

"Those boys are doing their part, every one of them, God love them. And to me, they're all heroes, whether they fall in battle or sit at a desk stateside. But you know this, Kitty, sure I've said it often enough: We're all fighting this war, dressed in a uniform or not. And where the part of the boys overseas is the fighting and the part of the boy stateside is to do the best job he can do to support them, our job is to remain proud and optimistic. We on the home front have to be the bright place those boys can come to in their minds. And we offer our own kind of ammunition: the belief that they're doing the right thing. We must support them fully in every way we can, and we must wait patiently for them to come home."

"And if they don't?" Kitty asked, bitterly.

Frank nodded. He sat still for some time, staring into his empty glass. Finally, he looked up at her and said, "We live but a short time, at the longest. How do we make our lives mean something? If we die in glory, with our minds and our hearts fixed on achieving a great goal, we have lived a life that mattered.

"What fate decides an illness, or some terrible accident? Who can guarantee any of us another day, whether we are here on Pine Street in Chicago, Illinois, or on the beaches of Sicily? The boys who are fighting this war know that they will make a difference today and in all the years to come. They know that, whether they come home or not, they have helped write a mighty page of history. They know it, it lives large inside them, and as hard as it may be for you to understand, I believe that even the youngest of them are resigned to it. It may seem selfish for us to enjoy ourselves when they suffer so. But part of the reason for us to do it is so that we can tell them about it. When you girls write those men about a meal you had or a walk you took or a movie you saw, you're giving them the experience to have with you. When you tell a soldier how proud you are of him, he is prouder of himself. Whenever those boys get a letter, they are for a few precious moments taken far away from a hellish place—sure you know they call letters from home ten-minute furloughs!

"But, Kitty, over there is where those boys want and need to be. If it doesn't start out that way, it ends up being that way. Men in combat love one another, and although they hate war, they love it, too. I experienced it myself. A soldier needs to believe with all his heart in his commander and his mission, and he needs for us to believe in him. How do we show him that we do? Not by mourning the fact that he's there but by cele-brating the life we are privileged to lead on account of his sacrifice."

Kitty bit at her lip; she felt dangerously close to bursting into tears.

"All right?" Frank asked gently.

She nodded.

"Off to bed, then, for the both of us, and may the good Lord help the one faces Margaret first."

"I'm not afraid of her," Kitty said.

"'Course you are, and so am I. She's a formidable woman. But she makes a lovely jelly roll."

When Kitty crawled into bed beside Louise, she felt her sister's wakefulness. "Good night," she whispered.

"Good night," Louise said. And then, "I heard everything Pop said. He's right, you know."

Kitty said nothing. She still wanted to believe that there were other ways to settle things than war after war after war. But when Louise took her hand, she squeezed it.

TWO DAYS LATER, WHEN KITTY CAME HOME from work, she thumbed through her pile of mail on the front hall table. There was another let-ter from Michael. He had used the same false name as last time, and the same boxy print, so different from his usual elegant script. Kitty slipped the letter into her pants pocket and took it upstairs to the bathroom to read it.

Dear Kitty,

Written in haste, but with great urgency. Please forgive and disregard last letter. Was awful tired. Okay now. Fine as wine, as J. would say. See you all and soon; I truly feel this can't go on much longer.

Much love to you, dear.

Michael

Well, now! That was better! Kitty sat on the edge of the tub and turned on the faucets for a bath, then realized it wasn't time to take a bath now. It was dinnertime, not bath time. Oh, she was tired! She couldn't even think straight. She used the toilet, washed her hands and face, and pushed her hair back from her forehead. Then she leaned in to the mirror to inspect herself. It seemed so long ago that she'd done this with such pleasure, such excitement, and to be frank, such great admiration. Now she looked at herself in a different way. She had dark smudges under her eyes; she had lost more weight. And oh, look at her hair, so dull and dirty. Aw, so what? Accentuate the positive. That weight loss came from a job that was giving her enough money to make a real difference. Her father had begun calling her Mrs. Rockefeller, and her mother had again taken her aside to thank her for the significant contribution she was making to the family.

Kitty read Michael's note one more time, then threw it away, as she had his last letter—she didn't want Louise to see either of them. *Can't go on much longer.* If only that were true. Kitty looked at her watch, as if that had anything to do with it, as if the war were a movie and would be over in twenty minutes. She had read an article that cautioned against thinking the war was all but won. In the Nazis' favor were Hitler's messianic control of the population, the natural will to survive, an army that remained strong and was yet unbroken, and the riches that had come from plundering Europe. Much of the money was gone by now, and the German army was in retreat, but still . . . The article had talked as well about the boys' attitudes. They were sick to death of fighting and dreamed often about how life would be when they returned home. But the catchphrase was *I'll do the job I want to do when I finish the job I have to do.*

There was an urgent knock on the door, and she opened it to find Tommy. "Hi, squirt!" She stepped into the hall and let him go in. "How are you?"

"Fine, thank you," he said quickly and slammed the door. He had lost more weight, too; she could see his shoulder blades through his shirt, and his collar gaped huge around his neck.

Tish was in the bedroom, sound asleep. She was lying crosswise on the bed, her mouth open slightly. One shoe was still on. She was beat, too. Kitty stood smiling, watching her sleep. Soon Louise would come home and sit in the living room with her feet up while she waited for dinner, exhausted. But at least she wasn't losing weight. She couldn't see her feet anymore.

Louise and Michael's baby. Everyone was counting the days. An early May delivery date had been predicted. A new baby and spring. Heaven. Even Frieda Schumacher, the bent-backed, bewhiskered old maid two doors down who scowled at everyone, had rung the doorbell last Sunday and thrust at Margaret a present wrapped in newspaper. "This is for your daughter's baby," she'd muttered and then stomped off the porch. "Thank you!" Margaret had called after her. She'd waved, her potato peeler in her hand. "Thank you . . . miss!"

" 'Twas such a shock, I forgot her name!" Margaret said later. Inside the box had been a beautifully knitted blanket, snow white, and soft as snow, too, and matching bonnet and booties. Louise had added them to her hope chest, and every now and then she took them out and lay them on the bed, as if the baby were in them. Her sisters often stood beside her at such times, each with her own vision. Kitty saw Michael's dimples, reborn; she saw chubby arms and legs waving excitedly. Tish said she thought the baby would have red hair, like Michael's mother, and an exceptionally calm demeanor. Louise said she had no idea how the baby would look, but imagine, a whole new *person* added to the world! She and Michael had decided on names: Mary Margaret for a girl. And for a boy? Michael Francis. The Second. This was what Tish called the doll they kept in the crib, Michael Francis O'Conner, always the whole name. For as far as she was concerned, a girl was not an option. "I simply won't have it," she'd told her sisters, her blue eyes wide and really, Kitty thought, kind of *greedy*.

"Okay," KITTY SAID, SIGHING. "Here it is." She read out loud to her sisters from Julian's letter:

"*April fourth, 1944*

"*Somewhere in the Pacific*

"*I'm sitting here in the tent with a cup of joe. I've been waiting for a quiet time to write this letter, and now that time is here. I just had a luxurious bath in a stream with two nets stretched across either end to keep out the alligators. Then I took a walk to enjoy the view: shattered coconut trees, overturned jeeps, and whatnot. Oh hell, I guess I'll skip the preview and go right to the feature.*

"*Kitty, it seems like I'll never be your kind of guy. You've changed, and I have, too. I'm not the man you said good-bye to at the train station. Or maybe we always were different and we had to be apart in order to see that. I do think of you. I think a lot about you and your sisters, too. The Heaney sisters, wowser, best of the Midwest. But everything back home seems like it's a movie or something, an out-of-focus movie at that. Maybe it would be best if you and I stopped writing. Seems like you might have more in common with that other guy; you kind of tipped your mitt when you mixed up letters that time. And to be frank, it seems like I have more in common with Tish. I hope it doesn't hurt your feelings for me to say so. Maybe you already know. But I can tell it's a strain for you to write to me, and it's hard for me to write to you, too. I just don't know what to say.*

"*Kitty, you know I'll always love you. But not that way. I think you wanted me to slip you some ice for the fourth digit before I left, but I just* didn't see us a married couple, and now I see I was right. I hope we'll still be friends.

"Julian

"P.S. Thanks for that picture you sent. Nice lid. You always did look swell in hats."

Kitty blinked back tears. She was surprised at how much this hurt. Oh, she'd known for some time that things were never going to work out the way she'd planned between Julian and her. But to have it so forthrightly presented to her! To have him be the one to initiate the breakup! "Oh, well," she said lightly. And then, to Tish, "He's all yours."

Tish shook her head. "Oh, no, I never meant to—"

"I don't mind, honest I don't. It just feels kind of funny." And now she began to cry in earnest.

Margaret came into the kitchen, her face full of concern, her hand to her throat. "Who died?"

All the sisters burst out laughing, and then Kitty said, "Just a relationship. Julian and me. But you know, he's grown very fond of Tish."

"What do you mean, he's grown fond of Tish? He can't go through my daughters like Kleenex!"

"It's okay, Ma," Kitty said. "Things were never quite right between us."

"Yes." Margaret sat heavily at the kitchen table. " 'Tis true."

"Cripes!" Kitty said. "Was anyone ever going to tell me?"

"I suppose Julian just did," Margaret said. "Ah, me." She rubbed her forehead.

Kitty stood up. "I'm going for a walk. Nobody come. I'm fine."

She threw on a coat and walked quickly down the stairs, down the block. In a short while she began to breathe more easily. So many men had told so many loved ones that they weren't the same man anymore. Well, she wasn't the same woman, either. Oh, it wasn't just because of the change in her affections. Rather it was because of the way her ideas about herself had begun to change. She had believed for so long that she knew exactly who she was and exactly what she wanted. She had seen her future as Julian's wife, a woman who would stay home and bear children and derive most of her satisfaction from whatever goals her husband accomplished. She had doodled "Mrs. Julian Stanton" thousands of times, eager for the day when she could sign her name that way legitimately. But now she was working in a place that gave her more independence, and she'd grown used to it. She felt stronger not only in her body but in her spirit. How to reconcile this new person emerging with the one she'd always been? How could a woman who swooned over a green-and-rose-plaid taffeta evening gown admire equally a well-made ratchet wrench? How could someone who relied on men to open doors for her have become a person who only yesterday crawled under the kitchen sink to make an adjustment so the faucet wouldn't wobble?

She had written to Hank about some of this, and in a letter back he had said he thought times like this could galvanize people into a certain kind of unity but could also make for unexpected changes in the individual, for strange contradictions. He said he himself had begun to feel the need to be alone most of the time. And yet he also felt a kind of love and compassion for humanity far greater than what he'd ever felt before. He found it hard to blame the war on any one person. He thought that, despite witnessing—and taking part in—such unimaginable violence, most soldiers would come home from the war wanting never to hurt anything again.

He told her about boys who came back from battle vacant-eyed, their hands shaking, who in a few hours' time were ready to smile and joke again and then eager to rejoin those at the front. He said that extinguishing life in another seemed to make you unspeakably grateful for your own, indeed for life in general. For a few hours after a battle, Hank said, everything the men looked at seemed caressed by their eyes. They were such young boys. They were such old men.

Oh, but Julian, who never told her things like this yet surely felt them. And now good-bye to Julian and his sweet kisses and his money and his wonderful good looks. Good-bye to the innocent time that had spawned their relationship. But good-bye also to the unease that had been there almost from the beginning, and the worry about how to explain Hank. She would write back to Julian when she got home. She would tell him that she understood, and that she would always love him, too. Because she would. Julian Stanton. "So long, sweetheart," she said softly, and a man passing by her stopped and said, "Sorry?"

"Only a little," she said and smiled.

She walked slowly, then, thinking that soon the first flowers would come pushing through the remaining patches of snow: the elegantly drooping snowdrops, the Easter-colored crocus. Not long afterward, tight little buds of lilac would burst open, and their scent would be everywhere. The air would soften and the days last longer, then longer still. There would be newspaper kites with bright rag tails flying high against blue skies, and twisted streams of water running in the gutters, where her brothers would sail their little boats. Soon the sound of shovels being scraped against the sidewalk would be replaced by the gritty sound of wagons being pulled down the block, kids with food-smeared faces being pulled along by some bossy older sibling. Crows would screech out their proprietary caws, cardinals would whistle, robins would hop heavily on the lawns in search of worms. Spring was coming, just as it always did, no matter how hard the winter that preceded it.

Now Kitty began walking quickly back toward home, for she wanted to share these thoughts with Hank in a letter. Indeed, she suspected she'd recalled such images just to tell him. And there was something else she wanted to tell Hank. She would say that spring would be the same as ever, but it would be altogether different this year, too, and it was because of him, did he understand?

He would understand.

If a sheet of paper were put before them, Kitty thought, she would draw something on it; Hank would study it and add to it. Then she would do the same. They would create something together that belonged to each of them equally, that *was* them equally. This was what she wanted to tell him. Also she wanted to tell him that Hattie had met a new man. That Margaret and Frank had gone out dancing for the first time in ages. She wanted to tell him that she would take him to Henrici's restaurant as soon as he got off the train in Chicago, the minute he stepped off the train, and then they'd go dancing at the Aragon Ballroom. They would take her brothers to Riverview Park to shoot the chutes and ride the roller coaster and ogle the fat lady and the tattooed man. Hank would love the boys and the boys would love him.

She wanted to tell him about the time they'd had a race outside in elementary school, and she had lost because she had tried to avoid stepping on the ants, because she liked ants, their industry and cooperation, did he like ants? Did he like Jo Stafford? Johnny Mercer? Did he like tobogganing in the winter, boating in the summer? Did he like her, still? Did he love her? Because guess what.

There was always so much that she wanted to tell him, so much that she *did* tell him. And each time she finished a letter, she would think, *That's it, sister. You're out of gas now. You'll never be able to think of something different to tell him tomorrow.* But she always did have something different to tell him. Except for the one thing she told him every time, in one way or another: *Oh, Hank. Be careful.*

"READ IT AGAIN," LOUISE SAID. The sisters were in bed, Tish at the foot and all but snoring, but Louise and Kitty awake—Kitty because her sister kept tapping her shoulder and whispering, "Hey? Kitty? Are you asleep? Hey? Are you awake?"

Louise was often restless like this at night now. Margaret said it always happened that way, it was Nature's plan. When it got close to the time for the baby's birth, the mother didn't sleep well anymore. "It's to get you ready," Margaret had told Louise. "You'll be leaping up and down all night for many weeks."

"I'll help with him," Tish had said, and Kitty had volunteered herself as well. But inside she was thinking, *Oh, no, I need my* sleep!

She needn't have worried: Louise had said she'd sleep in the living room with the baby at first; no sense in all of the family's rest being disturbed. "Good idea," Kitty had said quickly, and when Tish and Margaret had glared at her, she'd said, *"What?* It *is* a good idea!" But now Louise was wide awake and asking to hear again a certain paragraph she'd particularly liked from one of Hank's letters.

"I'd read it to myself if you'd let me," Louise said, and Kitty said nothing. Surely Louise knew why Kitty wouldn't hand over this letter—or any of Hank's—to her. There were too many personal things. Lovely, thrilling, personal things. Things that made Kitty soft at the center, that made her heart speed up. Things so wonderfully explicit they made her blush reading them. *And to feel your arms around my neck, your body moving beneath my own.* Oh! she couldn't even think of it!

"I'll read it one more time," Kitty said, "but then you have to leave me alone."

"I will," Louise said. "I'll go downstairs if I can't sleep after this."

Kitty tried to make a lot of noise, getting the letter from her dresser drawer. She wanted Tish to have to wake up, too. But it was no use. If that girl had been at Pearl Harbor, she would have snored right through it.

Kitty got the letter, settled in under the covers, and read:

"The other day, some old colonel told me, 'Soldiers measure their lives in months, if they're worth a damn as soldiers.' In my experience, it's more like days. One day. You might think that could suggest a terrible hopelessness, a disregard for life. Not so. Instead, you live for the day you're alive. You are more fully appreciative of every single thing: the taste of a cigarette, the moon coming over the horizon, the smell of wood smoke coming from some farmhouse, some guy sharing chocolate from home. Despite everything, our hearts yearn to be lifted, and they will find a way."

"Thank you," Louise said, and Kitty told her she was welcome. Then Louise lay down and punched her pillow into shape. She sighed, and Kitty saw two tears roll down her cheeks. "Don't you wish they could come home at night, though? Okay, go and fight all day if you have to, but just come home at night. Have a good hot meal and a bath and sleep in a bed. With us."

"Louise," Tish said sleepily.

"Yes?"

"Pipe down. And turn out that light!"

"Oh, *certainly*, Tish; yes, I will! Oh my goodness gracious, I'm so sorry for having awakened you." Louise looked over at Kitty and raised her eyebrows. Kitty nodded. *"Now!"* Louise said, and the sisters each grabbed one of Tish's legs and pulled her out of bed and onto the floor. An old trick, one that each of them had suffered many times.

"Judas Priest!" Tish yelled. "I told you guys I want to sleep! Now shut your heads and let me *sleep!*"

Here came footsteps down the hall. The girls leaped into bed, turned off the light, and lay quiet as stones.

"Not another word," Margaret said. "If you can't sleep, say the rosary. To yourself! One more sound from any of you and you'll all be down in the basement doing laundry. I have a full box of Duz and a mountain of ironing. 'Tis sheets and men's shirts, too!"

Now came a silence so thick you could almost slice it like bread.

ON MOTHER'S DAY NIGHT, KITTY AWAKENED to the sound of Louise moaning. She shot up in bed and looked for her sister but didn't see her. "Louise?"

"What?" Louise said. And then "Ooooooh. *Ow!*" She was lying on the floor beside the bed, clutching her stomach.

Kitty pulled hard at the covers and hung her head over the side of the bed.

Tish made a half-growling sound and yanked the covers back over herself.

"Oh, jeez!" Kitty said. "Louise, what are you doing? Are you having the baby?"

Now Tish leaped up. "*Where?*"

"Yes," Louise said. "It's coming!"

"Well . . . Well . . ." Kitty said, then hollered, "*Ma!*"

"No!" Louise said. "Don't call her! I don't want to have it yet."

"What do you *mean?*" Kitty got out of bed to kneel beside her sister. Again she hollered for her mother, then told Tish, "Go get her. Hurry!"

"No!" Louise said. And then she cried out again.

"MAAAAAAAAAA!" Kitty yelled, and she heard Margaret call back, "I'm coming, I'm coming! Frank, telephone the doctor, Louise is having her baby!"

Now came the pounding of the boys getting up and coming out into the hall and the sound of Margaret yelling at them to get back to their rooms and don't even think about coming out if they knew what was good for them, she'd tell them when they could come out, and they should stay in there without a sound, even if it took a month of Sundays, by God.

"Kitty!" Louise cried.

"Frank!" Margaret yelled. "Don't come with me! Go downstairs and call the doctor!"

Then their mother was in the girls' room and at Louise's side, and her voice was soft and low. "All right, now, darling. What are you feeling?"

"Oh!" Louise said. "Oh!"

"I know, I know it hurts, my love. But let's get you into bed, and we'll stay right here with you, you'll have your lovely baby soon, the doctor's on the way."

"I don't want to have it now!" Louise put her hand to her belly. "Don't! Go back!"

"Stop that now." Margaret signaled to her girls to help, and they all lifted Louise back to bed.

"Oof!" Margaret said, blowing her hair off her face and rubbing her back. "That's a big baby coming, God bless him!"

"But not now!" Louise sobbed. "Not noowwww!"

Margaret sat on the bed and took Louise's hand. "Louise, darling. The baby's coming whether you want it to or not. It's all right. We're all here, I and your sisters, and though we may not see her, the blessed Virgin Mary our mother, too. And the doctor's on the way."

"I want my baby to come tomorrow!" Louise said.

Margaret told Tish, "Go downstairs so you're there to let the doctor in. Open the door and stand there and don't leave. Tell your father to put some coffee on. Hurry up." Then, to Louise, who lay weeping, "Now, Coots, why don't you want your baby to come?" She pushed her daughter's hair back from her forehead and kissed it.

"It's *Mother's* Day," Louise said. "I want him to have his *own* day! Ow!"

"Now listen to me. What day could be better than this to have your baby? Take your mother's hand and settle down now, sure 'tis as natural as rain having a baby. Here we go. Bend your knees and let me have a look, there's a good girl." Moaning, Louise bent her knees up, and Margaret stuck her head under the sheet.

"How long have you been hurting?" she asked, laying the sheet neatly back over her daughter.

"For an *hour!*" Louise said.

"Ah. Well, then, 'tis his own day the baby will be having, don't you worry about that." To Kitty, she said, "Tell your father to cancel the doctor. We've time to take her to the hospital."

MICHAEL FRANCIS O'CONNER DID NOT HAVE RED HAIR; it was black, like Louise's. He did not have dimples; his fat cheeks were smooth and round. Nor did he seem to have a divine disposition: as Frank, Margaret, Tish, and Kitty stood crowded next to the other relatives looking at the babies in the nursery, they saw Michael screaming and kicking and waving his baby fists. His jaws trembled, and his face was red. Through the thick glass, they could make out his furious sounds—he was the only baby crying at the moment.

"Holy macaroni," Tish said. "He's *mad*."

"He's only hungry," Margaret said, and in a way that seemed involuntary, she rocked back and forth. "There now," she said softly. "You'll soon be with your mother." She clasped her hands to her chest. "Oh, the darling, darling boy," she said. "Frank, did you ever think we'd live to see the day?"

"Well, of course I did!" he said. "And see what a strapping young grandson we've got! Look at the size of him!"

Kitty didn't know what her father was talking about. The smallness of the baby made her feel weak in the knees, made her dry-mouthed. How could anyone take care of someone so tiny, so utterly defenseless? She didn't remember her brothers ever being so small. Surely they had to have been. But maybe looking at a baby as a sister and looking at a baby as a new mother—or future mother—was entirely different. Yes, that was it. One thing to hand over a tiny bundle to the one responsible for his care, another thing altogether to have that bundle handed to you!

Tish pressed her face to the glass and made loud kissing sounds. "Here we are," she said, in a high, singsong voice that made others stare and that embarrassed Kitty.

"Hush," she told Tish quietly, and her sister spun around and said loudly, "*You* hush!" and all the people laughed.

"I'm hungry myself," Frank said. "Let's go and tell Louise good-bye and get the uncles."

Because they were not old enough to visit, the boys had stayed home. They'd been instructed to clean their rooms, and then they'd get to go out to lunch and to the Oriental for a movie. Suddenly, all the news the Heaney family was hearing was good.

LOUISE WIPED TEARS AWAY FROM HER SMILING FACE, then told her family gathered around her, "All right. I'll read it to you now. I'll try not to cry again!"

Louise had gotten a letter from Michael, the one he'd written after hearing about the birth of his son. She sat up higher in bed and read:

"*May twenty-sixth, 1944*

"*Somewhere in England*

"*My darling Louise,*

"*So little time to tell you what might be the most important words I've ever said to you. I am so honored and so humbled at what you have done. You have given me a son, you have made us a family, and it is the thing I wanted most in my life from the moment I laid eyes on you. I cried when I heard, Louise, and I laughed, and I did a little dance and I whooped and hollered and I offered to buy every man in my unit a bottle of champagne, which of course is a pretty easy promise to make when you're in the middle of nowhere. Oh, how can I tell you? You have all my love, all my love, my darling, and you and Michael Junior have the truly heartfelt good wishes of every man here. I'm not the only one who cried upon hearing the news. It's funny how, in the midst of such darkness, our spirits could be lifted so high by news of this little fellow being added to our weary planet. Perhaps it's wrong to say this, but it's how I really feel: in him, it seems to me, lies all hope.*

"*I have to go, my love, and don't worry if you don't hear from me for a little while. I'll write again the instant I can. In the meantime, you tell our beautiful boy that his daddy holds him in his heart until he can hold him in his arms. And you, too, my darling, you, too, Louise.*

"*All my love, all my everything, forever,*

"*Michael*

"*Gosh, I hope you can read this all right. I got a doggone sliver in my finger and just can't seem to get it out—makes it hard to write. Regards to your family.*"

"'Tis a lovely letter," Margaret said.

"Let me take another picture," Frank said. "The boy's awake now and not screaming, let me catch it quick."

"Only one, and then Louise needs a nap," Margaret said.

"I'm all right, Ma. I rested long enough. I can help make dinner."

"You rest. I'll tell you when you're not tired."

"Can I rock Michael to sleep?" Tish asked.

"Yes," Margaret said, before Louise could answer.

"Can I keep the dog?" Binks asked. For days, he'd been asking if he could keep the little black dog that had come to live on the front porch of the house. The boys had fed him a few times, and now he wouldn't leave. Binks had named him Fala, after Roosevelt's dog.

"You don't know if he belongs to someone," Frank said. "You can't just take a dog in without at least trying to find his owner."

"But he just stays here! He doesn't go home!" Tommy said. He, too, wanted the dog. In truth, all of the family except Margaret did. But now even she relented, saying, "Oh, all right, you'll be the death of me with your constant harping on that little dust mop! You can bring him in, but before he takes one step in this house you put him in the laundry tub and bathe him. And then I want you to put up ads all over the neighborhood saying FOUND DOG. If no one claims him, you can keep him."

Binks's eyes grew wide. Then he ran downstairs yelling, "Fala! Fala! You can stay!"

Louise yawned, then settled into her pillows.

"You see?" Margaret said. "You need your rest!"

Tish took up the baby and began singing to him. Kitty watched her suspiciously, thinking this was just a ploy to get out of peeling potatoes. But it wasn't. Next to Louise, Tish had suddenly become the most motherly woman Kitty had ever seen.

Binks finished his letter to Julian and read it aloud to his sisters:

"You won't believe it, but I got a dog. It wasn't easy, too. His name is Fala and already he knows sit and come. When you see him you will like him a lot. He is real little. Joey Huggner has a big dog named Dandy and he joined the Dogs for Defense. His job will be barking to warn that someone's coming. Also he can rescue people and he might even pull a machine gun carrier.

"I got a haircut and Pop had the bowl crooked and now I look crooked too.

"Everything here is good but we all miss you like crazy. See you soon. Write back if you can, but if you're too busy it's okay.

"Love, Binks."

He looked up. "I could put in a picture if he has time to look at it."

"I think he'd love that," Kitty said.

"He definitely would," Tish told him. "He loves the drawings I send him."

Binks went to his room to draw his picture, and Tish read aloud from a letter from a medic stationed in an Army hospital in India:

"These Indians do anything and everything right smack-dab in the streets. They sleep. They shave. They eat and pray. And also they perform certain functions a gentleman like me wouldn't describe to a lady like you. But they do it in the gutters or sometimes even on the sidewalks. The place is just full of beggars.

"Yet there's incredible wealth among the squalor. And a lot of lofty re-

ligious thinking to counter the vice. Just these striking contrasts. There are beautiful mountains and stinking swamps. Wagons are drawn by Brahman bulls or coolies, but also there are modern streetcars and even Packards and Cadillacs. In a restaurant, I heard a native singer do 'Chattanooga Choo Choo' while the waiters ran around in their turbans and the busboys went barefoot. It's like some crazy dream.

"The temples and the gardens are really lovely, and the hovels are worse than anything I could ever describe. A beautiful white marble mosque is in the middle of this filthy city. They make you take your shoes off to go in there—it kind of makes you feel shy. Inside the gate there's a courtyard and a pool with goldfish and a fountain. People wash their faces with that water, and dip their fingers in it to brush their teeth. Inside, there are no pews or anything to sit on, and the people squat down, and then they bend and touch their foreheads to the floor. You know, when I saw that, I thought of this real fat lady who goes to my church, Mrs. Marion Effington, she calls herself by her whole name all the time, one of those stuffy old bats, but anyway I thought of how she would look bending over like that, her hat all falling off, and I started laughing and you can bet I got the evil eye.

"We live in bamboo huts with palm leaves serving as a roof. We have to put tents over our beds each night because the rain, rain, rain drips through—the mud is really something, too, because of all the rain. Quarters should improve as time goes on—cement floors, we're hoping for.

"Meanwhile, we carry on. The food is good. We pretty much get what we want. But you know what they say: there's no place like home. I've never understood how true that is until now.

"Well, cutiepuss, I've got to be off now. I sure do appreciate your letters. And I'll never forget that send-off you—

"Well, never mind about that," Tish said, and the color rose in her face. "Your turn, Kitty."

Kitty read from a letter she'd received from a sailor named Ralph Dowdy. He was a tall, rail-thin, brown-haired man she'd danced with one of the first times she went to the Kelly Club. He had the kindest brown eyes Kitty had ever seen. "You look like a minister," she'd said. And he'd laughed, astonished, and said that was what he was. "Didn't want to tell you right away," he'd said. "It scares some girls off." Kitty had told him she wasn't scared of ministers, but she was spoken for. And Ralph had said that figured. There'd be something plenty wrong with the world if a girl with her looks wasn't spoken for. Kitty had agreed to write him, and now she unfolded his V-mail and read:

"You know the artists' conceptions of ocean battles you see in magazines? Did you ever think they looked kind of phony? Well, I'm here to tell you that they're not. In fact, those renditions are far more subtle than the real thing. You should see what goes on. Let me try to describe it to you.

"In battle, the sea looks to be full of geysers, just these towering columns of water. Bursting shells really do turn a blue sky pitch-black. Flames surround gun muzzles, and ships appear to be on fire. And the noise! It was funny, the first time I heard that kind of noise I kept humming to myself, though of course I couldn't hear myself, I kept humming my favorite Chopin étude. It steadied me, somehow, in between visits I made to the men. Once, in the middle of what seems very much like hell, here comes a Jap bomber flying low and has the unmitigated gall to slide back his cockpit cover and thumb his nose at us! That guy got it, and I suppose from his point of view he went out in glory.

"Thanks for your last note, Kitty. I can't tell you how much mail means to us all. Any and all letters we get are read and reread, with true appreciation. Sounds like everything is good as good can be back home, and I wouldn't want it any other way. Pray for us all, and keep us in your thoughts as we hold you in ours."

Kitty sighed. Such starkly differing images, the view here at her own kitchen table versus what she imagined, reading such letters. Once it had seemed so exotic and exciting; now it seemed mostly sad. She was weary of it. And if she was, how must the boys feel?

"What's your letter from Michael say?" Tish asked Louise.

"This one I'm not sharing," Louise said. "But the other one I haven't even opened yet. It's short—let me see what he says."

Louise read the note to herself, then shared it with her sisters.

"June sixth, 1944

"Onboard ship

"Hi, honey—

"I sure hope this note gets to you. This will be the last letter for a while. Don't you worry about me, though, I am absolutely prepared for anything that may come. That's not because of my endless training, but because of you, darling.

"Keep sending those wonderful descriptions of our son, they're even better than the photographs. I swear I can see him, Louise. I looked at my hand the other day, and I 'saw' his on top of it. So tiny! Keep telling me, darling, tell me every single thing about him and you, you know I can never get enough.

"Gotta go, sweetheart, my best girl. Take care of yourself and the baby, and remember I love you with all my heart and I always will.

"Yours, Michael."

"Oh, Louise," Kitty said and reached for her sister's hand. He'd written the letter on D-day.

Louise pulled her hand away. "Don't. He's fine. I'm going to write him back now. I want him to have lots of letters when he's got time to read them again. You and Tish write him, too, would you? And then before we go to bed I want you to set my hair like you promised, Kitty. I want mine just like yours, I like that style."

Sometimes Kitty felt as though she and her sisters were walking together down a sidewalk, talking and laughing, oblivious to almost everything around them. But every now and then, the sidewalk disappeared, and before them was a chasm, deep and wide and black as the skies that young preacher described. Terrifying. But for the sisters, it was always temporary. However nightmarish the things they heard about in letters, or on the radio, or in magazines or newspapers, they awakened safe in their beds, the hope of morning upon them, and the peace. And in bed at night they talked about the men, yes, but mostly they talked about Sinatra and movie stars, hairdos and hemlines, ideas for what else to put in Louise's hope chest. Kitty had bought her two more nightgowns, one black and one pink. She'd given her long white tapers to put on her dinner table. And she'd given her war bonds, so Louise wouldn't yell at her about spending on the other things.

IT WAS BEASTLY HOT, AND KITTY WAS IRRITABLE. She pounded loudly on the bathroom door. "What are you doing in there?" she asked Binks.

"Walking the dog," he said.

"You've had *plenty* of time to 'walk the dog'!" Kitty said.

"Nuh-uh, it's hard."

"What are you talking about?" She rattled the doorknob.

Binks opened the door and unfurled his yo-yo. "See?" he said. "It just goes dead."

"Binks," Kitty said. "Do not practice your yo-yo tricks in the bathroom. People have to use the bathroom."

"I need privacy!"

"Well, find it somewhere else!"

"Where?" he demanded.

He had her there. But she gave one of Margaret's stock answers about how, if he used his brain as often as he used his mouth, he'd surely figure it out.

"Why are you so cranky all the time?" Binks asked.

"I'm not!"

But she was. Yesterday, at work, someone had told her about a woman who'd had the awful job of writing to her wounded son about his wife, who had died in childbirth, along with their little daughter. The woman had begged her son to trust in God. She'd tried to assure him that life would go on, that he would recover, though she had no idea the extent of his wounds—she knew only that he was unable to write the letter he'd sent himself, someone had had to do it for him. Her son did not recover. He had been shot through the spinal cord and was left quadriplegic. He died a week after hearing the letter about his wife. Kitty knew it was irrational, but she couldn't help thinking that, if the man had been with his wife, she wouldn't have died. And if the wife had delivered a healthy baby and been fine herself, maybe the young man wouldn't have died. Surely they were all in heaven now, but Kitty wanted them to be on earth. That whole little family, gone.

Also upsetting was the fact that Kitty had not heard from Hank in almost three weeks. She dutifully answered the letters she got from other boys, but she was heartsick, thinking that something had happened to Hank and it was just a matter of time before she would get word from his mother that he, too, had been injured—or worse. Hank had asked his parents to get in touch with Kitty if something did happen, and they had agreed. Then they had asked when they might meet this girl. One week after he set foot back in the country, Hank had promised; and Kitty had agreed to take time off from work to travel to San Francisco with him. But now she had a sick suspicion that that day would never come.

She went back downstairs and sat with her sisters at the table. Michael Junior was sleeping soundly in the laundry basket. Louise picked up a thick letter from Michael and looked at the postmark. "Texas!" she said, confused. She opened the letter, read a few lines quickly, then said, "Oh."

"What's he say?" Tish asked, and Louise held up her hand; she'd let them know after she looked at it first.

After she'd finished reading the letter, Louise said quietly, "Well, I kept asking him to tell me what it was really like over there. He finally did."

"What's it say?" Tish asked.

"I can't read this out loud. It's . . . I can't."

"Can I?" Tish asked.

Louise nodded. "But I don't want to hear it again. I'm going out in the parlor with Ma and Pop." She picked up the baby and quickly left the room.

Tish looked over at Kitty, her eyes wide. "Go ahead," Kitty said quietly. "Read it."

"*June twelfth, 1944*," Tish said, and Kitty said, "Six days after D-day."

"I actually *know* that," Tish said, then read on.

"*Somewhere in France*

"*Darling Louise,*

"*It's late afternoon, and so blessedly quiet. We're holed in behind the lines for a few days, awaiting supplies and replacements, and today I had the luxury of a haircut, a hot meal, and a bath, if you can call warm water in a helmet a bath. In the morning, I'll give this letter to a buddy of mine, Fred Jenkins, whose leg got messed up real bad and who's going home tomorrow. He'll mail it stateside, and that way we can bypass the censors, which we will certainly need to do if I'm to respond honestly to your persistent requests.*

"*I thought for a long time about whether or not to do this, and I hope I made the right decision. I think I understand why you keep asking me to tell you more, to say everything I can about how I'm feeling. You must believe that it will keep me from becoming one of those poor fellows that just break down. Or maybe you're right, maybe people at home should have more of an idea what it's really like here, they should have more of an idea of what war really means. I'll try to answer your questions, but believe me, I won't come close to telling you everything. There's just too much to say, and no words for some things anyway.*

"*Yes, I have killed a lot of men, I really don't know how many, but a lot. I don't usually see their faces when I do, but I see some afterward, and I certainly see plenty of our guys who have died in battle. Oh, Louise, it's more awful than you can imagine. You see a body curled as if in sleep sometimes, but there's that terrible stillness that lets you know it's not sleep, and it's some guy you saw laughing and smearing jelly on bread with the back of a spoon that morning. You see limbs blown off, arms, legs, and once I saw a head lying there with the eyes open, and I just didn't know what to do when I saw that. You see guys with terrible burns, one guy we tried to pull to safety and the skin on his legs just slid right off. You think, Skin doesn't do that! Skin doesn't* do that!

"*There are guys bleeding to death who don't know it, they're smiling, they're talking, they don't feel the pain because they're in shock, they ask you for some water and then they're dead. On D-day, I ran past a guy lying on his spilled guts with his eyes closed and his thumb in his mouth. Eisenhower's speech had been read to us over the loudspeaker by our commander when we crossed the channel that morning. What valor and inspiration were in his words—all about how we were embarked on a great crusade, that the hopes and prayers of liberty-loving people were going with us. We each got a copy of that speech, and I kept reading it, I pretty much memorized it, especially the part at the end where he said the tide had turned and we were marching together to victory. I took great pride in him saying he had full confidence in our courage, our devotion to duty, our skill in battle. I got gooseflesh when he asked for the blessing of Almighty God on "this great and noble undertaking." But how to reconcile that with spilled guts on a beach and flies in the eyes of some dead nineteen-year-old kid who traded his life for some words on paper?*

"*That guy I ran past, I'd talked to him on the way over. He was holding a tablet and frowning, trying to think of how to say what he wanted. He was writing to his sweetheart, a gal named Harriet, a real looker, he showed me her picture and she was wearing a bathing suit and posing like a pinup girl. Polka-dot two-piece, real curly red hair piled up high on her head, smiling as big as all outdoors. But he was frowning at that picture while writing to her, and I knew, because he told me, that he was writing a letter to be given to her in the event of his death. All of us have done that, sweetheart, written those letters and made out wills, and please don't let it scare you, it offers a kind of comfort to us, and anyway, we were told to do it. Funny how some things can't be said unless we're thinking we'll be dead when they are. My friend Jack showed me the letter he wrote to his son, telling him he was proud to have served his country, telling him to be a big boy, to take good care of his mother, she loved him so much, telling him it would be hard for him to understand why his daddy died, but he would, in time. I intend to write little Michael such a letter, too. I hope he'll never have to read it. Guys write their parents, their sisters and their brothers,* their best friends. One guy wrote a letter to his old cocker spaniel, and he was acting like it was a big joke, but I saw the tears in his eyes. Gosh, I just don't know how anything can ever be more precious than the words in those letters.

"So Harriet's boyfriend, Lou Silver was his name, he didn't make it, Louise, so few in the first wave made it out of the battle that day. One company of 197 men lost all but 7 or 8. Omaha Beach sure got the worst of it, so much went wrong—the paratroopers were all but massacred, the flotation devices on the tanks didn't work, and all but one sank with their crews. The landing crafts were just swamped because the waves were so high, we had to keep bailing water out of them and I was sure we'd never make it. None of the boats could get all the way to the beaches, and our ramp wouldn't go down so we had to jump over the side and some guys landed in water over their heads and their heavy equipment sank them, they drowned. Because of the weather, the air corps wasn't able to cover those of us who made it to the beach, and we were just pinned down there for over three hours. This after it had been drummed into us to get off the beaches, get off the beaches, die on the bluffs if you have to, but get off the beaches because if you don't, you will die there for sure.

"I know thousands made it out of there alive, but thousands didn't. And you keep seeing the guys you ran past, floating in water turned red by all the blood or sprawled out in the sand, you see them when you're awake and when you're asleep, dead in those sad and undignified ways, it sure isn't anything they show you in the training films. A dead guy killed in action is so much different from your old uncle Ned in his coffin. These guys are so young, and to see them dead, well, it's kind of ridiculous. I know what we're fighting for, it's as keen and continually present in my mind as my love for you and our child, Louise. But man alive, those long minutes before you go into battle, your stomach is churning and you're holding your weapon so tight and your mouth is sticking to itself and your heart is pounding so fast and you're thinking, What am I doing here, why did I ever enlist? But then there you go, go, go, run, run, shoot, duck, cover your head, run, crawl, and bullets are screaming past and mortar shells are coming in and guys are *yelling and falling all around you and sometimes they call out for their mother, and you quit thinking, you quit feeling, you have to, you move down into your guts and you just go. It's kill or be killed. That's all it is. Survival. And the enemy is thinking the same thing. Kill the Yanks. Kill them. All this hate on both sides for people you never met, you're killing people you never even saw before. I know this war is about what soldiers represent, I know that. We're fighting an idea, a wrong and deadly idea in the form of a person, and I know, too, a soldier's duty, he does what he's told without questioning, but a guy's face is different from an insignia, an enemy soldier's wallet falls out and there are his photos of his girl.*

"We see these things almost every day, dead men whose loved ones will soon learn they are never coming home. I think about some guy's wife out hanging sheets on the line in the warm summer air and the kid is asleep in the crib and then comes the telegram with the black stars. I heard about this one woman, she wouldn't answer the door, she saw them coming to deliver the telegram and she wouldn't answer the door, as long as she didn't answer the door, her son was still alive.

"You get used to it in a way, but in another way you know you never will. You sit around after battles lasting anywhere from minutes to weeks, and you smoke a cigarette and talk to your buddies, eat some grub, even joke around, play cards, but inside you are reeling. I am, anyway. We are all so far away from the kind of naïve exuberance we had when we first left, thinking we'd pick off the Krauts and the Japs like in a carnival game and come home heroes. Just such a different thing now. I don't ask the others about that, about how they feel now versus how they felt then. Or about how they feel at all, really, none of us does that. What we have to try to do is forget the sadness, the horror, the fear, the humanity—or lack thereof. I know one guy sent a terrible letter to his sweetheart, kind of yelling at her to stop saying how much she missed him. Tell me what you had for dinner, he said. Tell me about the movies you went to, what you wear every day. Tell me what you saw on the streetcar on the way to work, tell me some jokes. Some guys said they thought it was kind of rough, but he mailed it anyway, said she had to learn to cheer him up.

"I guess he's right, we need to keep a part of ourselves in some nice place, it's like our own private church inside us where we can go anytime. We need to have that connection to home. We share the food we get—those New York boys getting the Katz's salamis, are they ever popular!

"We listen to American music when we can, sometimes we get patched in real good. One night we heard Glenn Miller from a German station in Berlin, if you can believe it! How's that for an insult! I heard the Andrews Sisters sing 'Don't Sit Under the Apple Tree' at one of the USO shows we picked up, it was swell. And don't you, Louise Marie, don't you dare sit under any apple trees or anywhere else with anyone but me! I'm kidding you, honey, I know you won't. You are my angel now, truly, the thought of you lifts me up and away from everything here, you're better than a prayer. I swear I'll come home to you. It's funny how some guys know they're going to get it that day, they just wake up knowing it and oftentimes they're right, but what I know is that I'm coming back to you, I know it beyond a doubt, Louise, I just do. I don't know when, but I sure know how, as I've imagined it and described to you a thousand times before, your sweet arms around my neck, our first kiss after such a long time, boy, don't even get me started.

"I'm not going to read this over. I know if I do, I won't send it. I said an awful lot, probably way too much, and I apologize if the awful parts make you feel bad, sweetheart. I hope it wasn't the wrong decision to tell you these things. And I hope, too, that you'll understand that I can't ever do it again. Surely it's not good for you, and it's not good for me, either. Seems like a guy's got to store some things away. I can't imagine that when I come home I'll want to talk about any of this, I don't think any of us will. We'll all be so eager to put it behind us and start our new lives.

"Well, I've got to get moving. My powdered eggs await, aren't you jealous? Say hi to those gorgeous sisters of yours, punch your brothers, and give my love to your parents. I'll write again as soon as I can. Keep up your letters, too, darling. Sometimes we move so fast the mail has a hard time catching up to us, but then it does, and oh boy what a day that is. One day I got eight letters at once, and you'd have thought I won the Kentucky

Derby. It was better than the Kentucky Derby. I tap-danced all over my foxhole—Fred Astaire had nothing on me that day.

"*Yours always. Yours, Louise. Always.*

"*Michael.*"

Tish put the letter down and looked at her sister. Her face screwed up.

"Don't!" Kitty said. She wanted to cry, too, but she was afraid if Louise saw her sisters crying, she'd feel worse. "When Louise comes back in here, don't mention that letter unless she does."

"I don't think she'll come back in here tonight," Tish said.

"You're probably right. Who are you writing to tonight?"

"Just Julian." Tish looked down.

"Don't feel bad. Julian and I are all washed up."

"I know. Julian said. Only he said you were 'gebusted.'"

Kitty laughed. "Tell him I said hello."

"Who are you writing?" Tish asked.

"Butch Henderson," Kitty said and sighed. "And Emmet Thompson. And Roger Carlson."

"I'll bet you hear from Hank tomorrow," Tish said.

Kitty nodded. Sure she would.

AS IT HAPPENED, TISH WAS RIGHT. The next evening, the doorbell rang. It was nine o'clock, early enough that the family was awake, but late enough to make a person nervous about unexpected visitors. "Who could that be?" Margaret asked.

"I'll see," Frank told her, his voice deep and authoritative. But then, "Come, Fala," he said, revealing that he wasn't without apprehension himself. Not that Fala would do much. Frank always said the dog needed a muzzle to control his licking.

The sisters, seated as usual at the kitchen table, listened carefully as Frank walked to the door, then opened it. "Hello," he said, doubtfully.

"I'm sorry to come here so late," a man's voice began, and Kitty was off her chair and running.

"Hank!" Louise and Tish said together. Tish tightened her robe tie and patted her hair, and Louise rose so quickly she nearly upset the table. Together, they moved to the front door and began calling out greetings. The boys had come downstairs, and now they stood in a little huddle, silent and admiring. Hank talked to the family, but his eyes stayed fixed on Kitty, who had attached herself to his side and was weeping happily and pulling out her hairpins. "Wait," she was saying. "Don't look at me yet."

"Fat chance," Tish said.

"Let the man in, let the man in," Frank said. "Drinks all around!" Fala suddenly began barking, and Frank said, "Well, of course, I mean you, too! What good's a dog that can't drink?"

Kitty couldn't think of what to say. She was glad for her family and all the confusion, because she was rendered temporarily speechless. She thought of Molly Swanson at work, who'd said when her new husband came home on leave, she'd asked her girlfriend to open the door. When her friend had refused, Molly went to the door, opened it quickly to say, "Sorry, we don't need any eggs today," then slammed it shut. "Now why did I do that?" she'd asked Kitty. "Can you imagine? When I opened the door again, there he was with his feelings all hurt. Golly! Why did I do that?" Kitty had said maybe she was just overwhelmed. Molly had shrugged and said she guessed so. But her hubby was never going to let her live that down.

Now Kitty understood. When you were flooded with such emotion, you didn't think right—your feelings were jumping all over the place. When she'd set eyes on Hank, the only thing that had come to her to say was something that brought equal parts shame and exhilaration—she couldn't wait to confess it to her sisters tonight. All she could think of to say was, *Now I can grow my nails back!* Poor Hank. Barely across the threshold and she had him married and supporting her and her hands.

"ARE YOU SURE YOU DON'T WANT TO COME?" Kitty asked Louise. It was Saturday night, and Hank was going to take Kitty and her sisters to the State-Lake, then to dinner at George Diamond's Steak House, then to the Green Mill to hear jazz. Tish was downstairs waiting already, and Kitty had almost finished getting ready, even though Hank wasn't due to arrive for another twenty minutes. Every time she left him, she couldn't wait to see him again. Louise had been going to come but then had decided at the last minute to stay home. She needed to reline her dresser drawers, she'd said, she'd bought some pretty paper last week with tiny pink roses. But now she lay on the bed, Michael Junior sleeping in her arms.

Kitty came over, tightening an earring, and looked down at her sister. "Are they straight?" She pulled back her hair and turned from side to side.

"Are what straight?" Louise asked.

"My earrings!"

Louise looked carefully at one ear, then the other. "Yes. Yes, they are. You look very pretty."

"Scootch over," Kitty said.

After Louise made room for her on the bed, Kitty touched her sister's cheek. "You okay?"

"Sure I am." She forced a smile.

Kitty spoke gently. "Is it hard to have Hank home while Michael's still in the thick of it?"

"Oh, no, Kitty, gosh. I'm glad he's back. He flew his missions, he deserves to be back! I'm just feeling a little . . ." She pulled a letter from her pocket and gave it to Kitty. "I got this today."

Kitty unfolded the thin pages full of neat blue script and read:

Dear Michael Junior,

I'm asking your mother to hold on to this letter for when you're older. If you're reading it, it means I didn't make it back from the war.

You know, you picked the best person in the world to be born to, and I know that she will guide you well all your life. What I want to tell you are just a few things that I would have told you—probably over and over— had I had the great privilege to help raise you.

First of all, I want you to know that I believed in the cause for which I died. No war is won without sacrifice, and I think I can speak for every man I've met here when I say we knew exactly what we were doing and why. We fought for the country we left behind, and those in it, to preserve a way of life; and we fought to rid the world of a great evil.

Death is a hard thing to understand at any age, and perhaps under any circumstances. But I hope you will come to see that I did not die when my body left this earth. I live on as long as someone remembers me, and I know your mother will, and I know you will come to know me through her. And I live on because of you, Michael, for even though you are your own man, I am forever a part of you.

A few words of advice.

Tell the truth. Make it a habit. Nothing will erode your soul more than to live a life built on falsehoods.

Do not provoke a fight, but if you or your family are attacked, fight back honorably.

Make time for prayer and reflection; try to understand your value as a man on the earth but see, too, your proper place in the scheme of things. It may sound funny to say this, but I have come to see that we are all far more important and less important than we think.

If your mother marries another man, and I hope she will, I want you to give to that lucky fellow all the love and respect you would have given to me.

My biggest wish for you is that you enjoy this beautiful life you were given. For all its problems and difficulties, life is mostly a wonderful experience, and it is up to each person to make the most of each day. I hope you are successful in your life, but look to the heavens and the earth and especially to other people to find your real wealth.

Wherever I am, wherever you go, know that my love goes with you.

Your proud father,
Michael O'Conner

Kitty handed the letter back to her sister, her eyes full of tears.

"Aw gee, I'm sorry," Louise said.

"For what?"

"I made you cry."

Kitty wiped carefully under her eyes. "That's okay. But you know what? Guess what I want to tell you that I just *know*."

"That he'll make it back?"

Kitty nodded.

"I know that, too," Louise said. "I really do. It's just that when you get a letter like this, and you think about all the boys who wrote them who didn't make it back, or won't . . ." She shook her head. "And all their women who will be left alone and will never find another man like that one, because there's only one of each of us. I just can't get it right, Kitty, I just can't imagine it. A guy wakes up and eats breakfast, and it's his last day on earth, and he doesn't even know. He has no idea. Every guy over there knows men are going to be killed; every time they're in combat, they see men killed all around them, yet every guy thinks he's going to make it."

"I know," Kitty said. "Hope." She didn't want to go out anymore. She wanted to put on her pajamas and talk to her sister. She wanted to make them fried egg sandwiches to eat in bed.

"Oh, stop," Louise said, as though she were reading her sister's mind. "Go have fun. I'll come next time. Gosh, he's swell, that Hank. You're lucky to have found him."

Kitty shrugged.

"Knock it off," Louise said.

"What?"

"The nonchalance. You're nuts about him."

"We'll see."

"Look at me," Louise said. "Let's make sure you didn't smear your mascara. Do you like that mascara, anyway?"

"I do," Kitty said. It was new, an expensive brand she'd bought last week from Tish at the cosmetics counter where she worked. Even with Tish's discount, it was outrageous. "I'll put some on you," Kitty said. "Want me to?"

"I'm not going anywhere!"

"So?" Kitty looked at her watch. "I've got time. I'll put some on you. I'll show you how to do it."

"Okay," Louise said, and she sat up higher in bed, happy now.

Kitty headed for the bathroom to retrieve the black cake of mascara, the cunning little brush. *There,* she was thinking. *Now Louise is okay. Now I can have fun.*

The bathroom door was locked, and Kitty rapped lightly against it. "Who's in there?"

"Me," Binks said.

"Well, come out."

"Okay." The toilet flushed, and Binks banged the door open.

"Good boy," Kitty said.

"WAIT TILL I TELL JULIAN ABOUT THE GREEN MILL," Tish said. She straightened the piece of writing paper before her.

"He's been there," Kitty said.

"Did you go with him?" Tish asked.

Kitty spoke carefully. "We went there a long time ago." They had drunk sidecars, and at one point Julian had lifted her up in the air and kissed her. She'd bitten his ear, and the people around them had whooped and applauded. "Some hot tomato, huh?" Julian had said. "Eat your hearts out, fellas."

"We didn't have any fun, though," Kitty said.

"Well," Tish said happily, and Kitty felt sure she knew what her sister was thinking. *He didn't have fun with* you.

Kitty was glad for Tish and Julian. She wouldn't trade her situation with anyone. She was finally deeply, wildly, madly in love. She talked to Hattie about Hank almost every day, and last time she'd said, Wasn't it a miracle that she had found the one man for her? Wasn't it truly a miracle?

Hattie had said she was very happy for Kitty, but truth be told, she didn't really think it was a miracle. She'd said, "I know how you feel about him. It's how I felt about Will. But I guess I believe that there's a lot more than one man for me, and for you, and for every other woman. And more than one woman for every man."

Kitty didn't like thinking that way. But she guessed it was true. Still, when you were with the man you loved like crazy, you didn't have to acknowledge that there could ever be another you would love so well. You could pretend it *was* a miracle you'd found each other. You could relish the knowledge, however false, that no one else would ever do.

FALL AGAIN. LEAVES DRIFTED SLOWLY or, in a wind, blew down sideways. The days were warm and golden, and the nights made the tip of your nose cold. Michael Junior was almost able to sit up unsupported and adored his strained peas. Kitty sang him lullabies each night, and every time he reached up to touch her face, his eyes wide and wondering, she nearly wept. She understood now the attraction to babies, to children. Oh, did she. She understood with her mind and her heart and her gut.

Fala had learned to fetch the newspaper, and Frank took all the credit, though it was Tommy who'd taught the dog how. "Showed the little fellow once, and didn't he do it ever after!" Frank said, ignoring the number of times Tommy had done it before him.

Billy was working delivering newspapers, and was so well liked he made extremely good money in tips. He was saving for a car, he said; he was going to buy a new car as soon as they started making them again. "Better get a bigger piggy bank," Frank told him, and Billy said his money was at the bank. Earning interest. To which Frank said, uncharacteristically, nothing. Binks's baseball team had taken first place, and he slept with his trophy. Tommy's health was stable; his cheeks were pink again.

The war news was good, too, if you ignored the casualties. Paris had been liberated, and it seemed Hitler really was all but done for. According to the newspaper, he was hiding in his underground bunker, wavering between fits of rage and deep depression. He suffered from headaches, stomach cramps, and dizziness, and existed on an assortment of drugs. He was mentally ill, too, talking to his generals about the new armies he would raise, the secret weapons that would appear, the quarrels that would break out among the Allies, which would facilitate a victory for Germany. Meanwhile, his "army" was old men and children. Yes, Hitler was nearly defeated; it was just a matter of time. Then the Japs would get licked and the boys would come home. What a day that would be!

Meantime, the Nazis had boasted that Germany would eat, even if all the rest of Europe starved, but Michael wrote of seeing heartbreaking groups of refugees, of how he gave away most of his food to children who stood staring at him with their eyes wide, their bony hands clasped before them.

He wrote about the odd poignancy of coming across horses hit by artillery fire and lying dead in their harnesses at the sides of the roads. He told Louise about the mighty Russian army, how they and their American allies had at last met, and had drunk and danced together. He told her about Ernie Pyle's famous remark, made after the Americans arrived victorious in Paris and all the French girls were throwing flowers and kisses. Pyle was reported to have said, "Any guy that doesn't get laid tonight is a sissy." *Guess what?* Michael had written. *I'm a sissy, and I couldn't be happier about it.*

Julian wrote from Saipan that they were sending boys home who had been two years over. Those boys going back were overjoyed but also scared to death. When your days left grew shorter, you got very nervous about being hit. Later, from the Palau Islands, Julian wrote Tish, *Don't worry about me, kid. I'm taking it easy, making like a crab in the sand.*

The sisters wrote back: to them and to other soldiers they met here and there. Always letters going out and always letters coming in, all up and down the block. If someone saw someone else out on the porch taking mail from the box, they would call out, "Did you hear from him?" And if you said yes, they appropriated some of your joy and some of your relief, too.

It was different for Kitty now; her man was home. But of course she worried about those who remained. One night she moaned loudly in her sleep, dreaming about Julian being killed. When her sounds awakened her sisters and they in turn awakened her, she told them she'd been dreaming about some monster. Purple, with purple eyes. They were too tired to doubt her word. The next morning, Kitty went to the church and lit a candle for Julian. *Please don't let him die*, she whispered, then quickly added, *or get hurt, either.*

On an unseasonably warm November day, Hank and Kitty were having a late lunch of hamburgers at the dime-store lunch counter. They'd been shopping for clothes for Hank, casual clothes for his days off from work. He had gotten a job teaching flying—his time in the service had taught him valuable things that could be passed on to men who were still being trained to be sent overseas.

They were talking about the kind of life they'd lead after they were married. Hank had given Kitty a ring three days after he'd gotten home, one he said he'd bought the day after he met her. She still didn't quite believe him, but he insisted that it was true. "I knew instantly," he said. "And I wrote a buddy in California who's a jeweler and told him how much I had to spend. And he sent the ring to me, and I carried it in my pocket until I could give it to you."

It was a small, round diamond that Kitty wore, nothing so grand and glorious as she used to imagine she'd have. But it meant the world to her. She looked at it a thousand times a day, and every time she saw it, she felt a pleasant rush of love and anticipation for the happy life she dreamed she'd have with Hank. But now they were back to the same tired argument they'd been having for weeks. Hank wanted her to quit her job and find office work until they were married, then quit altogether. It was so different, the way Hank talked to her, so different from the way he had written her, when it seemed as though he wanted her to make up her own mind, and respected her for having the ability to do so. It was true that her first thought had been that she couldn't wait to quit. But now she had changed her mind. Ever since the talk she'd had with Frank when she was thinking about quitting the factory early on, she had understood the need for personal sacrifice, for the great satisfaction of putting someone before you. It mattered to her that Michael and Julian and millions of other boys were still fighting, and that what she did directly helped the effort. In addition, she cared more than she had realized about Hattie, about their daily conferences in the employee lunchroom, their friendship. And the thought of making so much less money was discouraging. Kitty still remembered the Depression and the gaunt, jobless men who used to go door-to-door selling apples and rags. Hank said she wouldn't need to make money, he would make money for both of them, as was right. And her moving in with him would lighten her family's financial burden: they wouldn't need her money so much. If they did need help, he would take care of it.

At first when he talked about her family not needing her help, Kitty had nodded, agreeing, thinking, *One less mouth to feed.* But then she thought of her place at the table, empty. She thought of her bed, where Tish and Louise would sleep without her, and she felt a terrible piercing pain. What would life be without her sisters to talk to, to laugh with, every night? So often she'd fantasized married life with the man she loved, but now what it really meant felt starkly and unpleasantly revealed. It was as though a stage set she'd believed was a real and lovely place had been shown for what it was: an illusion. In thinking always about what she would gain by being married, she had never thought about what she would lose. Her family sitting in the parlor eating popped corn and laughing at Jack Benny. The unplanned moments of humor and sweetness in a family, the security you felt at so clearly belonging somewhere. The history of all the members, so well known, the comfortable predictability of all the different personalities. It bothered Kitty to think of herself as a coward, a weak person who clung to her mother's skirts—or her sisters'. But maybe she was exactly that.

Oh, and there was more to it. There was the siren song of everything that life might *also* be. Not so much another man but another way of being. What if she advanced in her work life to make great sums of money—if not at the factory, then somewhere else? What if she took a chance on being something altogether different? Suppose she could become a stewardess and fly all over the world? When she had asked Hank about traveling, he'd laughed and said the farthest he wanted to travel was downtown. In fairness, he had been home for only two days when she'd asked him that. It hadn't been the time to talk to him about travel. Later, when the war was over, that would be the time to talk about it.

But he wanted children right away, too! Kitty just wasn't sure she was ready quite yet. She knew she wanted them someday, baby Michael had put her doubts to rest on that subject; she now knew that she wanted them very much. But later. For the time being, she didn't talk about how much she loved helping care for Michael, lest Hank put more pressure on her. She didn't smile at the way Hank held little Michael and sang to him. On one occasion, Hank had been the only one able to settle Michael down after he'd had a fussy day. "Oh, I just like babies," Hank had said. "I guess they like me back." He'd laughed as Michael cooed at him, making sounds so very much like conversation. The rest of the family had laughed, too, delighted, but Kitty had looked carefully away.

Kitty turned on her stool and told Hank, "I will quit my job eventually. Just not yet. You have to let me decide things, too. You can't tell me to do it now just because that's what you think is best. Don't I get a vote?"

Hank was quiet. Kitty could all but predict what he was going to say: Guys on the battlefield liked their women working in a defense plant. Once they got home, though, they wanted them back in skirts and away from other men. It was only natural. It was only right.

Hank said, "Waitress? More coffee?" and his voice had a tight, strained quality she'd never heard. Well. He was saying that same thing a different way. She looked over at the woman next to her, who looked away. *Don't get me involved, sister. This is your fight.*

Kitty sighed. "Let's go for a walk, Hank. Want to go for a walk?"

"Sure." He leaned over and kissed her forehead. His eyes softened, and Kitty's stomach leaped up. Oh, she adored him, she did. She took his arm as they began walking, thinking of Marcele Cox, who'd written in *Ladies' Home Journal,* "Many a woman will end her period of war work convinced that home, after all, is the place where she can make her best conquests and secure her most beautiful rewards." But Marcele had also written, "A husband is the person on the right side during the wedding ceremony, and on the right side forever after," and this had given Kitty considerable pause. It was all so confusing! She tightened her grip on Hank's arm, thinking the truest thing Marcele had written was this: "Marriage is love turned so the seams show." They'd show each other their truest, most honest selves, she and Hank, and they'd figure out a solution for everything.

By the time Kitty and Hank got off the streetcar, headed for dinner with Kitty's family, they had agreed that she would work at the factory for as long as she wanted. Period. The deal Kitty made privately with herself was that when she got pregnant, she would stop working. Oh, she could hardly imagine it. A child, made by Hank and her, living inside her. She'd been through pregnancy with Louise, but that was different. This would be her body changing and delivering into the world a real live baby, her and Hank's child. It was so scary! But it was wonderful to think about, too. A million lovely things to imagine about having a baby, being a mother. Once she was pregnant, then she'd tell him how all along she'd been thinking about how cute babies looked sitting in bathtubs, their tummies round and their faces alternating between wrinkled-brow befuddlement and wide smiles that nearly broke your heart. She would tell him how she used to stand over baby Michael, just watching him sleep, aching with love. How she leaned so carefully over the crib rail to gently touch his hand.

When Kitty and Hank came into the house, it was oddly quiet. There was the smell of pot roast in the air, and Kitty knew her mother had made a real apple pie. But it was too quiet. "Ma?" *Tommy's sick again,* she thought.

"Up here," Margaret called. And then, "Stay there, I'm coming down."

Kitty and Hank waited at the bottom of the steps. Margaret walked close to the wall and moved slowly, nearly apologetically. She was wearing her apron and twisting her hands in it. She had been crying.

Kitty put her hand to her chest. She couldn't breathe. "Tommy?" she whispered, and her mother shook her head.

"'Tis Michael," she said. "The telegram came this afternoon. Killed in action."

Hank took Kitty in his arms. For one moment, she leaned in to him, her eyes closed tightly. Then she ran upstairs.

Louise was in the bedroom. She sat on the edge of the bed, her family gathered around her. She was not crying, nor did it appear she had been. "Kitty," she said. "You're home. Did Ma tell you?"

Kitty nodded.

"He was trying to protect another guy," Louise said. "Isn't that just like Michael?"

Again, Kitty nodded. Her sister's preternatural calm unnerved her.

"Louise?" she said.

She smiled. "I'll get by. I'm all right. Say, did you know we're having pot roast for dinner?"

Kitty walked slowly over to sit beside her sister and put her arms around her. Louise took in one loud, gasping breath, and then it came. Kitty rocked her sobbing sister, weeping herself, and the rest of the family quietly left the room. Except for Tish. Tish moved to sit at Louise's feet and pressed her face into her sister's knees.

"You know what's funny?" Louise said. "I was worried about his splinter."

THAT NIGHT, KITTY WENT INTO the boys' room to see Tommy. He wouldn't come down and sit with the family; he said he wanted to be alone.

Kitty found him lying on his bed, facing the wall. Asleep? No. She tapped him on the shoulder, and he turned around. Not asleep and not crying, either. "Hi, Kitty," he said.

"Hi, honey. What are you doing in here?"

"Just thinking."

"Oh." She sat on the bed beside him and took his hand. "What are you thinking about? Will you tell me?" He nodded but didn't speak.

"Tommy?"

He looked into Kitty's face, considering. Then he said, "I knew Michael was going to die."

Kitty swallowed. It came to her that she should tell him he shouldn't say such things. But she believed him, and so she said, "You did?"

He nodded. "And I told God that if He would just let Michael live, I'd make a sacrifice for Him. And that's why I didn't eat. But it didn't work."

"Oh, Tommy. I hope you don't think . . . You don't think Michael died because of anything you did, do you? Or didn't do?"

"I just had this idea. But it didn't work."

Kitty nodded. Then, though she knew it was awful, she said, "Is Julian going to be okay?"

Tommy nodded gravely, and Kitty reached out to hold him. For a while she rocked him, he let her; and then she asked him to come downstairs with her, and he did. He didn't need to tell her not to say anything. He made himself a sandwich before he joined the family in the parlor.

"Dagwood Bumstead!" Frank said, admiring the huge creation.

And Margaret said, "Leave him alone and let him eat. He's overdue, God knows."

KITTY WAS LAST IN THE BATHROOM, and when she tried to throw her Q-tips away, they fell from the top of the overfilled trash can. She sighed; was there anyone in the house who would ever empty the bathroom garbage besides herself? She yanked the basket toward her, and more trash fell out. Now she'd have to pick up the soiled Kleenex and the—

A letter. Kitty unfolded the crinkled paper and read:

Darling Michael,

Tonight I had a vision. Bet you didn't know I was so talented. But I did, I had a real vision and here's what it was:

I saw me at the train station, holding the baby, waiting for you to arrive. I was wearing blue, and so was baby Michael, and you know he was just looking off so expectantly like he'd recognize you instantly. And the train came, and Michael, you were the first one off. And I walked up to you, and I was crying of course, and you kissed me and you kissed your son, and then you took him from me and we walked off together and we were all smiling, all three of us.

Oh, Michael, I long so for the day when that vision comes true. And you know when we do walk away, I will be so glad for you to hear not the sounds of gunfire but the sounds of church bells, and of people working in peace. I can't imagine that on that day I won't be thanking God for your safe return, I can't imagine I won't be thanking Him for the rest of my life. Oh, darling, I love you so, and I will completely, until my dying day.

Enough of that! I'm making myself tear up! Let me tell you a story about our beautiful son. This morning, as I gave him his bath

Well, for Pete's sake, hold on, darling, Ma is calling me. The phone just rang, and I have a terrible feeling it was Fala's owner. She'll want to confer with me about how to handle Binks. To be continued!

Kitty thought maybe she'd save this letter. But it wasn't what Louise wanted. She put the letter back in the trash. Soon, Louise would be getting her last letter from Michael. The "in the event of" letter. Kitty felt sure that neither she nor Tish nor anyone else in the family would ever see a word of that letter. Nor should they.

On JANUARY 1, KITTY AWAKENED EARLY. She'd been out late with Hank for New Year's Eve and had a throbbing headache, but she was going to honor her New Year's resolution right away. She had promised herself two things: one, to decide at last on a firm date to marry Hank, all her fears be damned; two, to get Louise out of the doldrums. She knew her sister would mourn Michael in some way forever, as would she, but Louise needed to go out, she needed to eat, she needed to smile again. She refused to go anywhere with her sisters or her parents. The only time she'd been out of the house was when Hank had talked her into going to the drugstore for an ice cream soda. He was like a brother already, she'd said. She could be with him. He helped, because he let her be herself.

Kitty looked down into Louise's sleeping face—such dark circles under her eyes! Kitty tapped her sister on the shoulder and whispered, "It's 1945! Happy New Year!"

"No," Louise said and turned over.

Downstairs, Kitty could hear Michael Junior babbling and Margaret speaking softly to him. "'Tis my nose you're wanting, is it? How about some banana first, young man!"

"The baby's up," Kitty said softly, and now Louise turned over.

"I'll go." She sat up at the side of the bed, her head hanging low.

Kitty touched her arm. "Ma's got him, Louise. She said she'd watch him all day so you and I could go downtown and see the decorations before they come down."

"I don't want to." Louise lay back down.

Kitty ripped the covers off her, and Tish shouted, "Cut it out! I'm trying to sleep!" She pulled the covers over her head.

"You come with me," Kitty whispered angrily to Louise. "This is enough! Now, I have something very important to tell you. You come with me right now."

Surprisingly, Louise sat up again and put on her slippers. "Where are we going?"

Kitty had no idea. She hadn't thought Louise would actually come with her. But reflexively, she said, "To the bathroom."

"Is it empty?" Louise asked.

"Yes. Come with me." Kitty followed her sister down the hall, her fingers crossed.

The door was closed, but the bathroom was empty. Kitty turned the lock and sat Louise on the toilet.

"What do you have to tell me?" Louise whispered. "Are you pregnant?"

"No!" Kitty said.

"Okay, then. I'm going back to bed."

Kitty pushed her sister back down. "Louise, you have to stop this. You have a son to take care of. You've got to get up and start doing things. You're the one who always says that the way to get through any crisis is to do something. Something definite and gay!"

"I know," Louise said. "I know, I know, I know! I owe it to Michael Junior to be happy. I owe it to Michael's memory to be happy. I owe it to the boys over there. I owe it to the family. But I'm not happy. I'm not! And I'm not going to pretend I am. My life is over."

Kitty knelt before her. "Oh, Louise. Your life isn't over. Gosh, you're only twenty-two years old!"

"It is over," Louise said. "Everything I dreamed of died with Michael. And don't tell me about all the brave widows starting over again. I'm not them. And they didn't lose Michael."

"Louise, listen to me. Everybody's tiptoeing around you, but I'm just going to tell you straight out that you're acting like a spoiled brat. Nobody can have a good time in the house because you're walking around with your tragic face. Nobody can laugh. Nobody can even smile. We don't any of us expect you to feel better overnight. But you've made no effort at all to get better! You don't think of anyone but yourself!"

"Kitty. Why can't you understand this? I lost *Michael*."

"You can find another Michael!"

Louise slapped her sister's face. Kitty stood and pressed her hand to her mouth. It came to her to slap her sister right back, but instead she did nothing. Said nothing.

Louise began to cry then, in a weary, absent sort of way. "Oh, I'm sorry. I'm sorry! It's just that it hurts so *much* and it never *stops*. I never should have told him I was pregnant. It put too much on him. It's my fault he died."

"It's not your fault! It's Hitler's fault!"

"It's mine, too. And the only thing that brings me any peace is to think about . . . I want so much to be with him."

Kitty knelt beside Louise and spoke softly. "What do you mean?"

She shrugged.

"Louise. Do you mean you want to die, too?"

She nodded.

Kitty swallowed. "Well, that's . . . Oh, but Louise, that's serious. I think you'd better tell—"

"Don't tell!" Louise said. "Please don't tell anyone I said that."

"But how can I not?"

"It's just that I don't see how I'll ever get close to living the only kind of life I ever wanted to live. I wanted Michael and our family and a home to care for. That's all. And now . . . I don't know. I want nothing."

"It's not true," Kitty said. "You might not be able to see it yet, but you'll overcome this, Louise; you'll even meet another man someday— and don't hit me again! But you will, honey. If you think about it honestly, can't you imagine meeting another guy? Not tomorrow, but someday? Someone you might want to marry and have a family with?"

"No. I won't."

"If he were a lot like Michael?"

"That would be worse. That's the thing. It really does feel hopeless to me, and I just get to thinking sometimes that I don't want to be here. I don't want to go on. Even with little Michael. Someone else would do a better job with him. He's so young, he'd get used to someone else."

Kitty set her jaw. "If you don't want me to tell anyone about the things you're saying, then you do something for me. You get dressed and you come out with me. You spend the whole day out with me. Okay? That's the only way I won't tell Ma and Pop exactly what you told me. I mean it!"

Louise sighed.

"We'll go see all the decorations. They're really pretty this year."

"Yes."

"This will make you feel better, you'll see. Sometimes when you feel really bad, it doesn't take as much to help you as you'd think it would. I mean, the sun is out, it's nice outside, Michael's down there eating his bananas and making Ma laugh. And the decorations are so pretty this year."

"You said." Louise stood and looked at herself in the mirror. "Yikes. I look like the wrath of God."

Kitty waved her hand. "Don't you worry about that. I can fix that in five minutes."

"Let Tish do it," Louise said, and Kitty felt too happy to be insulted.

LATE THAT NIGHT, KITTY SAT with her father at the kitchen table, sharing a piece of chocolate cake with him. There was a certain ritual when you shared things with Frank: two bites for him, one for the person "sharing." She didn't mind; she didn't want the cake so much as her father's company and advice. She hadn't told Frank what Louise had said about not wanting to live, but she had expressed concern about her. When the sisters had gone out that day, Louise had tried to appreciate the decorations, had tried to enjoy the time she had with Kitty, but she was dead behind the eyes, and in the end they had come home early, and Louise had gone to bed right after dinner.

"'Tis a terrible thing that's happened to her," Frank said. "'Twill take a long while for her to get over it. Truth be told, I don't know how she'll ever find a fellow good as Michael." He shook his head. "I never thought I'd say so, but I'm glad she did what she did, so that she has his child. Oh, I know how much harder it will be for her to find a husband, when he will have to take on another man's child; he will have to be a man of exceptionally good character. But she'll find him. In the meantime, we must all help her."

"I don't know how to help her," Kitty said. "Seems like nothing works."

"Give her time," Frank said. "And remember, Kitty, each of us in this family has one unique thing to offer Louise that no one else can give her. Close as she is to you, it wouldn't surprise me if what you give her isn't the thing that turns her around."

Kitty said nothing. She ate more cake. She'd had the same thought—she was the one who could best help Louise. She felt proud that her father thought so, too. It would come to her, the thing she could offer that would bring her sister back.

VALENTINE'S DAY, 1946

KITTY FINISHED FASTENING THE LAST of the many buttons on the back of Louise's wedding dress. Then she spun her sister around so that she could see herself in the mirror. "Look at you!"

"Look at *you*!" Louise said.

Kitty had to admit that she'd never looked lovelier. She wore a lavender bridesmaid's dress and a beautiful matching picture hat. Her shoes were covered in lavender lace. She was the only bridesmaid; Louise had wanted to keep the wedding small.

"I'm going to give you a minute alone," Kitty said. "You come out when you're ready."

"Gosh, I'm nervous!" Louise shook her hands.

"I know, Coots. But that's good luck. A bride is supposed to be nervous on her wedding day. Take your time."

In the church's vestibule, Kitty looked anxiously about. She needed to find the best man; the wedding was scheduled to begin in five minutes. Outside in the cold, on the church steps, Frank stood still as a statue, his back to her, his hands in his pockets. His head hung down; you could read some sadness there. But he'd be smiling like the jolly Irishman he was when he turned around, and Kitty had no doubt that at the reception he'd be the life of the party.

Hank came quickly into the vestibule and stood by Kitty. He looked Cary Grant handsome in his tuxedo; it made Kitty's throat hurt.

"Hey, you," she said. "Are you nervous?"

"Nah. You?"

"A little. My shoes have awfully high heels. I hope I don't fall!"

"Well, you never fall hard, do you?" He spotted Julian and called out, "Ah! My best man."

Julian was beaming, and his limp was barely noticeable. Kitty had been worried when he told Tish he'd be going down the aisle without his cane—he didn't want their daughter to be embarrassed. "Julian, she's two weeks old," Tish had said. But Julian was doing fine without his cane, at least so far. He kissed Kitty's cheek. "Hello, you gorgeous thing. You ready?"

She was not, really. Inside, something turned over. "Sure am!"

"Can I lean on you?" Julian asked.

"Of course."

"Don't tell."

"I never will."

Now the organ began playing, and Frank came into the vestibule. For one moment, he rested his eyes on Kitty, and there was in his gaze such deep affection that Kitty had to look away lest she cry. Then Frank turned his attention to the bride, to whom he offered his arm, held out straight and steady and sure.

KITTY STARED INTO THE MIRROR and adjusted her bangs one more time. She freshened her lipstick and powdered her nose. She hoped she wasn't wildly off the mark with her lipstick; her vision had deteriorated further still.

In the living room, she called Louise to give her one more chance to come along. The last reunion of their high school, classes of 1940–1945. Again, Louise said no. Then, laughing, she said, "Why do you want to go and hang around with all those old goats? Come over here, we're going to have a cookout, everybody's coming. The kids, the grandkids, the great-grandkids . . ."

"Maybe I'll come later," Kitty said.

"Want me to send Hank to pick you up?"

"I'll take a cab."

"Don't be silly; I'll send Hank. I'll have him pick you up at the high school. What time?"

Kitty looked out the window. Across the street, a young couple pushed a baby in a stroller. They had a little yellow puppy, too; it bit at the leash. A golden? A Lab? So many new young families had moved in; the neighborhood had almost completely turned over. "I just want to say hello," Kitty said. "I don't imagine I'll be there more than an hour or two. So few are coming this time; I believe they're expecting only twenty or so. But I'll say hello, and maybe I'll dance. I still love to dance, you know."

"Well, do a dip for me," Louise said. "I'll have Hank get you at eight-thirty. What are you wearing?"

"Oh, just a black bouclé suit. Cream blouse. Pearls. And black heels, a nice Italian leather."

"You're going to kill yourself wearing those heels!"

"And die a happy death," Kitty said, and then, "Hey? I'll bet Kyle Leverett will be there, he's still around. You used to have a big crush on him."

Louise laughed. "*No!* I'm not coming with you. I'd rather remember Kyle as he was. What a good-looking fellow! Those eyes! And what a football player he was, too. Didn't he marry Kate Marshall?"

"Oh, they got divorced years ago."

"How do you know? Did he come after you again? He always had a big crush on *you.*"

"He had a crush on all three of us!"

"Lots of boys did," Louise said proudly. "The Dreamy girls, remember?"

"Kyle did call me, once. Gosh, it was years ago. But we never got together."

"Some catch," Louise said. "I heard he's worth millions. See if he still can do that thing with the nickel."

"I will," Kitty said. Louise was mixing Kyle up with Tom Bender—he was the one who pulled a nickel from his nose—but she wouldn't tell her sister that. No point in correcting every single thing. Soon enough Hank would have to decide how best to care for his wife; some of the things she was beginning to do were dangerous: forgetting to turn off the stove burner, getting lost in the neighborhood when she went out for walks. Mostly, though, she was doing well enough. Her doctor had said it was likely cancer or a heart attack would get her before dementia would. "Imagine being happy to hear news like that," Louise had said, and they'd laughed and laughed.

Kitty ordered a cab to take her to the high school and all the way there answered questions that the young man who was driving put to her. What was school like then? What had she done for a living? Had she lived here all her life?

A young historian! It was refreshing; most young people didn't give a damn about her or her generation. For them, World War II was that Hitler thing, if they even knew that much. She answered the young man's questions dutifully: school was far more disciplined and the kids learned a lot more. She had been a fashion writer, had written for many newspapers and magazines. And yes, she had lived here all her life, though she had traveled a great deal.

"Got any kids?" the driver asked.

"No," Kitty said. "I've got a lot of nieces and nephews, though. And great-nieces and -nephews!"

The driver regarded her in the rearview mirror. "Bet you were a looker," he said.

Kitty laughed. "People always used to tell me I looked just like Rita Hayworth."

"Who's that?" the man asked, and Kitty said, "Oh, she was a real famous movie star. Back then."

"Did you come from a big family?" the cabbie asked, and Kitty said yes, adding that there were a lot of big families in those days. And she was lucky; all her siblings were still alive but for her sister Tish, who had died at forty-one of breast cancer. Her brothers all lived in California, but she and her sister Louise had stayed here in Chicago. Kitty told the driver that the house where he'd picked her up was the place she and her family had lived.

"There were *six kids* in that place?"

"And only one bathroom," Kitty said, smiling.

"That's too small a house for that many people!"

"It was big enough," Kitty said. "People then didn't mind sharing."

"I can't wait to have a family," the man said, and Kitty said yes, she believed there was something to it.

"*Here* we go," he said, pulling up at the high school. He got out of the cab to open the door for her, then offered his hand so that he could help pull her out. She needed a little help getting out of cars; sometimes it was awfully embarrassing—once, her skirt had ridden up right past her girdle. She thanked the driver and asked how much she owed. "Aw, that's okay," he said, smiling. "Wasn't much of a ride."

"I insist," she said, her chin raised high. She paid him and tipped him well. He offered to help her into the school, but she told him no, she was just fine. She walked in alone.

KITTY STOOD OUTSIDE THE AUDITORIUM, waiting for Hank's car. Here it came, the long blue sedan, ten years old and looking brand-new. Maybe twenty thousand miles on it. Hank got out and opened the door for her, and she settled herself on the wide bench seat. "You should have heard the band," she told him, when he got back behind the wheel. "Just a bunch of young kids, but they're really good, and they were playing all those old songs. 'I'll Be Seeing You,' 'Don't Get Around Much Anymore.'"

"'Long Ago and Far Away'?" Hank asked, smiling. "That's my favorite."

"Mine, too," Kitty said. "But no, they didn't play it."

"Did you dance a lot?"

"Not at all. Nobody asked me."

"*What?*"

Kitty laughed. "Oh, you know, almost no one dances anymore. They just listen."

Hank pulled into a parking place and turned off the engine. "Let's go in there and dance. Shall we?"

Kitty looked doubtfully at him.

"Come on!"

"Oh, all right," Kitty said. "But no Lindy Hop!"

"A fox-trot's as fast as I can go, believe me."

They walked back into the auditorium. Most of the people had gone; only about six or seven remained, sitting at tables with plastic glasses of wine and little sandwiches on paper plates, the lettuce wilting now. The musicians were beginning to pack up. But Hank got their attention, and the bandleader came over and crouched down at the edge of the stage to listen to what he said. The man smiled and looked over at Kitty, said something to the rest of the band, and they took up their instruments.

Hank walked across the floor and took Kitty gently into his arms. Oh, he was still a wonderful dancer. His steps were smaller, but his carriage as erect as ever, and he knew just how to hold a girl. A girl! A girl of eighty-five!

" 'Long ago and far away,' " Hank sang softly along, then smiled down at her. "Ah, Kitty. How'd we get so old?"

"Beats me," she said.

"You know, I want to ask you something: Didn't you ever want to marry *any*one?"

"Once I did," Kitty said.

Hank was quiet and then he asked, "Who?"

She thought for a minute; they were so old now, what could it matter? But then she said, "Oh, there was a man I met in Italy when I was thirty-five. I guess that would have been my last chance for a traditional life, you know, home and kids."

"But you didn't really want kids, either."

And now she lied again, the old, practiced lie, said so often that it almost seemed like truth. "No," she said, "I never really did. I only liked the fantasy. When it was time for the reality . . . Well, you know."

"Yes," he said, and there was such sorrow in it.

"But you've been happy, Hank," she said, and she sounded more schoolmarmish than she meant to. What she really meant to do was not to tell him he'd been happy but to ask if he had been.

He stopped dancing. "You know there was only ever one girl for me, Kitty. And that was you."

"Oh, stop it."

"It's true. May I tell you just one more time how very much I loved you?"

She swallowed with difficulty. For heaven's sake, no tears! She put her cheek up next to his and began to move them about on the floor.

"Stop leading!" he said. And then, "Okay, I won't talk about it anymore, but I meant what I said."

"Oh, Hank. It was such a different time. It was a setup for romance, really: all those handsome young men in their uniforms, going off to war, all the love letters. And all the hopes about what would happen when the war was finally over."

"And the music!" Hank said, and they laughed and finished dancing as the song ended, "Just one look and then I knew, / That all I longed for long ago was you."

Kitty stepped away. "Thank you for that lovely dance."

Hank bowed; oh, his hair was so thick and silvery and beautiful. "Thank *you*," he said and took her arm. They walked out, their steps echoing in the all but empty room.

When he helped her into the car, Hank caught sight of a bracelet Kitty was wearing that had slipped from beneath her sleeve. "Is that . . . ?"

"Uh-huh." He had given it to her a short while after he'd come home from the war. They'd been walking by a jewelry store; she'd admired it in the window, and he'd gone right in and bought it.

"I'm so glad you still wear it sometimes," he said.

The truth was, she never took it off. "Louise must be wondering where we are," she said.

When Hank turned to back up the car, she saw that he was grinning.

"What's funny?" she asked.

"I'm just glad you still have that bracelet," he said. "It must be over sixty years old!"

Sixty-two years. She turned to stare out the window and made herself speak lightly. "Well, Hank. You know this: there are some things you never say good-bye to."

They drove home through a light rain. At one point, the car skidded slightly, and Hank reached over to put his arm across her, though her seat belt was buckled securely. "You all right?" he asked, staring straight ahead.

For a moment, she didn't answer.

"Kitty?"

"I'm fine, Hank."

She didn't look at him, either; nor did she speak again until they got to the house, where Louise stood at the open door, smiling, waiting for them both.

ACKNOWLEDGMENTS

I AM TRULY INDEBTED to the staff at the Chicago and Oak Park Public Libraries for assistance in the research I did for this novel. Especially helpful were the following: Mark Andersen, Mary Dempsey, Amy Eshleman, Noreida Hague, Margaret Kier, Kathy Mielecki, Carolyn Mulac, and Rashmi Thapliyal Swain.

I want also to acknowledge the generosity of my uncles, Frank Hoff and William Loney, who shared memories of the war and of the times. Both men served overseas in World War II, and both came home with medals.

My father, Arthur Hoff, also served in the war, and his wife—my mother, Jeanne Loney Hoff—wrote letters to him from the home front (where she, like the young women in the novel, shared a bed with her sisters). My parents were called numerous times with questions— sometimes about K rations or field conditions, sometimes about hemlines and forties mascara, sometimes about FDR or Marlene Dietrich or *Amos 'n Andy.* My aunts, Helen DeNet, Patricia Thornton, and Catherine Quigley, provided juicy details about flirting on streetcars, the content of V-mail, and which sister was the worst to sleep next to.

I stand in awe of my relatives for their kindness, patience and recall. And their character. This novel is nothing if not an expression of admiration for the people who so uncomplainingly took up the extraordinary burdens and sacrifices of a necessary war.

ELIZABETH BERG is the author of sixteen novels, including the *New York Times* bestsellers *We Are All Welcome Here, The Year of Pleasures, The Art of Mending, Say When, True to Form, Never Change,* and *Open House,* which was an Oprah's Book Club selection in 2000. *Durable Goods* and *Joy School* were selected as ALA Best Books of the Year, and *Talk Before Sleep* was short-listed for the ABBY Award in 1996. The winner of the 1997 New England Booksellers Award for her work, Berg is also the author of the nonfiction work *Escaping into the Open: The Art of Writing True.* She lives in Chicago.

ABOUT THE TYPE

Minion is a 1990 Adobe Originals typeface by Robert Slim-bach. Minion is inspired by classical old-style typefaces of the late Renaissance, a period of elegant, beautiful, and highly readable type designs. Created primarily for text setting, Minion combines the aesthetic and functional qualities that make text type highly readable with the versatility of digital technology.